The best of
Janet Dailey

D0415009

CONTENTS

Bed of Grass
Page 5

Heart of Stone
Page 189

BED OF GRASS

BED OF GRASS

BY

JANET DAILEY

MILLS & BOON LIMITED
15–16 BROOK'S MEWS
LONDON W1A 1DR

First published 1979
Australian copyright 1979
Philippine copyright 1980
Reprinted 1980
This edition 1984

© Anne Weale 1979

ISBN 0 263 74708 5

Set in Linotype Baskerville 11 on 12 pt.
09—0584

Made and printed in Great Britain by
Cox & Wyman Ltd, Reading

CHAPTER ONE

WITH efficient, precise motions, Valerie Wentworth folded the lingerie and laid it in the suitcase. Tucking a strand of toffee-coloured hair behind her ear, she walked back to the open drawer of the dresser for more. There was a determined line to the sensuous curve of her lips and a glint of purpose in light brown eyes. Her complexion had a hint of shocked pallor under the pale gold tan of her skin.

A woman stood in the room watching Valerie pack. Her expression was not altogether approving of what she saw. In her forties, her figure had the solid build of middle-age and her brown hair was beginning to become frosted with grey. Her mouth was pinched into lines that discouraged smiles.

'I still say you're a fool, Valerie Wentworth, to go tearing off to Maryland like this.' The acerbic tongue of the older woman repeated an earlier claim.

'He was my grandfather.' Valerie didn't pause in her packing as she walked to the closet and began stripping clothes from the hangers. 'He didn't have any other family but me.'

'Elias Wentworth didn't want you around when he was alive. What makes you think he'd want you at his funeral?' came the challenging retort.

'He isn't in a position to say what he wants, is he?' A trace of anger was in Valerie's voice, an anger caused by the reference to the estrangement between herself and her grandfather. 'And nothing you can say is going to make me change my mind, Clara,' she warned.

'That sanctimonious old man turned his back on you seven years ago, at a time when you needed him most.' Clara Simons reminded her sternly. 'Him and his self-righteous ways,' she murmured under her breath with a sniff of contempt. 'Despite all the letters you wrote him, you haven't so much as received a Christmas card from him in all this time. He disowned you. Blood ties meant nothing to him. After the way he treated you, I wouldn't think they'd mean anything to you either.'

A tailored suit in a rich dark blue fabric was the closest Valerie came to a mourning dress; her stringent budget couldn't absorb the cost of a new dress. She was inwardly grateful that changing customs no longer made black mandatory at family funerals.

'Granddad took me in and raised me after my parents died,' she replied to Clara's comment. 'I owe him something for that.'

'What utter and complete nonsense!' the woman scoffed at her logic. 'How can you feel obligated to that heartless, straightlaced coot? Anyone with an ounce of compassion would have stood beside you seven years ago. They might not have approved of what you'd done, but they would have stood with you and not turned a scared girl like you were out in the cold to fend for herself with no money and no place to go.'

'You didn't know me when I was a young girl, Clara,' stated Valerie. 'I was a wild, irresponsible thing, always into trouble. My escapades would have greyed any young man's head. When I was thirteen, I started smoking cigarettes—I used to sneak off to the stables to smoke. Once I almost set the whole place on fire. I heard Granddad coming and threw a burning cigarette away, and it landed in some hay. If Granddad hadn't spotted it, the stable would have gone up in flames and the horses with it. Granddad had every right to be enraged with me. It scared me when I realised what I'd almost done, but despite the spanking I got, it didn't stop me.'

'Every youngster experiments with cigarettes at some time in their life.' Her friend attempted to rationalise Valerie's behaviour. 'In your case, I wouldn't be surprised if you got into trouble just to gain that insensitive man's attention.'

'You don't understand.' Valerie sighed and turned to face the woman who had become her friend, her family, and her surrogate mother over the last five years. 'It wasn't just the smoking. I drank his drink until he finally had to lock it up in the safe. I'd take one of his thoroughbred horses and go night-riding. I don't know how many times I led a lame horse home after a midnight gallop. They were valuable animals, his livelihood, and I treated them like toys.'

'Children can be thoughtless at times,' Clara admitted, her defence of Valerie not quite as vigorous as before, but still steadfast in her loyalty.

'There was more.' She was driven to make a full confession, needing to expose her guilt. 'I used to steal money from him to hitchhike into Baltimore and go to movies or just buy things. Sometimes I'd be gone all weekend, but I never told him where I'd been. Can you imagine what I put him through?'

'You're being too hard on yourself,' was the stubborn insistence. 'Don't forget that I know what a frightened, love-starved girl you were when I met you.'

'Love-starved,' Valerie repeated thoughtfully. An ache that still hadn't receded after seven years flickered in her tawny eyes. 'Perhaps,' she conceded, since it was the easiest explanation. 'But I'll never forget the anguish that was in Granddad's face the day I told him I was pregnant.' In her mind's eye, she could still see the look of knife-stabbing pain he had given her. 'He was such a moral, upright man that he felt shamed and disgraced by what I'd done. When he demanded to know the father and I belligerently refused to tell him, it was the last straw that broke him.'

Tears burned her eyes at the memory of that stormy scene. She hid them in a flurry of activity, hurriedly folding the blouse to her blue suit and laying it in the suitcase.

'But to throw you out——!' Clara refused to consider her grandfather's actions as justified.

'For a long time, I resented him for abandoning me, even hated him,' Valerie admitted. 'But I was eighteen. Turning me out was probably the best punishment he could have given, because it made me responsible for myself. Now I know the heartache of worrying over a child, and I only regret that I never had the courage to go back and tell Granddad how sorry I was for the anguish he suffered because of me.'

'And that's your reason for going to his funeral,' Clara concluded, crossing her arms in front of her in a stance that suggested disapproval and challenge. 'It's an empty gesture, don't you think? And a costly one, too, considering the wages you'll lose.'

'Mr Hanover has given me the time off and I'm entitled to two days of compassionate pay.' She tried to dodge the issue as she closed the suitcase and locked it with a decisive snap.

'What about the other three days you'll be taking off?' The pointed reminder pinned Valerie to the spot. 'You won't be getting paid for them. And there's the cost of driving all the way to Maryland, too.'

'I'll just have to cut back on a few things.' She was determined not to consider the financial ramifications of her decision to attend her grandfather's funeral. Somehow she'd weather it.

'Humph!' Clara breathed out the sound. 'You're barely making ends meet now.'

'That's my problem.' Valerie opened a second, smaller suitcase and set it on the bed. 'You can't talk me out of going, Clara. You're just wasting your breath.'

Walking to the dressing table, she opened a different drawer and took out a half a dozen sets of little-boy-sized under-pants and socks. When they were in the second suitcase, she began adding pyjamas and slacks and shirts.

Clara watched in silence for several seconds, her expression growing more disgruntled. 'If you must go, there's no sense in carting Tadd along with you.'

'He'll think it's a vacation like all his school-friends take in the summer,' Valerie reasoned.

'Well, you won't think it's a vacation while you're driving there and back with that bundle of energy bouncing all over the car seats,' her friend declared. 'What will you do with him when you get there? A six-year-old boy isn't going to understand about funerals ... or sit through one.'

'I don't have much choice.' Valerie glanced at the second single bed in the room, a twin to her own, except for the worn, stuffed teddy bear resting against the pillow. She was aware of the validity of Clara's argument.

'I'll look after him,' Clara volunteered. There was a grudging quality to her voice, an impatience that she hadn't been able to persuade Valerie not to go.

Valerie glanced at her friend, her strained features softening as she looked at the stern-faced woman. For all her gruffness, Clara had become her rock. She had been the cook in a restaurant Valerie had stumbled into a week after leaving her grandfather's home. She had been frightened, broke and hungry, looking for any kind of job that would put food in her stomach. Clara had taken pity on her, paid for the meal Valerie couldn't afford, persuaded the owner to hire Valerie as a waitress, and taken her to her apartment to live until she could afford a place of her own, which wasn't until after Tadd was born.

'If school wasn't over for the summer, Clara, I might accept your offer,' Valerie replied, and shook her head in refusal, brown curls swinging loosely about her shoulders. 'As it is, you've barely recovered from your bout of pneumonia. The doctor insisted you had to rest for a month before going back to work at the restaurant. Looking after Tadd twenty-four hours a day could never be classified as a rest.'

'What about Tadd's father? Will you be seeing him when you go back?' A pair of shrewd blue eyes were watching her closely.

A chill of premonition shivered over Valerie's shoulders. Her hands faltered slightly in the act of folding one of Tadd's shirts. The moment of hesitation passed as quickly as it had come and she was once again poised and sure of her decision.

'Probably,' Valerie admitted with a show of indifference. 'Meadow Farms adjoins Granddad's property, so some member of the Prescott family is bound to put in an appearance at the funeral. I don't know whether it will be Judd or not. He runs the Farm now so he may not consider the funeral of an insignificant horsebreeder to be worthy of his time, neighbour or not. He may deputise someone else to represent the family.'

'No woman ever completely forgets the man who takes her virginity, especially if she eventually bears his child. Do you still care about him, Valerie?' came the quiet, but piercing question.

A wound that had never completely healed, twisted Valerie's heart squeezing out a bitter hatred that coated her reply. 'I wouldn't have married Judd Prescott if he'd begged me— though he's never begged for anything in his life. He takes what he wants without ever giving a damn about anybody's feelings. He's ruthless, hard, and arrogant. I was a fool to ever think I was anything more to him than a means to satisfy his lust,' she coldly berated herself.

'That's why I never told Granddad who the father of my baby was. I knew he'd go over to Meadow Farms with a shotgun in his hand, ranting and raving about family honour and scandal, and I would rather have been stoned than see Judd Prescott's derisive amusement at the thought of being forced to marry me.'

The suppressed violence in Valerie's denial and rejection of Tadd's father brought a troubled light to Clara's eyes. There was an uneasy look to her expression, but Valerie was too caught up in her own turmoil to notice the gathering silence that met her denunciation. She continued folding and packing her son's clothes into the suitcase.

'Do you know, I believe there's a sensible solution to our problem?' Clara said after the long pause.

'What problem?' Valerie glanced briefly at her friend. There was none as far as she was concerned.

'I'm going crazy sitting around my apartment doing nothing and you're going to have your hands full trying to cope with Tadd on this trip.' It was more of a statement than an explanation. 'A change of scenery would do me good, so I'll ride along with you to Maryland. Naturally I'll pay my share of the expenses.'

'I can't let you do that,' Valerie protested. 'I'd love to have you come with me—you know that. But you've done so much for me already that I couldn't take any money from you for the trip.'

Clara shrugged her wide shoulders, her gaze running over Valerie's shapely, petite figure. 'You aren't big enough to stop me.' Turning towards the door, she added over her shoulder, 'I'll go pack and fix some sandwiches to take along on the trip. I'll be ready in less than an hour.'

Before Valerie's lips could form an objection, Clara was gone. A half-smile tilted her mouth when she heard her apartment door closing. Arguing with Clara was useless. Once she had made up her mind about something, not even dynamite could budge her.

Valerie didn't like to contemplate what her life might have been like if she hadn't met the other woman. It hadn't simply been food, a place to live or a job that Clara had given. She had encouraged Valerie to take night courses in secretarial work, acquire skills that would obtain a better paying job to take care of herself and Tadd.

Many times Valerie had thanked God for guiding her to this woman who was both friend and adviser, supporter and confidante. This gesture of accompanying her made her doubly grateful. Although she hadn't admitted it, she was apprehensive about going back for the funeral. There were a lot of people to be faced, including Judd Prescott.

Walking to the single bed in the corner, Valerie picked up the teddy bear to put in the suitcase. A combination of things made her hold the toy in her arms—the notification a few hours earlier of her grandfather's death, her hurried decision to attend his funeral, her discussion with Clara and the memories attached to her departure from Maryland seven years ago.

Those last were impossible to think about without Judd Prescott becoming entangled with them. Her interest in him had been sparked by a remark

Days had gone by without her seeing him before she had finally realised that Judd was avoiding her. Hurt had grown into indignation and finally a smouldering anger. Her injured pride had demanded revenge. She began haunting the edges of the Meadow Farms stableyard, hoping to catch Judd alone.

At the sight of a luxury sports car that Judd usually drove, coming slowly up the paddocked drive to the stable, Valerie had set her fleet-footed horse on a route that would intersect the car's path before it reached its destination. Jumping her mount over a paddock fence, she had halted it in the middle of the road to block the way. The car's brakes had been applied sharply to bring it to a skidding stop before hitting her.

Judd had come storming out of the driver's side of the car, his features stone-cold with rage. 'What the hell were you trying to do? Get yourself killed?' His icy gaze had flicked to the lathered horse, dancing nervously under her tight rein. 'And if you don't give a damn about yourself, you have no business abusing blooded animals that way. His mouth will be raw if you don't quit sawing on those reins.'

'Don't tell me how to ride a horse! And what do you care what happens to me anyway!' Valerie had flamed. 'At least I know what kind of a low, contemptible man you are! You take a girl's virginity, then drop her cold! !'

'I didn't want it.' Judd had drawn out the denial through clenched teeth. 'Considering the reputation you have, I thought you'd lost it years ago.'

Valerie had gone white with rage at his insulting

remark. She had jabbed her heels into the sides of her hunter, sending it lunging at the tall, insolent man. He had stepped to the side and she had begun striking at him with her riding crop. Catching hold of the end, Judd had pulled her from the saddle. Her horse had then bolted for home pastures.

After he had twisted the riding quirt out of her grip, he had crushed her twisting, kicking body against him. 'You little she-cat, I should use this on you!' His savagely muttered threat had made Valerie struggle all the more wildly, cursing and swearing at him, calling him every name she could think of. He had laughed cruelly, 'Your language would put a stablehand to shame!'

An animal-like scream of frustration had sounded in her throat, but immediately his mouth bruised her lips to punish them into silence. The dominating quality of his kiss had subdued the rest of her until the only twisting Valerie did was to get closer to his leanly muscled frame.

When his mouth ended its possession of hers, she had whispered, 'Make love to me again, Judd.'

'You damned little temptress.' But his voice had been husky with passion, the smouldering light in his green eyes fanning her trembling desire.

Valerie had received the answer she wanted when he swept her off her feet into his arms and carried her to a secluded bed of grass that was to become their meeting place during the following months.

What Valerie had lacked in experience, she had made up for in willingness. Under the guidance of a master in the art of love, she had learned rapidly. Over the course of time it had become evident to her that Judd desired her as much as she desired him. Secure in this knowledge, it had never bothered her that he didn't take her out anywhere. Besides, there had been her grandfather's wrath to be considered if he knew about the two of them.

Even when she first suspected she was pregnant, she wasn't worried. Nor later, when she hitched a ride to Baltimore to a medical clinic for confirmation of her condition, was she apprehensive. She had been certain Judd would be as pleased as she was about the news and be moved to propose.

She had been saddling a horse to ride over to Meadow Farms when her grandfather had walked up. 'Where you going?' he had demanded.

Valerie had responded with a half truth, patting the sleek neck of the bay horse. 'I thought I'd take Sandal out for a canter, maybe over towards Meadow Farms.' Just in case he would see her heading in that direction.

'The place will probably be bustling with activity, what with the party and all.' He commented in a disapproving way.

'What party?' It had been the first Valerie had heard about one.

'The Prescotts are having one of their lavish society affairs tonight.' His eyes had narrowed on her in accusing speculation. 'And don't you be getting any ideas about crashing it. No granddaughter of mine is going to get involved with such carrying-on.'

'Yes, Granddad.' Despite the feigned meekness of her tone, a vision had already begun to form of

Judd possessively holding her hand while he introduced her to friends and family at the party.

Wrapped in her romantic imaginings, Valerie had ridden off to the secluded place in the wooded pasture where they always met, but Judd hadn't been there. Even though the meeting hadn't been prearranged, she had been positive he would appear. Within minutes after she had dismounted, he rode into the clearing.

There had been so many things she wanted to tell him in that instant—how ruggedly handsome he was, to finally admit how much she loved him, about the baby—their baby, and how ecstatically happy she was. But something had made her keep all that inside. She had even turned away when he dismounted and plucked a green leaf from a low-hanging branch.

'It's a beautiful day, isn't it?' she had observed instead.

'Beautiful,' had come his husky agreement from directly behind her.

When his hands circled her waist to cup her breasts and draw her shoulders against his chest, Valerie had breathed in sharply and released it in a sign of pure pleasure. Her head had lolled backwards against his chest while his mouth moved against the windblown waves of her caramel hair.

'How do you always know when I come here?' she had murmured, the wonder of it something she had never questioned before.

'A fire starts burning inside of me, here.' His hand had slid low on her stomach to indicate the location, his mouth moving against her hair as he spoke.

Valerie had turned in his arms, in answer to the flames he had started within her. Hungrily he had begun devouring her lips and she had felt herself begin to surrender to his appetite. But she had wanted to talk. Finally she had dragged her lips from the domination of his, letting his mouth wander over her cheek and ear and nibble sensuously at her throat.

'I thought you wouldn't come today,' she had said weakly.

'Why?' Judd had sounded amused.

'Because of the party.' Her limbs were turning to water.

'That isn't until tonight.' He had dismissed its importance, but made no suggestion that she should attend.

Valerie had understood why no invitation had been given to her grandfather. He was not in the Prescotts' social or financial sphere. Besides, he was morally opposed to drinking and dancing. He would have considered it an offence to be invited, not a courtesy.

'I've never been to a party like that before.' Valerie had tried not to be too open about seeking an invitation. 'It must be grand. I suppose the women will be wearing diamonds and beautiful gowns.'

'In all their clothes, none of them will look lovelier than you do without any.' Even as he spoke, his hands were unbuttoning her blouse.

Valerie had attempted to gently forestall his

efforts. 'Why didn't you invite me?' Her question had been light, not betraying how much she wanted to go.

'You wouldn't like it.' His mouth had worked its way to the hollow of her throat, tipping her head back to allow greater access.

'How do you know?' She had strained slightly against his hold.

Judd had lifted his head, ebony hair gleaming in the sunlight. Behind his lazy regard, impatience had shimmered. A firmness had strengthened the line of his mouth.

'Because it isn't your kind of party,' he had replied in a tone that said the discussion was at an end.

At that moment fear had begun to gnaw at Valerie's confidence. Proud defiance had been present in the way she returned his look.

'Maybe you aren't inviting me because you've made arrangements to take somebody else,' she had challenged.

'It isn't any of your business.' A cold smile had touched his mouth as it began to descend towards hers.

Hurt by his attitude as much as his words, Valerie had tried to draw out of his arms. Her blouse had gaped open in the front and his gaze had roamed downward to observe the creamy globes of her breasts nearly spilling free of her lacy bra. His hand had moved to help them, but she managed to stop it.

'Please, I want to talk, Judd,' she had insisted.

'Why waste energy with words when it can be put to more pleasurable use?' he had argued, and pressed her hips against his so she could feel his urgent need for her.

With a sickening rush of despair, she had realised that they had seldom talked when they met. They had made love, rested, and gone their separate ways. Their past communications had always been physical, never vocal. Valerie had suddenly seen what a fool she had been to think otherwise.

'Let me go!' She had pushed angrily at his chest, the yellow lights in her pale brown eyes flashing warning signals of temper.

'What's this little display of outrage about?' Judd had eyed her with cynical amusement, holding her but no longer forcing her close to him. 'After as many times as we've made love together, it's a little late to be playing hard to get.'

Her temper had flared, adrenalin surging through her muscles to give them strength, and she broke out of his encircling arms.

'That's all I mean to you, isn't it?' she had accused. 'I'm just someone to roll around on the grass with, someone to satisfy your lusts. To you, I'm nothing but a cheap little tramp. I'm not good enough for you to be seen in public with me!'

'You'd better sheathe your claws, tigress. You're the one who invited me into your bed of grass,' Judd had reminded her with deadly calm.

A couple of long jerky strides had carried Valerie to the place where her horse was tethered. She had gathered up the reins and mounted before turning to face him.

'I hope you go to hell, Judd Prescott.' Her voice

had begun to tremble. 'And I hope it's a long, hot trip!'

Putting her heels to her mount, she had turned and galloped the horse towards her grandfather's farm. Tears had drenched her cheeks with hot, salty moisture. All her rosy dreams had shattered that day when she had realised Judd had never felt more than desire for her.

An hour later she had informed her grandfather that she was pregnant, immune to his wrath when she refused to tell him it was Judd who had fathered the life she carried. It had been almost a relief when he had ordered her out of the house. She had put as much distance between her and Maryland as possible.

That was how she had ended up here in Cincinnati, Ohio, living in the same apartment complex as Clara, with an illegitimate six-year-old son, and a job as secretary to an industrial plant executive.

Her cheeks felt hot and wet. She lifted a hand that had been clutching the teddy bear and touched her fingers to her face. They came away wet with tears. The wound inside her was as raw and fresh as it had been seven years ago. She scrubbed her cheeks dry with the back of her hands and blinked her eyes to ease the stinging sensation.

'Mom!'

A four-foot-tall whirlwind came racing into the bedroom. It stopped its motion long enough for her to gaze into a pair of hazel eyes predominantly shaded with olive green. Hair a darker shade of brown than her own fell across his forehead, crowding into his yes.

'Clara said I was to come into the house. You said I could play outside until you called me,' he declared in a breathless rush, already edging towards the door again. 'Can I go back out? It's my turn after Tommy's to ride Mike's Big Wheels. What are you doing with Toby?' He saw the teddy bear in her arms.

'I was just packing him in your suitcase,' she explained. 'We're going on a trip, remember?'

Tadd momentarily forgot his turn on the Big Wheels. 'Where's Maryland?'

'It's a long way from here. We'll have to drive all day,' Valerie laid the teddy bear on top of his suitcase. 'We'll be ready to go soon, so you'd better wash your face and hands and change into those clean clothes.' She pointed to the coloured tee-shirt and jeans lying on the bed.

Tadd made a face when she told him he had to wash. 'Why are we going to Maryland?'

'Because your great-grandfather has died and I want to go to his funeral,' she answered patiently.

'Why?'

Valerie concealed a sigh. She was never certain whether his questions were asked out of genuine interest or an excuse to postpone something he didn't want to do.

'When I was your age, I didn't have a mommy, so your great-grandfather took care of me. I cared about him the way you care about me. That's why I want to go to his funeral.'

'Did I know him?' Tadd tilted his head to one side, his expression showing only innocent curiosity.

'No.' Valerie shook her head.

Her teeth nibbled at the inside of her lower lip. She had written to her grandfather about Tadd's birth, but had never received any form of acknowledgement. None of the letters she had regularly sent had ever been answered.

'Do I have a grandfather?' He altered the subject slightly.

Valerie hesitated. The only relations Tadd had that were still living were on the Prescott side. But, for the time being, it was better if he didn't know about them. The time would come soon enough for him to learn about his heritage.

'No.' Not legally, she defended her lie.

'If you died, there wouldn't be anybody to take care of me, would there? I'd be an orphan,' he stated with a round-eyed look.

'Clara would look after you,' Valerie reassured him, bending to kiss his forehead before he could dodge away. 'Go and wash.' She administered a playful spank to his backside as he scampered towards the bathroom. 'You'd better hurry, too,' she called the warning after him. 'Clara's coming with us and you know how upset she gets if people aren't ready on time.'

CHAPTER TWO

VALERIE had done most of the driving, with Clara
spelling her for an hour every so often to give her a
rest. They had travelled well into the night before
stopping at an inexpensive motel along the highway
for a few hours' sleep. The morning sun was in their
faces, its light shining on the countryside of Maryland.

'How long before we get there, Mom?' Tadd
piped the question from the back seat and leaned
over the middle armrest to hear her answer.

'To save the wear and tear on your vocal cords,
Tadd, we should have tape-recorded that question
when we started out.' Behind the searing dryness of
Clara's voice, there was a hint of amused tolerance.
'You must have asked it a thousand times.'

'How long, Mom?' he repeated.

'Not long. We'll be seeing the lane to the farm
any minute now.' Valerie discovered her hands
were gripping the steering wheel until her knuckles
were white.

Seven years had brought some changes to the area
where she had once lived, but they had just driven
past the entrance gates to Meadow Farms. Charcoal
black fences marked off its paddocks. Just over that
far hill near that stand of trees was the place where
she used to meet Judd. It was one place she would
have preferred to forget.

'That's a fancy-looking place,' Clara observed, but her eyes were on Valerie when she shot her a startled look.

'Yes,' she agreed nervously. 'It's the Prescott place.' She knew she was confirming what Clara had already guessed.

'Look at all the horses!' Tadd breathed, pressing his face against a side window. 'Did they ever let you ride them when you were a kid, Mom?'

'I didn't ride any of those, but your grandfather owned horses. He raised them,' Valerie explained, shifting the subject away from the breeding farm they were passing. 'I used to ride his.'

'You can ride?' There was a squeak of disbelief in his voice. 'Gee, I wish I had a horse.'

'Where would you keep it?' Clara wanted to know. 'It's too big for the apartment. Besides, you're not allowed to have pets.'

'When I get big, I'm going to move out of there and get me a horse,' Tadd stated, his tone bordering on a challenge.

'When you get big, you'll want a car,' Clara retorted.

'No, I won't.' After the confinement of the car for almost twelve hours, Tadd was beginning to get irritable. Usually he enjoyed arguing with Clara, but he was starting to sound mutinous.

'Here's Granddad's place.' Valerie distracted his attention as she turned the car on to a narrow dirt lane.

A sign hung from a post on the left-hand side. The paint had faded, but enough of the letters were still distinguishable to make out the name 'Worth

Farms', a shortened appellation of Wentworth. Board fences flanked the lane. Once they had been painted white, but the sun had blistered it away, leaving the wood greyed and weathered. Half a dozen mares with foals could be seen, grazing in the green carpet of grass in the pasture.

'Look, Tadd.' Valerie pointed to the opposite side of the car from where he was sitting. 'There are horses here, too.'

But not for long, she thought to herself. With her grandfather gone, they would be sold off, and the farm, too. It was difficult to accept that the place she had always regarded as home would soon belong to someone else. It was a sorrow, a resigned regret. Valerie had no hard feelings against her grandfather for disinheriting her; she had given him ample cause as a teenager.

'Can we stop and see the horses, Mom?' Tadd bounced anxiously in the back seat, not satisfied with the slowed pace of the car that gave him a long time to watch the sleek, glistening animals.

'Later.' Valerie qualified her refusal.

'Promise?' he demanded.

'I promise,' she agreed, and let her gaze slide to Clara whose shrewd eyes were inspecting the property. 'The house and barns are just ahead.' The roofs and part of the structures were in view.

'Are you sure there'll be somebody there?' Clara questioned with dry scepticism.

'Mickey Flanners will be there. I know he'll let us stay long enough to wash and clean up. We can find out from him the details about the funeral arrangements and all,' she explained, and smiled briefly. 'You'll like Mickey,' she told her friend. 'He's an ex-jockey. He's worked for Granddad for years, taking care of the horses and doing odd jobs around the place. He's probably looking after things now until all the legal matters are settled and the farm ... is sold.' Again she felt the twinge of regret that this was no longer her home, not when her grandfather was alive nor now. She covered the pause with a quick, 'Mickey is a lovable character.'

'Which means he's short and fat, I suppose.' The cutting edge of Clara's statement was blunted by her droll brand of humour.

'Short and pudgy,' Valerie corrected with a twinkling look.

As they entered the yard of the horse farm, the barns and stables were the first to catch her eye. Although they were in need of a coat of paint, they were in good repair. Valerie hadn't expected differently. Her grandfather had never allowed anything to become rundown. The two-storey house was in the same shape, needing paint but well kept. The lawn was overgrown with weeds and in dire need of mowing.

Her sweeping inspection of the premises ended as her gaze was caught by a luxury model car parked in front of the house. A film of dust coated the sides, picked up from dirt roads. A tingling sensation danced over her nerve ends. Her mouth felt dry and she swallowed convulsively.

'Did you really used to live here, Mom?' Tadd's eager voice seemed to come from a great distance.

'Yes.' Her answer was absent.

'I wish I did,' was his wistful response.

Automatically Valerie parked beside the other car. It could belong to any number of people, she told herself, a lawyer, a banker, someone from the funeral home, just anyone. But somehow she knew better.

The car's engine had barely stopped turning before Tadd was opening the back door and scrambling out. Valerie followed his lead, but in a somewhat dazed fashion. A small hand grabbed hold of hers and tugged to pull her away from the house.

'Let's go see the horses, Mom,' Tadd demanded. 'You promised we would.'

'Later.' But she was hardly conscious of answering him. An invisible magnet was pulling her towards the house, its compelling force stronger than the pleadings of her son.

'I want to go now!' His angry declaration fell on deaf ears.

The screen door on to the front porch opened and a man stepped on to the painted board floor. The top buttons of his white shirt were unfastened, exposing the bronze skin of his hair-roughened chest. Long sleeves had been rolled back, revealing the corded muscles of his forearms. The white of his shirt tapered to male hips, dark trousers stretching the length of his supply muscled legs.

But it was the unblinking stare of green eyes that held Valerie in their thrall. Fine lines fanned out from the corners of them. Harsh grooves were etched on either side of his mouth, carved into sun-browned skin stretched leanly from cheekbone to jawline. His jet black hair was in casual disorder that was somehow sensuous.

Her heart had stopped beating at the sight of Judd, only to start up again at racing speed to send the blood pounding hotly through her veins. The seven years melted away until they were no longer ago than yesterday. Untold pleasures were no farther away than the short distance that separated them. That chiselled mouth had only to take possession of hers to transport her to the world of secret delights.

The compulsion was strong to take the last few steps to reach that hard male body. Valerie would have succumbed to it if the small hand holding hers hadn't tugged her arm to demand her attention. Reluctantly she dragged her gaze from Judd and glanced down to the small boy at her side. Only a few seconds had passed instead of years.

'Who's that man?' Tadd frowned, eyeing Judd with a look that was both puzzled and wary.

Valerie couldn't help wondering what would happen if she told him Judd was his father. But of course she couldn't, and didn't. Tadd's question had succeeded in bringing her to her senses. That aching rawness of desire for Judd hadn't diminished over the years of separation, Valerie realised that painful truth, but she was equally determined not to become enslaved by that love as she had been seven years ago.

Her gaze swung back to Judd, her amber-flecked eyes masked. 'It's a neighbour, Judd Prescott.' Her voice sounded remarkably calm.

A muttered sign came from Clara, issued low for Valerie's ears alone. 'I didn't think it was your lovable Mickey.' Her comment implied that she had guessed Judd's identity the minute he had stepped out of the house.

Valerie didn't have time to acknowledge her friend's remark, for Judd was walking down the porch steps to greet her. He extended a hand towards her.

'Welcome home, Valerie.' His low-pitched voice carried little other expression than courtesy. 'I'm sorry your return is under these circumstances.'

His words of sympathy were just that—words. They carried no sincerity. A bitter surge of resentment made her want to hurl them back in his face. One look at his hard features cast in bronze told her he was incapable of feelings, except the baser kind.

Valerie swallowed the impulse and murmured a stiff, 'I'm sorry, too.'

Unconsciously she placed her hand in his. When she felt the strong grip of his fingers closing over her own, she was struck by the irony of the situation. She was politely and impersonally shaking hands with a man who knew her more intimately than anyone ever had, a man who was the father of her child. There wasn't any part of her that the hand she held hadn't explored many times and with devastating thoroughness. She felt the beginnings of a trembling desire and withdrew her hand from his before she betrayed it.

'I'm Tadd.' Her son demanded his share of the attention.

Her hand drifted to his small shoulder. 'This is my son,' she told Judd, and watched his reaction.

He didn't seem surprised by her announcement, nor was there any suspicion in his expression that he was looking into the face of his child. Valerie supposed that she saw the faint resemblance between the two because she knew and was looking for it.

'Hello, Tadd.' Judd bent slightly at the waist to shake hands with the boy. It was a gesture minus the warmth of affection or friendliness, prompted only by courtesy.

At first Tadd seemed slightly overwhelmed by the action. Then a smile of importance widened his mouth. 'Hello,' he replied.

Valerie realised it was the first time an adult had ever shaken hands with him; usually they rumpled his hair and tweaked his chin. No wonder he was looking so proud and important! She was almost angry with Judd for being the one to treat Tadd as something other than a pet, because she knew he meant nothing by it. She stifled the rush of antagonism and turned to introduce him to Clara.

'Clara, this is Judd Prescott. He owns the land that adjoins my grandfather's.' The explanation was unnecessary, but Valerie made it to show Judd that she hadn't found him important enough to discuss with her friend prior to their arrival. 'This is my friend Mrs Clara Simons.'

'I'm pleased to meet you, Mrs Simons.' Judd issued the polite phrase and shook Clara's hand.

'Likewise, I'm sure.' Clara returned the polite phrasing, while the two of them eyed each other like a pair of opponents taking the measure of the other's strengths and weaknesses. Tension seemed to crackle in the air.

'I didn't expect to see you here when we arrived, Judd.' Valerie's brittle comment was a challenge to explain his presence on the farm. 'I thought we'd find Mickey instead.'

'Did you?' The gleam in his eyes seemed to taunt her statement, but Judd went on smoothly without waiting for a reply. 'Mick is here. I just stopped by to check on things and see if there was any way I could be of assistance.'

'A neighbourly call, hmmm?' Clara's sharp voice questioned his motive with mockery.

But he remained unscathed by the jibe, his cat-green gaze swinging to the stoutly built woman unperturbed. 'Something like that,' he agreed. Turning to one side, he called towards the house. 'Mick? Valerie has arrived.'

'You don't say!' came the muffled exclamation in a lilting tenor voice that Valerie remembered well, and seconds later a short squat figure came bustling out of the house. Mickey looked older and wasn't as agile as she remembered. The wispy crop of hair on his head still reminded her of straw, but it was thinner. 'As I live and breathe, it's Valerie!'

'Hello, Mickey.' She smiled, unaware of the warmth and affection her expression held or the way Judd's eyes narrowed into green slits at the unconsciously alluring transformation.

With slightly bowed legs, Mickey Flanners was built so close to the ground that he appeared to tumble down the steps to greet her. A head shorter than she was, he clasped one of her hands in the powerful grip of both of his. She realised that his hands still had the strength to control the most fractious of horses.

'I got word yesterday afternoon that you was coming for the funeral, but I didn't know how soon you'd get here.' His knowledge was of horses, not subjects like grammar and speech, but his brand of reckless Irish charm made it easy to overlook.

'We drove practically straight through,' Valerie explained. 'We stopped here before going into town to rest and find out the details about the funeral arrangements. I thought you would know about them.'

'Of course I do. You——' Mickey began, only to be interrupted by Tadd.

'You aren't even as tall as my mom. When are you going to grow up?' he wanted to know.

'Mind your tongue, Tadd!' It was Clara who snapped out the reproval, but Valerie just smiled and Mickey laughed, never having been sensitive about his size, and Judd's green eyes simply observed.

'To tell you the truth, me lad,' Mick adopted a poor imitation of an Irish brogue and winked at Valerie, 'I don't intend to ever grow up,' he confided to Tadd in a loud whisper. 'Wouldn't you like to stay little like me all your life?'

Without hesitation, Tadd made a negative shake of his head. 'No, I want to grow tall like him.' He pointed at Judd.

Valerie caught her breath at the amused twitch of Judd's mouth. But he didn't know it was his son who wanted to grow up like him. At the rate Tadd was growing out of his clothes, she guessed he probably would top the six-foot mark like Judd.

'Well, if that's the way you feel about it, there's nothing I can do.' Mickey looked properly crest-

fallen, but laughter danced in the eyes he turned towards Valerie. 'Where's your luggage? I'll carry it in
the house for you.'

'We were planning to stay at a motel in town.'
Valerie's instinctive response was a protest.

'A motel?' Mickey stepped back. 'Eli would have
my hide if I let you and the boy stay at a motel! I
mean—if he was alive,' he corrected with a sobering
look. 'You're the only family he had. There's no
sense in sleeping in a strange place when your old
bedroom is empty.'

'Our luggage is in the trunk of the car and the
keys are in the ignition,' Clara offered the information while Valerie was still absorbing Mickey's reply.

He had made it sound as if her grandfather would
have wanted her back. And he had known about
Tadd, and obviously hadn't kept it a secret or
Mickey would not have taken his presence for
granted. For that reason alone Valerie wasn't going
to argue about staying, discounting the fact that she
could ill afford the cost of the motel room.

Mickey's ebullient spirits could never be battened
down for long. They surfaced again as he obtained
the key from the ignition and walked to the rear of
the car to unlock the trunk. He began unloading
the suitcases, chattering continuously.

'When you left here, Valerie, old Eli seemed to
lose heart. He didn't quit or anything like that.
He'd never give up his horses, but he just didn't
seem to have the enthusiasm any more.' Mickey
paused to glance around the place. 'For the last
three years he's been talking about painting every-

thing, but he never got around to it. The truth is I don't think he had the money to hire it done and neither one of us were spry enough to paint it ourselves. And you know your grandfather, if he couldn't pay cash for what he wanted, he did without.' He set the last suitcase on the ground. 'Is this all of them?'

'Yes,' Valerie nodded.

He glanced down at them. 'Guess I'll have to make two trips.'

'I'll help you carry them inside, Mick,' Judd volunteered, as the ex-jockey had expected him to do. Judd was aware of his tactics, but appeared tolerant.

'Thanks, Judd.' Mickey picked out the heaviest suitcases and handed them to him.

That was when Valerie noticed that Tadd had tagged along after Judd. He tipped his dark head way back to look up at him, a determinedly adult look on his childish face.

'I can carry one,' he insisted.

'Do you think so?' Judd's glance was indulgent and tolerant, but indifferent. He nodded towards Valerie's make-up case. 'That one looks about your size. Can you handle it?'

'Sure.' Tadd picked it up with both hands. It bounced against his knees as he walked behind Judd towards the house.

'I'll tell you one thing, Valerie,' Mickey was talking again as he led the way up the porch steps and into the house. 'Your granddad sure perked up when he found out he had a great-grandchild. Proud as a peacock, he was, passing out cigars to anybody that came within hailing distance.'

A lump entered her throat. Her grandfather had been proud; he hadn't been ashamed when he learned of Tadd's birth. Why hadn't he let her know? She would have brought Tadd for him to see. Hadn't he realised that she had expected her reception would be a door slamming in her face?

'Ain't got no coffee made,' Mick added. 'But I guess you could make a pot while we take the luggage to your rooms. Ain't nothing been changed since you left, so the fixings are where they always were. You know what old Eli said, "a place for everything and everything in its place",' he quoted the old adage that her grandfather had recited many times.

'A cup of coffee is just what I need,' Clara stated briskly. 'You go and fix some, Valerie, while I see to our luggage and hang our clothes up before they're permanently wrinkled.'

Valerie was left downstairs to make her way to the kitchen while the rest of them climbed the steps to the second floor bedrooms. She hadn't realised how tense she had been in Judd's presence until she was free of it. Her severely controlled nerves seemed to almost shudder in relief when she stood alone in the simple farm kitchen. She had wanted that fiery attraction between them to be dead, but it wasn't—not for her.

She heard footsteps approaching the kitchen, more than one set, and began filling the coffee pot with water. She turned off the taps as Judd entered the kitchen, followed closely by Tadd and Mickey.

'I saw the bedroom where you slept as a little kid,

Mom,' Tadd announced, bouncing over to the counter to stand on tiptoe to see what she was doing. 'Mickey showed it to me. He said it was the same bed you used to sleep in. Can I sleep in it, Mom?'

'Yes, you may sleep in my bed if you want to,' she agreed, and turned to open the cupboard on her left.

Her gaze encountered Judd's. She had the disturbing sensation that she had just given permission to him instead of her son. The canister of coffee was where it had always been kept. Her shaking hands lifted it down to the counter-top as she turned to avoid the glitter of his eyes.

'When can we go see the horses?' Tadd reverted to his previous theme.

'Later on. I told you that before,' Valerie replied with a hint of impatience creeping through.

'But it is later,' he reasoned. 'And you promised.'

'Tadd, I'm making coffee.' She shot him a warning look not to pursue the issue and his lower lip jutted out in a pout.

'So it's horses you're wanting to see, is it, lad?' Mickey's lilting voice brought the light of hope back into Tadd's hazel-green eyes.

'Yes, would you take me?' he asked unashamedly.

'First I have to find out how bad you want to see them,' Mick cautioned, and walked over to open a cupboard drawer. 'You can either have a piece of candy,' he held up a chocolate bar, 'or you can come with me to see the horses. Which will it be?'

Except to glance at the candy, Tadd didn't hesitate. 'The horses.'

Mickey tossed him the chocolate bar. 'Spoken like

a true horseman! Your great-granddaddy would have been proud to hear you say that.'

Tadd stared at the candy. 'Aren't you going to take me to see the horses?'

'Of course, lad.' Mickey reassured him with a wink. 'But you'll be needin' some energy for the walk, won't you?'

'You mean I can have both?' Tadd wanted to be sure before he tore off the paper wrapping around the bar.

'Isn't that what I just said?' Mick teased, and moved towards the back door. 'Come along, lad. And don't you be worrying about him, Valerie. I'll watch over him the same as I watched over you.'

Valerie had enjoyed watching Mickey work his Irish charm on her son. It wasn't until the door shut that she realised she had been left alone in the kitchen with Judd. What was keeping Clara? she wondered desperately, but was determined not to lose her composure.

'Mickey has always had a way with children,' she said into the silence, not risking a glance at Judd as she spooned the coffee grounds into the percolator basket.

'That's because there's a little bit of truth in the fact that he's never grown up.' Judd had moved closer. Valerie was fully aware of his disconcerting gaze watching her. He leaned a hip against the counter a few feet from where she worked and became part of her line of vision. 'I knew you were coming,' he said with studied quietness.

She glanced up, the implication of his words jolting through her. Judd had meant that he had known she was coming the same way he had always known when she would be at their meeting place, and she didn't want to know that.

Deliberately she pretended that she was unaware of a hidden meaning to his comment. 'Word gets around fast, doesn't it? I did tell the hospital when they called that I'd be coming as soon as I could. I suppose everyone in the area knows it by now.' She put the lid on the coffee pot and plugged the cord into a socket. Out the kitchen window she could see Tadd skipping alongside Mickey on their way to the barns. 'I suppose you've finally got married and have a family of your own now.' She turned away, trying not to picture Judd in the arms of some beautiful debutante.

'No, to both of those.' An aloofness had entered his chiselled features when she glanced at him. 'You've matured into a beautiful woman, Valerie.' It was a statement, flatly issued, yet with the power to stir her senses as only Judd could.

'Thank you.' She tried to accept it as merely a compliment, but she didn't know how successful she had been.

'I'm sorry your husband wasn't able to accompany you. I would have liked to meet him,' he said.

'My husband? Who told you I was married?' Except for startled surprise, there was little expression in her face.

'Your grandfather, of course.' He tilted his head to one side, black hair gleaming in a shaft of sunlight.

Valerie realised that she should have guessed her grandfather would come up with a story like that in order to claim his great-grandson without feeling shame.

'That was rather a foolish question for me to ask, wasn't it?' she commented dryly.

Judd didn't make any comment to that. 'I suppose he wasn't able to get time off from his job.'

Valerie was toying with the idea of revealing her grandfather's lie and correcting Judd's impression that she was married. When she had decided to keep Tadd shortly after he was born rather than give him up for adoption, she had accepted the fact that she would have to live with the illegitimacy of his birth and not hide behind a phoney wedding ring.

Before she could tell Judd that she had no husband and never had, Clara walked into the kitchen. She glanced from Valerie to Judd and back to Valerie.

'Where's Tadd?' she asked.

'Mickey took him out to see the horses,' Valerie explained.

'Is the coffee done?' Clara sat down in one of the kitchen chairs, making it clear that she wasn't budging. 'Will you be staying for coffee, Mr Prescott?' Behind the question was a challenge to explain the reason why he was still here.

'No, I don't believe so.' Amusement glinted in his green eyes at the belligerently protective attitude of the older woman. His attention returned to Valerie. 'The funeral home will be open from six until eight this evening so your grandfather's friends can come to pay their respects. You're welcome to ride in with me if you wish.'

'It's kind of you to offer, but we'll find our own

way,' Valerie refused in the politest of tones.

He inclined his head in silent acceptance of her decision. Bidding them both an impersonal good-bye, Judd left. Neither woman spoke until they heard the roar of a powerful engine start up at the front of the house.

'Well?' Clara prompted.

'Well what?' Valerie was deliberately obtuse.

'Well, what did he have to say?' Clara demanded in gruffly autocratic tones.

'Nothing really, if you mean any reference to our former ... relationship.' Valerie removed two cups from the cabinet above the stove.

'Did he say anything to you about Tadd?'

'No. Judd thinks I'm married. It's a story Grand-dad cooked up.'

'Did you tell him differently?' Clara wanted to know, an eyebrow lifting.

'I started to when you walked in,' admitted Valerie, and shrugged. 'I suppose it's just as well I didn't. Whether I'm supposedly married or single, it doesn't change anything.'

'Are you going to tell him that Tadd is his son?'

'If he asks me, I will. What difference does it make?' Valerie said diffidently. 'He has no legal right to Tadd—I've seen to that. There isn't any-thing he could do if he wanted to, which I doubt.'

'But he still gets to you, doesn't he?' Clara's voice was understanding and vaguely sad.

'Yes,' Valerie sighed. 'After all this time, I'm still not immune to him. He's a rotten, insensitive brute, but he would only have to hold me to make me for-get that.'

'Don't let him hurt you again, honey.' It was almost a plea.

Shaking the honey-dark mane of her hair, Valerie curved her mouth into a weak smile. 'I'm not going to give him the chance!'

CHAPTER THREE

AT a quarter past six that evening Valerie slowed the car to park it in front of the funeral home of the small Maryland community. A few cars were already in the lot.

'Is this where we're going?' Tadd was draped half in the front seat and half in the back.

'Yes.' Valerie glanced at him briefly. His little bow tie was already askew and his shirt was coming loose from the waistband of his trousers. 'Clara, would you mind tucking his shirt in and straightening his tie?'

'Hold still!' Clara ordered when he tried to squirm away. 'I don't know if it's a good idea to bring him along.'

'He's old enough to understand what's going on,' Valerie replied calmly.

'Are we going to a funeral?' Tadd asked.

'No, Granddad's funeral is tomorrow,' she answered patiently.

'What's a funeral?' At his question, Clara sniffed, a sound that indicated Valerie was wrong to believe Tadd knew what was going on.

'A funeral is when a person dies and all his friends and family come to say goodbye to him. Do you remember when your turtle died? We put him in a box, buried him in the ground and asked God to take care of him for you because you couldn't.'

'Is that a funeral?' Tadd was plainly fascinated by the discovery.

'Yes, that's a funeral.' Valerie parked the car next to the curb. 'Let's go inside. Remember, Tadd, you promised me you'd be good.'

'I will.' He tossed off the agreement as he eagerly climbed out of the car.

The hushed atmosphere inside temporarily impressed Tadd. He stood quietly at her side, holding her hand while Valerie spoke to the funeral director. Several of her grandfather's friends had already arrived. Some Valerie remembered; others she didn't.

Tadd had little interest in the condolences the strangers offered. He was too busy looking around him in awed silence. He mutely nodded at Judd when he arrived and came over to speak to him and Valerie.

Valerie realised she was clenching her jaw in tension and tried to relax. 'Granddad was acquainted with just about everybody in the area, wasn't he?' she remarked.

'Everyone didn't agree with his strict code, but they respected him,' Judd stated. 'Have you had a chance to go up front?'

Valerie glanced towards the satin-lined casket. 'No. Each time I started, someone stopped to offer their sympathies.'

'Come on.' His arm curved impersonally behind her to rest his hand on the small of her back.

The heat of his touch seemed to send a fire racing up her spine. She was powerless to resist his guidance. Her fingers curled tightly around Tadd's small hand, bringing him along with her.

At the open casket Judd stopped, and Valerie looked on her grandfather's image for the first time in seven years. He looked old and tired lying there, in need of the rest he had obtained. She wanted to tell him how much she loved him and how sorry she was for hurting him, but she had said both many times in the letters she had written him, so she guessed he knew.

Tadd was trying to peer inside. 'Mom, I can't see,' he whispered loudly in irritation.

Bending down, Valerie lifted him up. His arm rested on her shoulder, his face close to her own. 'That's your great-grandfather.' She had felt the need to tell him something.

'Gee!' Tadd breathed, and turned a questioning scowl on her. 'How come we didn't bury Fred in a box like that?' he asked loudly.

A smile played at the edges of her mouth. His nonchalance at death seemed somehow right. She wasn't going to scold him for being disrespectful.

'We couldn't find one that small,' she answered, and it satisfied him.

As they turned to walk back where the other mourners were talking, Judd gave her a questioning look, his eyes cool and distant. 'Who's Fred?'

'A pet turtle,' she admitted, unable to keep from giving him a faint smile.

'I should have guessed,' he murmured dryly, shared amusement glittering briefly in his look.

More friends of the family arrived. Judd made no attempt to remain at her side as Valerie greeted them. Almost immediately he drifted to one side, although Valerie was aware that he was never very far away from her.

It wasn't long before the newness of Tadd's surroundings wore off. He became increasingly restless and impatient with the subdued conversations. He fidgeted in the folding chair beside Valerie's and began violently swinging his feet back and forth to kick at his chair rung. The clatter of his shoes against the metal was loud, like a galloping horse.

'Don't do that, Tadd,' Valerie told him quietly, putting a hand on his knee to end the motion.

He flashed her a defiant look, 'I want to,' and continued swinging his feet without letup.

'Stop it, Tadd,' she repeated.

'No!' he retorted in open belligerence, and found himself looking into a pair of cold green eyes that wouldn't put up with such rebellion.

'Do as your mother tells you, Tadd,' Judd warned, 'or you'll find yourself sitting alone in your mother's car.'

Tadd pushed his mutinous face close to Judd's. 'Good.' Olive-green eyes glared into a brilliant jade green pair. 'I want to sit in the car,' Tadd declared. 'I don't want to stay here in this dumb ole place.'

'Very well.' Judd straightened, taking one of Tadd's hands and pulling him from the chair.

'No, wait.' Valerie rushed out the halting words. 'Tadd is tired and irritable after that long trip,' she made excuses for her son's behaviour, and glanced anxiously at Clara. 'Maybe you'd better take him back and put him to bed, Clara.' She opened her bag and took out the car keys. 'Here.'

'And how will you get back?' her friend challenged in a meaningful voice.

It didn't seem proper to Valerie to leave yet. Mickey Flanners was standing only a few feet away, chatting with a horse trainer.

'Mickey?' When he turned, Valerie asked, 'Is it all right if I ride back to the farm with you?'

For an instant she thought Mickey glanced at Judd before answering, but she decided she had been mistaken. 'Sure,' his agreement came immediately.

Judd released Tadd's hand as Clara walked over to take him with her. Tadd glanced at Valerie. 'I'll be there soon,' she promised.

It was more than an hour later when Mickey asked if she was ready to leave. Valerie agreed and was required to say no more as Mickey began relating a steady stream of racehorse gossip as they walked out of the funeral home. Only one car was parked in the area where Mickey was heading towards and Judd was behind the wheel.

'Where are you parked?' Valerie interrupted him with the question.

'I thought you knew.' His startled glance was strictly innocent of deception. 'I rode in with Judd.'

'No, I wasn't aware of that.' There was a hint of grimness in her voice, but she didn't protest.

Mickey opened the front door on the passenger side for her. She had barely slid in when he was telling her to, 'Move over.' She found herself sitting in the middle, pressed close to Judd. For such a small man, Mickey Flanners seemed to take up a lot of room.

Judd appeared indifferent to the way her shoulder kept brushing against his as he reversed the car into the street. It was impossible to avoid the accidental contact with him unless she hunched her shoulders forward and held herself as stiffly as an old woman, and she refused to do that.

The expensive scent of male cologne filled her lungs and interfered with her breathing. Mickey continued his non-stop banter, which was a source of relief to Valerie, for without it, she was certain Judd would have been able to hear the erratic pounding of her heart.

When Judd had to swerve the car to avoid a pothole, Valerie was thrown against him. Her hand clutched at the nearest solid object to regain her balance. It turned out to be his thigh. His muscles contracted into living steel beneath her hand. She heard him sharply inhale a curse and jerked her hand away as if she had suddenly been burned.

She recovered enough of her poise to offer a cool, 'I'm sorry.'

His bland, 'That's quite all right,' made her wonder if she had only imagined that he had been disturbed by her unconsciously intimate touch.

Her grandfather's house was a welcome sight when Judd slowed the car to a stop in front of it. Mickey didn't immediately climb out. Instead he leaned forward to take a look at Judd.

'There's some of Eli's good brandy in the house. Will you come in, Judd, and we'll have one last drink to old Eli?' A second after he issued the invitation he glanced at Valerie. 'That is, if you don't mind. After all, it is your grandfather's house and his brandy.'

'It's as much your house as it is mine,' Valerie insisted. What else could she say? Mickey had worked for her grandfather long before she was born. His years of loyalty far outweighed her less than exemplary relationship with her grandfather, regardless of the blood ties.

'In that case, will you come in for a little while, Judd?' Mickey repeated his invitation.

There was an instant's hesitation from Judd. Valerie felt his gaze skim her profile, but she pretended an ignorance of the look. She hadn't seconded the invitation because she didn't want to give him the impression that she desired his company. Neither did she seek to avoid it because she didn't want him to know he still exerted a powerful attraction over her.

'Thank you, Mick, I'd like that,' he agreed finally. 'But I'll only be able to stay a little while. I've got a sick colt to check on.'

'Oh? What's wrong with it?' Mick opened his car door and stepped out.

As Valerie partially turned to slide out the passenger side, the skirt of her grape-coloured dress failed to move with her, exposing a sheer nylon-covered thigh and knee. She reached to hastily pull the skirt down, but Judd's hand was there to do it for her. In the confusion of his touch against her virtually bare leg, Valerie didn't hear his explanation of the colt's problem. She managed to push his hand away, an action that was at odds with her sensual reaction.

The warmth that was in her cheeks when she stepped out of the car wasn't visible in the fading sunset of the summer evening. It was a languid night, heavily scented with the smell of horses and hay and a sprinkling of roses that grew next to the house.

Mickey waited for Judd to continue his discussion of horses and their ailments. Valerie started immediately towards the house, not rushing her pace as one would fleeing, although it was what she wanted to do. In consequence, Judd was there to reach around her and open the porch door.

Hearing the return, Clara appeared from the living room. She had already changed into her nightgown, its hem peeping out from the folds of her quilted robe. A pair of furry slippers covered her feet. At the sight of the two men following Valerie inside, Clara stopped and scowled. Only Valerie, who knew her, was aware it was a self-conscious and defensive expression for being caught in that state of dress.

'What are you staring at?' Clara demanded of Mickey in her most rasping and abrasive voice. 'Haven't you ever seen a woman in a bathrobe before?'

'Not in a good many years.' Mickey recovered from his initial shock, his cheeks dimpling with mischief. 'I'd forgotten what a tempting sight it could be.'

'Watch your tongue!' Clara snapped, reddening under his sweeping look.

Hiding a grin, Mickey turned aside from the bristling woman. 'I'll get some glasses from the kitchen. Why don't you go on into Eli's office, Judd? I'll be along directly.'

'Don't rush on my account,' Judd replied.

Valerie felt his glance swing to her when Mickey left the room, but she didn't volunteer to show him to her grandfather's office/study. Instead she walked into the living room to speak to Clara, denying any interest in where he went or when.

'Is Tadd asleep?' she asked Clara.

'Finally, after throwing a holy fit to see the horses again,' was the gruff response.

'I'll go and look in on him.' Her sensitive radar knew the instant Judd turned and walked towards the study.

'Leave him be for now,' Clara insisted 'You might wake him, and I don't care to hear him whining again about those horses.' She shot a look in the direction Judd had taken and whispered angrily, 'You could have warned me you'd be inviting them in when you got back. I wouldn't have been traipsing about the place in my robe if I'd known.'

'I had no intention of inviting them in,' Valerie corrected. 'In fact, Mickey was the one who invited Judd, not me.'

'It's neither here nor there now,' Clara muttered. 'I'm going up to my room where I can have some privacy.'

Valerie was about to say that she'd come along with her when Mickey appeared at the living room entrance. Clara scurried towards the staircase under his dancing look.

'I'll be up shortly,' she called after Clara, then asked Mickey, 'Did you want something?'

'I know you're tired and will be wanting to turn in, but will you have one small drink with us to the old man?' He wore his most beguiling expression as he raised an arm to show her he carried three glasses.

The haunting loneliness in his blue eyes told Valerie that he truly missed her grandfather and wanted someone who had been close to Elias Wentworth to share his sense of loss with. Her glance flickered uncertainly towards the study where Judd waited.

'Very well,' she agreed, and wondered whether she was a sentimental fool or a masochist.

Judd's back was to the door, his attention focused on the framed pictures of thoroughbred horses that littered one panelled wall of the study. Valerie tried not to notice the way he pivoted sharply when she and Mickey entered, or the almost physical thrust of his gaze on her. She walked to the leather-covered armchair, its dark brown colour worn to patches of tan on the seat and arms.

'I've got the glasses,' Mickey announced. 'All we need is the brandy.' He walked to the stained oak desk and opened a bottom drawer. 'Up until a few years ago Eli used to keep his liquor locked up in the safe.'

Valerie's fingers curved into the leather armrest at Mickey's unwitting reminder of her past misdeeds. Her grandfather had kept it locked away to prevent her from drinking it. To this day, she didn't understand why she had done it. She hadn't liked the taste of alcohol and had usually ended up getting sick.

'Eli never touched a drop himself,' Mickey went on as he held the bottle up to see how much was in it. 'He was an alcoholic when he was younger. He told me once that it wasn't until after his wife died that he gave up drinking for good.' He poured a healthy amount of brandy into the first water glass.

'Only a little for me,' said Valerie, understanding at last why her grandfather had been so violently opposed to drinking.

'Eli swore he kept liquor in the house purely for medicinal reasons.' When he reached the third glass, Mickey poured only enough brandy in to cover the bottom. 'Personally, I think he kept it on hand to befuddle the brains of whoever came to buy a horse from him.'

Picking up two of the glasses, Mickey carried the one with the smallest portion to Valerie and handed the other to Judd. Judd took a seat on the worn leather-covered sofa that was a match to her chair. Mickey completed the triangle by hoisting himself on to the desktop, his short legs dangling against the side.

'To Eli.' Judd lifted his glass in a toast.

'May he rest in peace,' Mickey added, and drank from his glass. Valerie sipped her brandy, the fiery liquid burning her tongue and throat, conscious that Judd's gaze seldom wavered from her. 'Yeah, old Eli never smoked or drank,' Mickey sighed, and stared at his glass. 'They say a reformed hellion is stricter—and he sure was with you, Valerie. I remember the time he caught you with a pack of cigarettes. I thought he was going to beat the livin' tar out of you.'

'I caused him a lot of grief when I was growing up.' She lifted her shoulders in a dismissing shrug.

'You were a chip off the old block,' the ex-jockey smiled away her self-criticism. 'Besides, you gave him a lot of pleasure these last years.' His comment warmed her. 'Remember how Eli was, Judd, whenever he got a letter from her?'

'Yes,' Judd answered quietly.

At his affirmative reply, her gaze swung curiously to him. 'Did you visit Granddad? I don't remember that you came over when I was still living here.'

He rotated his glass in a circle, swirling the brandy inside. He seemed to be pretending an interest in the liquor while choosing how to word his answer.

'Your grandfather had a yearling filly that I liked the looks of a few years ago. Her bloodline wasn't bad, so I offered to buy her,' Judd explained with a touch of diffidence. 'After a week of haggling back and forth, we finally came to an agreement on the price. It was the first time I really became acquainted with Eli. I like to think that we had a mutual respect for each other.'

'After that, Judd began stopping by once or twice a month,' Mickey elaborated. 'Your granddad would get out his letters from you and tell anybody who would listen how you were.'

Apprehension quivered through Valerie that Judd might have seen what she wrote. Of course, she had never told her grandfather the identity of Tadd's father, not even in the letters. Not that she cared whether Judd knew, but she didn't like the idea that he might have read the personal letters intended only for her grandfather. Mickey's next statement put that apprehension to rest.

'He never actually read your letters aloud, but he'd tell what you said. All the time he'd be talking, he'd be holding the envelope with your letter inside it and stroking it like it was one of his horses.'

'I wish ... I could have seen him before he died.' But she hadn't thought she would be welcomed.

'I wanted to call you when he was in the hospital,' Mickey told her. 'But Eli told me that in your last letter you'd said you and your husband were going to take a Caribbean cruise. I didn't know he was so sick or I would have got in touch with you anyway.'

'On a cruise?' Valerie frowned.

'That's what he said,' Mickey repeated.

'I didn't go on any cruise,' she denied before she realised that it was another story her grandfather had made up.

'Maybe he got your letters confused,' he suggested. 'He kept them all, every one of them. He hoarded them like they were gold. He carried them around with him until they stuck out of the pockets of his old green plaid jacket like straw out of a scarecrow.'

'He did?' Valerie was bemused by the thought. The idea that he treasured her letters that much made her forgive him for making up those stories about her.

'He sure did. As a matter of fact, they're all still in his jacket.' Mickey hopped down from his perch on the desk and walked to the old armoire used as a storage cabinet for the farm records. The green plaid jacket hung on a hook inside the wooden door. 'Here it is, letters and all.'

As he walked over to her, Mickey began gathering the letters from the various pockets, not stopping until there were several handfuls on her lap. Some of the envelopes had the yellow tinge of age, but all of them were worn from numerous handlings.

Setting her brandy glass down, Valerie picked up one envelope that was postmarked five years ago. She turned it over, curious to read the letter inside, but the flap of the envelope was still sealed. A cold chill raced through her.

'No!' Her cry was a sobbing protest of angry and hurt disbelief. She raced frantically through the rest of the envelopes. All were sealed. None of the letters had ever been read. 'No! No! No!' She sobbed out bitter, futile denials of a truth too painful to accept.

'What is it?' Mickey was plainly confused.

'What's wrong?' Judd was standing beside her chair. He reached down and took one of the envelopes.

'Look at it!' Valerie challenged through her tears.

When he turned it over and saw the sealed flap that had no marks of ever having been opened, his darkly green, questing gaze sliced back to her. In each of her hands she held envelopes in the same unopened condition. Her fingers curled into them, crumpling them into her palms. In agitation she rose from the chair, letting the letters in her lap fall to the floor. She stared at the ones in her hands.

'It isn't fair!' In a mixture of rage and pain, Valerie cast away the envelopes in her hands. She began shaking uncontrollably, her fingers still curled into fists. 'It isn't fair!'

Scalding tears burned hot trails down her cheeks. The emotion-charged feelings and tempers maturity had taught her to control broke free of the restraints to erupt in a stormy display.

'Valerie!' Judd's quieting voice had the opposite effect.

The instant his hands gripped her shoulders and turned her around, she began pummelling his shoulders with her fists. Sobbing in earnest, she was like the tigress he had once called her, with tawny hair and topaz eyes, wounded and lashing out from the hurt.

'He never opened them. He never read any of my letters,' she sobbed in frustration and anguish.

Indifferent to the hands on her waist, she pounded Judd's shoulders, hitting out at the only solid object in the vicinity. Her crying face was buried in his shirtfront, moistening it and the lapel of his jacket.

Somewhere on the edge of her consciousness she was aware of concerned voices, Mickey's and Clara's. Only one penetrated and it came from Judd.

'Let her cry. She needs the release.'

She heard the door close. There was silence but for the sounds of her own sobbing. When the violence within subsided, she cried softly for several minutes more. Her hands stopped beating at the indestructible wall of muscle and clutched the expensive material of Judd's jacket instead. His arms were around her, holding her closely in silent comfort. Gradually she began to regain her senses, but there were still things that needed to come out.

Lifting her head far enough from his chest to see the buttons of his shirt, she sniffed, 'He hated me.' Her voice was hoarse and broken as she wiped the wetness from her cheek with a scrubbing motion of her hand.

'I'm sure he didn't,' Judd denied.

'Yes, he did.' Valerie bobbed her head, a caramel curtain of rippling hair falling forward to hide her face. 'He couldn't stand the thought of having me as a granddaughter, so he made up a fictitious one, complete with stories about marriage and vacation cruises. It was all lies!'

His hand raked the hair from one cheek and tilted her face up for his glittering study. 'What are you saying?' he demanded with tight-lipped grimness.

Golden defiance flashed in her eyes, a defiance for convention and her grandfather. 'I work for a living. I couldn't afford a trip on a rowboat. I'm not married—I never have been. Tadd is his great-grandchild, but without the legitimacy of a marriage licence.'

'Damn you!' His head came down, his mouth roughly brushing across a tear-dampened cheek to reach her lips. 'I've been going through hell wondering how I was going to keep my hands off somebody else's wife.' He breathed the savagely issued words into her mouth. 'And all the time you weren't even married!'

The hungry ferocity of his kiss claimed her lips, devouring their fullness. Her battered emotions had no defences against his rapacious assault and he fed on her weakness. She was dragged into the powerful undercurrent of his passion, then swept high by the response of her own senses. The flames of carnal longing licked through her veins to heat her flesh. This consuming fire fused her melting curves to the iron contours of male form. Not content with the domination of her lips, Judd ravaged her throat and the sensitive hollows below her ears.

His hand moved slowly down her back, unzipping her dress, but when the room's air touched the exposed skin, it was the cool breath of sanity that she had needed. She pushed out of his arms and took a quick step away, stopping with her back to him. She was trembling from the force of the passion he had so easily aroused.

At the touch of his hand on her hair Valerie stiffened. Judd brushed the long toffee mane of hair aside. His warm breath caressed her skin as he bent to kiss the ultra-sensitive spot at the back of her neck and desire quivered through her.

'You're right, Valerie.' His fingers teased her spine as he zipped up her dress. 'This isn't the time or the place, not with your grandfather's funeral tomorrow.'

'As if you give a damn!' Her voice wavered under the burning weight of resentment and bitterness. She dredged up the parting phrase she had used seven years ago. 'Go to hell, Judd Prescott!'

She closed her eyes tightly as she heard his footsteps recede from her. When she opened them they were dry of tears and she was alone. A few minutes later Clara came slopping into the room in her furry slippers.

'Are you all right now?' she questioned.

Valerie turned, breathing in deeply and nodding a curt, 'Yes, I'm fine.' The letters were still scattered on the linoleum floor, and she stooped to pick them up. 'Granddad never opened them, Clara.'

'That doesn't mean anything. He kept them, didn't he? So he must have felt something for you,' her friend reasoned, 'otherwise he would have burned them.'

'Maybe.' But Valerie was no longer sure.

'What did Prescott have to say?' Clara bent awkwardly down on her knees to help Valerie collect the scattered envelopes.

'Nothing really. I told him I wasn't married and that Tadd was illegitimate, so he knows Granddad was lying all this time,' she replied with almost frightening calm.

'Did you tell him he was his father? Is that why he left in such a freezing silence?'

'No. He never asked who Tadd's father was. I'm just a tramp to him. I doubt if he even believes I know who the father is,' she said, releasing a short bitter laugh. The postmark of one of the envelopes in her hand caught her eye. It was dated two days after Tadd's birth, unopened like the rest of them. 'If Granddad never opened any of my letters, how did he know about Tadd?'

Clara stood up, making a show of straightening the stack of envelopes she held. 'I phoned him a couple hours after Tadd was born. I thought he should know he had a great-grandson.'

'What ... did he say?' Valerie unconsciously held her breath.

Clara hesitated, then looked her in the eye. 'He didn't say anything. He just hung up.' The flickering light of hope went out of Valerie's eyes. 'I was talking to Mickey today,' Clara went on. 'It wasn't until a year after Tadd was born that he told everybody he had a great-grandchild.'

'I suppose so there was a decent interval between

the time I supposedly was married and Tadd was born,' Valerie concluded acidly. 'Damn!' she swore softly and with pain. 'Now all of them think Tadd is five years old instead of six.'

'I know it hurts.' Clara's brisk voice tried to offer comfort. 'But, in his way, I think your grandfather was trying to keep people from talking bad about you.'

'I'm not going to live his lies!' Valerie flashed.

'You don't have to, but I wouldn't suggest going around broadcasting the truth neither,' the other woman cautioned. 'You might be able to thumb your nose at the gossip you'd start, but there is Tadd to consider.'

Valerie released a long breath in silent acknowledgement of her logic. 'Where's Mickey?' she asked.

'He went out to the barn, said there was a place for him to sleep there where he could be close to the horses,' Clara answered.

'I'm tired, too.' Valerie felt emotionally drained, her energy sapped. Exhaustion was stealing through her limbs. She handed the letters to Clara, not caring what she did with them, and walked towards the stairs.

CHAPTER FOUR

A BEE buzzed lazily about the wreath of flowers lying on the coffin and a green canopy shaded the mourners from the glare of the sun. Valerie absently watched the bee's wanderings. Her attention had strayed from the intoning voice of the minister.

At the 'Amen', she lifted her gaze and encountered Judd's steady regard. Her pulse altered its regular tempo before she glanced away. The graveside service was over and the minister was approaching her. Valerie smiled politely and thanked him, words and gesture that she repeated to several others until she was facing Judd.

'It was good of you to come.' She offered him the same stilted phrase.

His carved bronze features were expressionless as he inclined his head in smooth acknowledgement. A dancing breeze combed its fingers through his black hair as he drew her attention to the woman at his side, ushering her forward.

'I don't believe you've met my mother, Valerie,' he said. 'This is Valerie Wentworth.' An inbred old-world courtesy prompted him to introduce the younger to the elder first. 'My mother, Maureen Prescott.'

'How do you do, Mrs Prescott.' Valerie shook the white-gloved hand, her gaze curiously skimming the woman who had given birth to this man.

Petitely built, she had black hair with startling wings of silver at the temples. Her eyes were an unusual shade of turquoise green, not as brilliant as her son's nor as disconcerting. She was attractive, her face generally unlined. She conveyed warmth where her son revealed cynicism. Valerie decided that Maureen Prescott was a genteel woman made of flexible steel.

'Judd was better acquainted with your grandfather than I, but please accept my sincere sympathies,' the woman offered in a pleasant, gentle voice.

'Thank you.' Valerie thawed slightly.

'If there's anything you need, please remember that we're your neighbours.' A smile curved the perfectly shaped lips.

'I will, Mrs Prescott,' she nodded, knowing it was the last place she would go for assistance.

Others were waiting to speak to her and Judd didn't attempt to prolong the exchange with her. As he walked his mother towards the line of cars parked along the cemetery gates, Valerie's gaze strayed after them, following their progress.

When the last of those waiting approached her, Valerie almost sighed aloud. The strain of hearing the same words and repeating the same phrases in answer was beginning to wear on her nerves.

She offered the man her hand. 'It was kind of you to come,' she recited.

'I'm Jefferson Burrows,' he said, as if the name was supposed to mean something to her. Valerie looked at him without recognition. He was of medium height, in his early fifties, and carried himself with a certain air of authority. 'I was your grand-father's attorney,' he explained.

'I'm pleased to meet you, Mr Burrows.' She kept hold of her fraying patience.

'This is not perhaps the proper time, but I was wondering if I might arrange to see you tomorrow,' he said.

'I'll probably be fairly busy tomorrow. You see, I stored many of my personal things at my grand-father's, childhood mementoes, etcetera,' she explained coolly. 'I planned to sort through them tomorrow and I'll be leaving the day after to return to Cincinnati. Was it important?'

'I do need to go over your grandfather's will with you before you leave.' There was a hint of pomposity that she had implied he had made a request that was not important.

'There's a provision for me in his will?' Her response was incredulous and sceptical.

'Naturally, as his only living relative, you are one of the beneficiaries of his estate.' His tone was repri-manding. 'May I call in the morning? Around ten o'clock, perhaps?'

'Yes. Yes, that will be fine.' Valerie felt a bit dazed.

As she and Mickey drove away from the cemetery a short time later, she saw the attorney standing be-side the Prescott car talking to Judd. After having previously been convinced that she would be disin-herited, Valerie had difficulty adjusting to the fact that her grandfather had left a bequest for her in his will.

It was even more difficult for her to accept the

next morning after Jefferson Burrows read her the will. She stared at the paper listing assets and liabilities belonging to her grandfather and the approximate net worth of the estate. All of it, except for a cash amount to Mickey, had been left to her.

'You do understand,' the attorney said, 'that the values on the breeding stock and the farm are approximate market prices, but I've been conservative in fixing them. Also, this figure doesn't take into account the amount of tax you'll have to pay. Do you have any questions?'

'No.' How could she tell him she was overwhelmed just at the thought of inheriting?

'You're fortunate that your grandfather wasn't one to incur a lot of debts. The only sizeable one is the mortgage on the farm.'

'Yes, I am,' Valerie tried to answer with some degree of poise.

'I know this inheritance doesn't represent a large sum of money,' he said, and she wondered what he used as a standard of measure. There was money for Tadd's education and enough left over that she wouldn't have to work for a year if she didn't want to. 'But I'm sure you'll want to discuss it with your husband before you make any decision about possibly disposing of the property.'

'I'm not married, Mr Burrows,' she corrected that misconception immediately.

He raised an eyebrow at that, but made no direct comment. 'In that case, perhaps I should go over some of the alternatives with you. Deducting taxes and the bequest to Mr Flanners, there isn't sufficient working capital to keep the farm running.

Of course, you could borrow against your assets to obtain the capital, but in doing so, you would be jeopardising all of what you inherited.'

'Yes, I can see that,' Valerie agreed, and she didn't like the idea of risking Tadd's future education.

'I would advise that you auction all the horses to eliminate an immediate drain on your limited resources and to either lease or sell the land.' He began going into more detail, discussing the pros and cons of each possibility until Valerie's mind was spinning in confusion. It was a relief when he began shoving the legal papers into his briefcase. 'It isn't necessary that you make an immediate decision. In fact, I recommend that you think about it for a week or two before letting me know which course of action you would like to pursue.'

'Yes, I'll do that.' She would need that much time to sort through all the advice he had given her.

After he had gone, she broke the good news to Clara, but even then it didn't really sink in. It wasn't until after lunch when the dishes were done and she and Tadd and Clara had walked outside that the full import of it struck her.

Valerie looked out over the pastures, the grazing mares and colts, the stables and barns, and the house, and she was dazzled by what she saw.

'It's mine, Clara,' she murmured. 'I inherited all of this. It's really and truly mine.'

'Do you mean it's yours like the car is?' Tadd asked, sensing the importance of her statement, but not understanding why.

'The car belongs to me and the bank,' Valerie

corrected him with a bright smile. 'I guess the bank has a piece of this, too, but I have a bigger one.'

'Does that mean we can live here?' His eyes rounded at the thought.

'We could live here if we wanted to,' she agreed without thinking, since it was one of the choices.

'You're forgetting you have a job to go to in Cincinnati,' Clara inserted dryly.

'I'm not forgetting.' Valerie shook her head, then turned her bright gaze on the older woman. 'Don't you see, Clara, I have enough money that I could quit my job?'

'Now you're beginning to sound like some heiress,' observed Clara in a puncturing tone.

'I wouldn't be able to quit working for ever,' Valerie conceded, 'but there's enough money here for Tadd to have a college education and to support us for a whole year besides.'

'Are we really going to live here, Mommy?' Tadd was almost dancing with excitement.

'I don't know yet, honey,' she told him.

'I want to. Please, can we live here?' he asked breathlessly.

'We'll talk about it later,' Valerie stalled. 'You run off and play now. Don't go near the horses, though, unless Mickey is with you,' she called as he went dashing off.

'You shouldn't be raising the boy's hopes up,' Clara reprimanded. 'You know you can't live here permanently.'

'Maybe not permanently, but we could stay here through the summer.' At the scoffing sound, Valerie outlined the idea that had been germinating in her mind. 'It would be a vacation, the first time I'd be able to be with Tadd for more than just nights and weekends. And I'd like him to know the freedom of country life.'

'What would you do with yourself out here?' Clara wanted to know.

'There's a lot that could be done. First, the horses would all have to be auctioned. And Mr Burrows suggested that I might get a better price for the farm if I invested some money in painting the buildings and fences. The lawn would need to be cleaned up and maintained. There's something to be gained from staying the summer. Besides, it would take time to sell or lease the place,' she reasoned. 'What are we talking about anyway? Just two and a half or three months.'

'What about your job? You are supposed to be back to work on Friday,' Clara reminded her.

'I know,' Valerie admitted. 'I'll just have to see if Mr Hanover won't give me leave of absence until the fall.'

'And if he won't?'

'Then I'll have to find another job.' Valerie refused to regard it as an obstacle. 'This time I'll have enough money to support myself until I find a good one.'

'It seems to me you have your mind all made up,' Clara sniffed, as if offended that her counsel hadn't been sought.

'The more I think about it, the more I like it,' Valerie admitted. 'You could stay, too, Clara. The doctor said you had to rest for a month. Why not here in the fresh air and sunshine?'

'If you're set on staying here, I might too.' There was something grudging in the reply. 'I'm just not sure in my mind that you're doing the right thing.'

'Give me one good reason for not staying the summer,' Valerie demanded with a challenging smile.

'Judd Prescott.' The answer was quick and sure.

The smile was wiped from her face as if it had never been there. 'He has nothing to do with my decision!' she snapped, her eyes flashing yellow sparks.

'Maybe he doesn't, but he's someone you're going to have to contend with,' Clara retorted. 'And soon, it appears.' Her eyes narrowed, gazing in the direction of the pasture beyond Valerie.

Hearing the drum of galloping hooves, Valerie turned to see a big grey hunter approaching the yard. His rider was instantly recognisable as Judd. Alertness splintered through her senses, putting her instantly on guard.

Tossing its head, the grey horse was reined in at the board fence. Judd dismounted and looped the reins around the upright post. He crossed the board fence and walked towards the two women with ease that said it was a commonplace thing for him to be stopping by. His arrogant assumption that he would be welcomed rankled Valerie.

'What do you want, Mr Prescott?' She coldly attempted to put him in his place as an uninvited trespasser.

His hard mouth curved into a smile that lacked both humour and warmth as he stopped before her. 'I have some business that I want to discuss with you, *Miss* Wentworth.' Sardonically he mocked her formality.

'What business would that be?' she challenged, her chin lifting.

His gaze skimmed her once over, taking in the crisp Levis and the light blue print of her cotton blouse. His look belied his previous statement that his purpose was business not personal.

'I understand that Mr Burrows was here to see you this morning,' he replied without answering her question.

'And where did you get that piece of information?' Valerie demanded.

'From Mr Burrows,' Judd answered complacently. His mouth twisted briefly at the flash of indignation in her look. 'I asked him to call me after he'd informed you of your inheritance.'

'Just what do you know about my inheritance?' She was practically seething at the attorney's lack of confidentiality.

'That you grandfather left everything to you.'

'I suppose Mr Burrows supplied you with that information, too.' Irritation put a razor-sharp edge to her tightly controlled voice.

'No, your grandfather did,' Judd smoothly corrected her assumption.

'I see,' she said stiffly. 'Now that we have that straightened out, what did you want?'

'As I said, I have some business to discuss with you regarding your inheritance.' His gaze flicked to the onlooking Clara. 'In private.'

'There isn't anything you have to say to me that I would object if Clara heard,' Valerie stated.

'But *I* object,' Judd countered. 'If you want to discuss my proposal with Clara after I'm gone, that's your business, Valerie. But my business is with you, and you alone, with no third party listening in.'

Valerie held her breath and counted to ten. Was it really business he wanted to discuss or was it some trick to get her alone? There was nothing in his expression to tell her the answer.

'Very well,' she agreed, however ungraciously. 'Shall we walk, Mr Prescott? Then you won't have to worry about anyone eavesdropping on your so very private business conversation.'

'By all means let's walk.' Amusement glittered at her sarcasm.

Valerie started off in the direction of the pasture fence where the grey hunter was tied. When they had travelled what she considered a sufficient distance, she glanced at him.

'Is this far enough?' she questioned.

He glanced over his shoulder at Clara, a taunting light in his eyes when their gaze returned to Valerie. 'For the time being,' he agreed.

'Then perhaps you would be good enough to state your business.' Her nerves felt as tight as a drum and the pounding of her heart increased the sensation.

'I don't know if you have had time to decide what you want to do about the farm, whether you're going to keep it or sell it,' Judd began without hesitation. 'I'm willing to pay whatever the market price is for the farm if you decide to sell.'

So it was business, she realised, and was angered by the disappointment she felt. 'I see.' She couldn't think of anything else to say.

'I offered to buy the place from your grandfather, but he wouldn't sell. It isn't a money-making concern, Valerie,' he warned. 'Your grandfather has a good stallion in Sunnybrook, but his mares are less than desirable. I tried to convince him that he should be more selective in the mares he bred to the stallion, but he needed the stud fees and couldn't afford to buy better bred mares.'

But Valerie's thoughts had strayed to another area. 'Why did Granddad tell you he was leaving all this to me?'

His gaze narrowed with wicked suggestion. 'Do you mean did he know that you and I were once lovers?' She hadn't expected him to word her suspicion so bluntly. The uncomfortable rush of colour to her cheeks angered her. Turning her back on Judd, she walked to the pasture fence, closing her hands over the edge of the top rail.

'Did he guess?' she demanded, letting him know that she had never told her grandfather.

'No. If he had, he'd probably have chased me off his land with a load of buckshot,' he answered.

'I ... wondered,' Valerie offered in a weak explanation for her question.

'You look more like the Valerie I remember, standing there with your lion's mane of shiny hair around your shoulders and those tight-fitting jeans that show off your perfectly rounded bottom.'

If he had stripped her on the spot, Valerie couldn't have felt more naked. She pivoted around to face him, hiding the area he had described with such knowledge from his roaming gaze. Leaning against the fence, she hooked the heel of one boot on the lowest rail.

'I think you said it was business you wanted to discuss,' she reminded him with flashing temper.

He looked amused. 'Have you given any thought to selling?'

Despite his compliance with her challenge, Valerie didn't feel much safer. 'I'm considering it ... as well as several other possibilities.'

'Such as staying on here permanently?' he suggested.

'I don't think that's possible,' she rejected that with a brief shake of her head. 'As you mentioned, the horses barely pay for themselves, so it would be difficult for me to earn a living from the farm.'

'You could always sell the horses and lease all the land except the house.' Judd took a step towards the fence, but it was angled away from her, posing no threat.

'I could,' Valerie conceded, 'but the income from a lease wouldn't be enough to support us. I'd need a job and there aren't many openings for a secretary in this community, especially well-paying ones. It's too far to commute to Baltimore. For that reason leasing practically cancels itself out.'

'Don't be too certain that you wouldn't have enough money from a lease,' he cautioned. 'The right party might be willing to pay what you need.'

He began wandering along the fence row, gazing out over the land as if appraising its worth. Valerie watched him, confused by the possibility he had raised. She didn't know whether he was telling her the truth or dangling a carrot under her nose to

lead her into a trap. Or had there been a hidden
suggestion in his words that she hadn't caught?

Before she could puzzle it out, Judd was asking,
'Do you mind if we walk on a little farther?' His
sideways look of question held a bemused light. 'I'd
like to get out from underneath the eagle eye of that
battleaxe.'

'Do you mean Clara?' Valerie was startled but
not offended by his mocking reference to her friend.
Without being aware of moving she began following
him, matching his strolling pace.

'Yes,' he admitted. 'She reminds me of one of those
buxom warrior maids in a German opera. All she
lacks are pigtails, a spear and an armoured breast-
plate.'

Valerie visualised Clara in such a costume and
couldn't help smiling at the image or the aptness of
his description. 'Does she make you uncomfortable?'
she asked.

Judd stopped, his level gaze swinging to her with
a force that rooted her to the ground. 'You make me
uncomfortable, Valerie.'

His hand lifted, the back of his fingers stroking
the line of her jaw before she could elude them. The
light touch was destroying. When his fingertips
traced the length of the sensitive cord in her neck all
the way to the hollow of her throat, her breath was
stolen by the traitorous awakening of her senses. She
sank her white teeth into the softness of her lower
lip to hold back the words trembling on her tongue,
unsure whether they would come out a protest or an
invitation.

Taking her silence as acceptance, Judd moved

closer. He hooked a finger under the collar of her blouse and followed its line to the lowest point where a button blocked his way, but not for long. A languorous warmth spread over her skin when his hand slid inside her blouse to climb and claim the rosy mountain of her breast. He bent his head to kiss the lip her teeth held captive. They abandoned it to his sensual inspection. Her heart throbbed with aching force under his sweet mastery. Inflamed by his slow burning fire, Valerie trembled with passion.

Satisfied with her initial response, Judd began nuzzling her cheek and eye, his tongue sending shivers of raw desire through her as it licked her ear. The heady male smell of him stimulated her already churning emotions. Of their own free will, her lips were nibbling and kissing the strong, smooth line of his jaw.

'I'll lease the place from you, Valerie,' Judd muttered against her cheek, 'and pay you whatever you need to live on.'

His offer stopped her heartbeat. 'Would you visit me?' she whispered, wanting to be sure she hadn't misunderstood.

'Regularly.' His massaging hand tightened possessively on her breast as he gathered her more fully into his encircling hold. He sought the corner of her lips, his warm breath mingling with hers. 'Night and day.'

With shattering clarity, his true proposition was brought home to her. Leasing the land was only a means to give her money—money that would oblige her to be available whenever he felt the urge for her company. She inwardly reeled from the thought with pain and bitterness.

Her lips escaped his smothering kiss long enough to ask a choked, 'Would the lease be ... long-term or ... short?'

'Any terms, I don't care.' Impatience edged his voice. 'After seven years, I want to make love to you very slowly, but you drive me to the edge of control,' he muttered thickly, his mouth making another foray to her neck.

Sickened by the weakness that made her thrill to his admission, Valerie lowered her head to escape his insatiable kisses and strained her hands against his chest to gain breathing room. Judd didn't object. It was as if he knew how easily he could subdue any major show of resistance from her. This arrogance was the whip to flog her into a cold anger.

'I'll tell you what my terms are, Judd.' She lifted her head slowly, keeping her lashes lowered to conceal the hard, topaz glitter in her eyes until she was ready for him to see it. 'My terms are ...' she paused, taking one last look at her fingers spread across his powerful chest before lifting her gaze to his face, '... no terms.'

As his green eyes began to narrow at her expression, she struck with feline swiftness. Her open palm lashed across his cheek in a stinging report, to be immediately caught in the vice-grip of his fingers.

'I won't lease you the land, the buildings, or my body,' she hissed. 'I will not become your chattel!'

She tried twisting her wrist out of his hold, but Judd wrapped it behind her back. Her other hand met the same fate and she was completely trapped in the steel circle of his arms. Deliberately he ground her hips against his, making her aware of his aroused state that had nothing to do with the anger blazing in his expression.

'You spitting little hellcat,' he jeered. 'You haven't changed. Seven years may have given you a certain amount of poise and sophistication, but underneath you're the same passionate and untamed she-devil. You want me to make love to you as much as I do.'

'No!' Valerie rushed the vigorous denial.

His upper lip curled into a taunting smile as if he knew how hollow her denial was. 'Yes, you do,' he insisted with infuriating complacency, and let her go. 'Sooner or later you'll admit it.'

Turning away smoothly, he began walking towards his horse, leaving Valerie standing there with a mouthful of angry words. She ran after him, trembling with rage.

'You'll rot in hell before I do,' she told him in a voice shaking with violence.

His green eyes flashed her a lazy, mocking look before he slipped between the rails of the board fence with an ease that belied his six-foot frame and muscled build. The tall grey horse whickered as he approached. Valerie stopped, staying on the opposite side of the fence, her hands doubled into impotent fists.

Unhooking the reins from the post, Judd looped them around the horse's neck and swung into the saddle with an expert grace. The big grey bunched its hindquarters, eager to be off at the first command from its rider, but none came. Judd looked down at her from his high vantage point in the saddle.

'I meant it when I said I wanted to buy this place,' he said flatly. 'If you decide to sell, I want you to know my interest in purchasing it is purely a business one. No other consideration will enter into the negotiations for the price.'

'I'm glad to hear it.' She struggled to control her temper and sounded cold as a result. 'Because any offer from you with strings attached will be rejected out of hand!'

His half-smile implied that he believed differently. If there had been anything within reach, Valerie would have thrown it at him. Before she could issue a withering comment to his look, her attention was distracted by the sound of someone running through the tall pasture grass.

It was Tadd, racing as fast as his short legs could carry him straight towards Judd. A breathless excitement glowed in his face, the mop of brown hair swept away from his forehead by the wind he generated with his running.

'Is that your horse?' The shrill pitch of his voice and his headlong flight towards the horse spooked the big grey. It plunged under Judd's rein, but his dancing hooves and big size didn't slow Tadd down. 'Can I have a ride?'

'Tadd, look out!' Valerie shouted the warning as the grey horse reared and it looked as if Tadd was going to run right under those pawing hooves.

In the next second he was scooped off the ground and lifted into the saddle, Judd's arms around his waist. Her knees went weak with relief.

'Hasn't your mother taught you that you don't run up to a horse like that?' Judd reprimanded the boy he held, but Valerie noticed the glint of admiration in his look that Tadd had not been afraid. 'It scares a horse. You have to let them know you're near and walk up slowly.'

'I'll remember,' Tadd promised, but with a reckless smile that reminded Valerie of Judd. 'Will you give me a ride? I've never been on a horse before.'

'You're on one now,' Judd pointed out. 'What do you think of it?'

Tadd leaned to one side to peer at the ground, his eyes slightly rounded as he straightened. 'It's kind of a long way down, isn't it?'

'You'll get used to it.' Judd lifted his gaze from the dark-haired boy to glance at Valerie. 'I'll give him a short ride around the pasture.'

'You don't have to,' she replied stiffly, and tried to figure out why she resented that Tadd was having his first ride with Judd, his father, and not her. 'Worming your way into Tadd's favour won't get you anywhere with me.'

A dangerous glint appeared in his look. 'Until this moment that hadn't occurred to me. I have a whole flock of nieces and nephews who are always begging for rides, and I lumped your son into their category. I know you're disappointed that I can't admit to a more ulterior and devious motive.'

Their exchange was sailing over Tadd's head. He couldn't follow it, but he had caught one of the things Judd had said. 'Are you going to really give me a ride?' he asked.

'If your mother gives her permission,' Judd told him in silent challenge to Valerie.

At the beseeching look from her son, she nodded

her head curtly. 'You have my permission.'

'Thank you,' Judd mocked as he reined the spirited grey away from the fence.

At a walk, they started across the grassy field. Tadd laughed and nearly bounced out of the saddle when the horse went into a trot, but he didn't sound or look the least bit frightened. After making a sweeping arc into the pasture, Judd turned the horse towards the fence and cantered him back to where Valerie was waiting.

With one hand, he swung Tadd to the ground. 'Remember what I told you. From now on, you'll *walk* up to a horse.' Tadd gave him a solemn nod of agreement. With a last impersonal glance at Valerie, Judd backed his mount away from the small boy before turning it towards its home stables.

'Come on, Tadd,' Valerie called to him. 'Let's go to the house and have something cold to drink.'

He lingered for a minute in the pasture watching Judd ride away, a sight that pulled at Valerie, too, but she resisted it. Finally he ran towards her and Valerie wondered if he knew any other speed. He ducked under the fence as if he had been doing it all his life. He skipped along beside her, chattering endlessly about the ride.

'Where did you two disappear to?' Clara asked when Valerie reached the houseyard. Her question bordered on an accusation.

'I went for a ride,' Tadd chimed out an answer, unaware he wasn't the second person Clara had meant.

'We just walked along the fence,' Valerie answered, realising a bushy shade tree had blocked her and Judd from Clara's sight.

'What was his business?' The tone was sceptical that there had been any such reason.

'He offered to buy the place,' Valerie answered, and murmured to herself, 'among other things!'

CHAPTER FIVE

AFTER much discussion and debate, Valerie persuaded Clara that the three of them should spend the summer on her grandfather's farm. She refused to be intimidated by Judd's proximity as a neighbour. This was the only chance she would ever have to show her son what it had been like for her to grow up in this house. And perhaps it would be the only time she would have to devote solely to Tadd while he was in his formative years.

Eventually she swayed Clara into going along with her. Once the agreement had been reached, they had to tackle the problem of arranging things in Cincinnati to be absent for possibly three months.

Clara's married sister agreed to send both of them more clothes from the apartments, forward their mail, and see that everything was locked up. Valerie's telephoned request to her employer for an extended leave of absence received a notification of her dismissal, as Clara had warned. But all in all, the arrangements were made with minimal complications.

Amidst it all was the decision of what to do about the farm and consultation with Jefferson Burrows, the attorney. At the end of the following week Valerie came to the decision she had known all along she would have to make. After confiding in Clara, she sought out Mickey at the stables.

Valerie came straight to the point. 'I wanted to let you know, Mick, that I've decided to sell the farm.'

Sitting in the shade of the building, cleaning some leather tack, the retired jockey didn't even glance up when she made the announcement. He spat on the leather and polished some more.

'Then you'll be selling the horses?' he asked.

'Yes, I'll have to,' she nodded.

'Since you're not keeping the place, you'll be better off to sell them soon,' Mickey advised. 'Were you going to have an auction?'

'Yes. Mr Burrows, the lawyer, said if I decided to sell the horses, an auction could be scheduled within two weeks,' she explained.

'It won't give you much time to do very much advertising,' he shrugged, 'but word has a way of getting around fast among horsemen. I'm sure you'll have a good turn-out. As soon as you set the date, I'll call some of my friends in the business and start spreading the word.'

'Thanks, Mick.'

'It's the least I can do. There is one thing, though.' He put the halter aside and stood up. 'You see that bay mare grazing off by herself?'

Valerie glanced towards the paddock he faced and saw the bay mare he meant, a sleek long-legged animal with a chestnut brown coat with black points.

'She's a beauty,' Valerie admired.

'Don't put Ginger in the auction,' Mickey said, and explained, 'She's the best get out of old Donnybrook, but she's barren, no good for breeding at all. She's got no speed, but she's a good hack, might even make it as a show jumper. But you'd never get your money's worth out of her in a breeding sale. If I was you, I'd advertise her as a hunter and try to sell her that way.'

'Thanks, I'll do that,' she promised. His thoughtfulness and ready acceptance of her decision made her feel a little guilty. This farm and these horses were practically like his own. He had lived here and taken care of all the animals here, many of them since birth. Now they were being sold and he was out of a job and a place to live. 'What will you do, Mickey? Where will you go?'

'Don't worry about me, Valerie,' he laughed. 'I've had a standing offer from Judd for years to come to work for him taking care of his young colts. He claims that I'm the best he's ever seen at handling the young ones.'

The mention of Judd's name made her glance towards the paddock again to conceal her expression. 'Judd wants to buy this,' she said.

'Are you going to sell it to him?' he asked, not surprised by her statement.

'It depends on whether or not I get an offer better than the one he makes.' Common sense made her insist that it didn't matter who ultimately purchased the property. She wouldn't be here when they took possession.

'If Judd has set his mind on buying it, he'll top any reasonable offer you get,' Mickey grinned. ''Cause once he makes up his mind he wants somethin', he seldom lets anything stand in his way till he gets it.'

It was a statement that came echoing back a week

later. Valerie was walking out of the bank in town just as Judd was coming in. Courtesy demanded that she speak to him, at least briefly.

'Hello, Judd,' she nodded with forced pleasantness, and would have walked on by him, but he stopped.

'Hello, Valerie. I saw the auction notice.' His tone sounded only conversational.

'For the horses? Yes, in less than two weeks from now,' she admitted. His gaze was inspecting her in a most bemused fashion. Valerie had the feeling a strap was showing or something, and her hand moved protectively to the elastic neckline of the peasant-styled knit top. 'Is something wrong?' she queried a bit sharply.

'You look very cool and proper with your hair fixed like that,' Judd answered. It was pulled away from her face into a loose chignon at the back of her head.

'It's a very warm day. I feel cooler if my hair is away from my neck,' Valerie replied as if her change of hairstyles required an explanation.

'It's attractive, but it isn't exactly you,' he commented in a knowing voice. Without skipping a beat, he continued, 'I suppose once all the legal arrangements are completed after the auction you'll be leaving.'

'We're staying a little longer.' She didn't see the need to tell him she would be there for the summer. He would discover it soon enough, so there was no point in informing him in advance.

'We?' A jet-dark brow lifted at the plural.

'Yes—Tadd, Clara, and myself,' Valerie admitted.

'The old battleaxe isn't leaving either, huh?' But the way he spoke the word was oddly respectful. Then his manner became withdrawn. 'I must be keeping you from your errands. Will you be at the auction?'

'Yes.' She was a bit puzzled by his behaviour and curious why he hadn't mentioned anything about buying her land.

'I'll probably see you there,' he said.

Valerie had the feeling she was being brushed off. She lifted her chin stiffly, smiled a cool, 'Probably,' and walked away.

Between that brief meeting in town and the auction, she didn't see Judd. She ignored the knotting ache in her stomach and told herself she was glad she had finally convinced him that she wanted nothing to do with him. She was positive Judd had only pursued her at the beginning of her return because he had thought she would be easy. Now he knew differently. She wasn't easy and she wasn't available.

But the way her heart catapulted at the sight of his familiar figure in the auction crowd made a mockery of her silent disclaimers of interest in him. It was a bitter admission to recognise that she was still half in love with him.

The stable and house yard was littered with cars, trucks, and horse trailers. There seemed to be an ocean of buyers, lookers, and breeders. Around the makeshift auction ring was an encircling cluster of people jostling to get a look at the brood mare up for bids.

Valerie looked for Tadd and saw him firmly holding on to Mickey's hand, as if concerned he might get separated from his friend in the shuffle of people. Another look found Judd working his way through the crowd towards the trailer being used as the auctioneer's office.

A horse neighed behind her, a nervous sound that betrayed its agitation at the unusual commotion going on around it. Valerie turned to watch a groom walking the horse in a slow circle to calm it, crooning softly. All the horses looked sleek and in excellent condition, thanks to Micky's unstinting efforts.

She glanced back to the auction ring where the rhythmic droning voice of the auctioneer was making his pitch. She walked in the opposite direction to the relative peace and quiet of the stables. Here the fever pitch of activity was reduced to a low hum as the grooms Mick had handpicked for the day prepared the brood mares and colts for the sale.

The warm air was pungent with the smell of horses. Straw rustled beneath shifting feet. Valerie wandered down the row of stalls, pausing to stroke the velvet nose thrust out towards her. She stopped at the paddock entrance to the barns and gazed out over empty pastures.

'It looks strange, doesn't it, not to see any mares grazing out there with their foals,' Judd commented with an accurate piece of mind-reading.

Valerie jumped at the sound of his voice directly behind her. 'You startled me,' she said in accusing explanation.

'Sorry,' he offered, but she doubted that he meant it. 'Is the auction going well?'

'So far,' she shrugged, and turned to look out the

half-door to the pasture. 'It's bedlam out there,' she said to explain her reason for escaping to the barns.

'A lot of buyers is what sends the prices up,' Judd reminded her. 'And, from the sound of the bidding on the number fourteen mare, Misty's Delight, she's going to bring top dollar.'

'Misty's Delight,' Valerie repeated, and released a short, throaty laugh. 'When I saw the names on the sale catalogue I didn't know any of the horses. Granddad called that mare, Misty's Delight, by the name of Maude. As far as I'm concerned, they aren't selling Black Stockings. They're auctioning Rosie, or Sally or Polly.'

'Yes, I'm glad your grandfather isn't here. Those mares were his pets, and the stallion, Donnybrook, was the most precious to him of them all,' Judd admitted.

'If Granddad was here, there wouldn't be a sale. There wouldn't be any need for one,' Valerie sighed, and turned away from the empty paddocks. 'But there is. And I'm selling. And I'm not going to have any regrets.' she finished on a note of determination.

'Have you listed the farm for sale yet?' he asked, taking it for granted that she was selling it.

Since it was true, she didn't see any point going into that side issue. 'In a way,' she answered, and explained that indecisive response. 'It won't officially be listed for another couple of weeks.'

'Why the delay?' He studied her curiously.

'I had a couple of appraisals from two local real estate agents,' Valerie began.

'Yes, I know,' Judd interrupted. 'I saw them, and I'm prepared to buy it for two thousand more than the highest price they gave you.'

She took a breath at his handsome offer and nibbled at her lip, but didn't comment on his statement. 'They suggested I'd be able to get about five thousand more if I painted all the buildings. So I'm going to take some of the profits from the horse sale and have everything painted.'

'I'll match that, and you can forget about the painting,' he countered. 'I'd just have to do it all over again in the Meadow Farms' colours.'

Leaning back against a wooden support post, Valerie eyed him warily, unable to trust him. She knew how vulnerable she was; she had only to check her racing pulse to be reminded of that. So she was doubly cautious about becoming involved in any dealings with him.

'Tell me the truth, Judd, why are you so determined to buy Worth Farms?' she demanded, her mouth thinning into a firm line.

A brow arched at her challenge as he tipped his head to one side, an indefinable glint in his eyes. 'Why are you so determined to believe that I have some other reason other than business?'

'Don't forget that I know you, Judd Prescott,' she countered.

The corners of his mouth deepened. 'You know me as intimately as any woman ever has, considerably more so than most,' he taunted her with the memory of their affair.

Her cheeks flamed hotly as conflicting emotions churned inside of her. 'I meant that I know you as a man.'

'I should hope so,' Judd drawled, deliberately misinterpreting her meaning.

'In the general sense,' she corrected in anger.

'That's a pity.' He rested a hand on the post she was leaning against, but didn't move closer. 'Meadow Farms needs your grandfather's acreage, the pastures, the grass, the hayfields. The stables and barns can be used for the weanlings and the yearlings. The house can be living quarters for any of my married help who might need it. If the old battleaxe had inherited it, I would still want to buy it. Have you got that clear, Valerie?' His level gaze was serious.

'Yes,' she nodded, a stiff gesture that held a hint of resentment.

'Good.' Judd straightened, taking his hand from the post and offering it to her to seal their bargain. 'Have we got a deal?'

'Yes.' Wary, Valerie hesitated before placing her hand in his and added the qualification, 'On purely a business level.'

'Strictly business.' He gripped her hand and let it go, a faint taunting smile on his lips. 'The matter is in the hands of our respective attorneys. We've agreed on the price, so the only thing left is for me to pay you the money for your signature deeding the land to me.'

'There's just one thing,' Valerie added.

'Oh? What's that?' Judd asked with distant curiosity.

'I'm not giving you possession of the house until the first of September. The barns, the stables, the pastures, everything else you can have when we sign the papers, except the house,' she told him.

'And why is that?' He seemed only mildly interested.

'Because that's how long we'll be staying. I want to have this summer with Tadd,' Valerie explained with a trace of defensiveness. 'With working and all, I haven't been able to spend much time with him up until now. He's been growing up with baby-sitters. I've decided to devote this summer to him and begin working again this fall when he goes back to school.'

'In that case, the house is yours until the first of September,' Judd agreed with an indifferent shrug. 'Are there any other conditions?'

'No.' She shook her head, her long toffee hair swinging freely about her shoulders.

'Then everything is all settled,' he concluded.

'I guess it is.'

It all worked as smoothly as Judd had said it would. The matter was turned over to their attorneys. There wasn't even a need for Valerie to see Judd. When all the estate, mortgage, and legal matters were completed, Jefferson Burrows brought the papers she needed to sign out to the house and gave her a cheque. The property became Judd's without any further communication between them and the documents gave her possession of the house until the first of September. It was all strictly business.

Something jumped on her bed, but the mattress didn't give much under its weight. 'Mom? You'd better get up,' Tadd insisted.

Valerie opened one sleepy eye to identify her son and rolled on to her stomach to bury her head under a pillow. 'It's early. Go back to sleep, Tadd.'

His small hand shook her bare shoulder in determined persistence. 'Mom, what's that man doing on
a ladder outside your window?' he demanded to
know.

'A ladder?' she repeated sleepily, and lifted her
head from under the pillow to frown at the pyjama-
clad boy sitting on her bed. 'What are you talking
about, Tadd?'

His attention was riveted on her bedroom window. A scraping sound drew her bleary gaze as well.
The sleep was banished from her eyes at the sight of
a strange man wearing paint-splattered white over-
alls standing on a ladder next to her window.

'What's he doing there, Mom?' Tadd frowned at
her.

There wasn't a shade at the window, nothing to
prevent the man from looking in and seeing her.
Valerie was angered by the embarrassing situation
she was in. She tugged the end of the bedspread
from the foot of the bed and pulled it with her. It
was white chenille with a pink rose design woven in
the centre. She sat up on the side of her bed with
her back to the window.

She picked up the alarm clock on the small table.
Its hands pointed to seven o'clock. She began wrapping the bedspread around her sarong fashion, fighting its length as her temper mounted. Pushing her
sleep-rumpled hair away from one side of her face
and tucking it behind her ear, she rose from the
bed.

Tadd followed. 'What's he doing there?' he repeated.

'That's what I'm about to find out!' she snapped, flinging a corner of the bedspread over her shoulder in a gesture unconsciously reminiscent of a caped Crusader.

She stalked to the staircase and hitched the bedspread up around her ankles to negotiate the steps. Part of the white bedspread trailed behind her like a train and she had to keep yanking it along to prevent Tadd from tripping on it.

As she slammed out of the screen door on to the porch, another similarly clad stranger was walking by carrying a stepladder. At the sight of Valerie, he stopped and stared.

'Would you mind telling me what's going on here?' she demanded, ignoring his incredulous and slightly ogling look. 'And where are you going with that ladder?'

'Don't look at me, ma'am.' The man backed away, absolving himself of any blame. 'I just do what I'm told. The boss said I was to come here and I'm here.'

'Where is your boss? I want to speak to him.' Valerie forgot to hitch up the spread before starting down the porch steps and nearly tripped.

'He ... he's on the other side of the house,' the man stuttered as one side of the spread slipped, revealing the initial curving swell of one breast before Valerie tucked the material back in place.

She had taken one step in the direction the flustered man had indicated when she heard the cantering beat of horse's hooves and looked to see Judd riding up on the big grey. She stopped and glanced back at the man.

'You can go on about your business now,' she snapped.

'Yes, ma'am!' He scurried off as if he had been shot.

Tadd stood on the porch, one bare foot resting on top of the other. He was watching the proceedings with innocent interest. curious and wide-eyed. Like his mother, his attention had become focused on Judd who was dismounting to walk to the house. Valerie stepped forward to confront him.

'Would you like to explain to me what these men are doing here at this hour of the morning?' she demanded, her nostrils distending slightly in temper.

'I came by to let you know I'd hired a contractor to paint the place. I think I'm a little late.' As he spoke, his gaze was making a leisurely inspection from her tousled mane of honey-dark hair down her bedspread-wrapped length and returning for an overall view of her alluring déshabille.

At the touch of his green-eyed gaze on her bare shoulder and its lingering interest on the point where the white material jutted out to cover her breast, Valerie tugged the spread more tightly around her. She realised that he was very much aware she was naked beneath it.

'A little late is an understatement,' she fumed. 'I woke up this morning to find a man outside my bedroom window on a ladder!'

'If I'd known you slept in the altogether, I would have been the man on the ladder outside your window,' Judd drawled with soft suggestiveness.

An irritated sound of exasperation came from her

throat. 'It's impossible talking to you. I'll speak to the contractor myself and tell him to come back at a decent hour!' As she started to take a step, her leg became tangled in the folds of the bedspread.

Judd reached out with a steadying hand on her arm. 'I think you'd better go back into the house before you trip and reveal more of your considerable charms than you'd like.' He lifted her off her feet and into his arms before she could suspect his intention. The bedspread swaddled her into a cocoon that didn't lend itself to movement.

'Put me down!' Valerie raged in fiery embarrassment.

A lazy smile curved his mouth as he looked down at her. 'I hired house painters, not nude artists. Not that I wouldn't object to having a private portrait of you.'

She caught sight of Tadd staring at them with open-mouthed amazement. 'Will you stop it?' she hissed at Judd, and he just chuckled, knowing she was at his mercy.

'Will you open the door for me, Tadd,' he requested in an amused voice as he carried Valerie on to the porch.

Tadd scampered forward in his bare feet to comply, staring at Valerie's reddened face as Judd carried her past him. He followed them inside, letting the screen door close with a resounding bang. In the entry-hall, Judd stopped.

'Now will you put me down?' Valerie demanded through clenched teeth, burning with mortification and a searing awareness of her predicament.

'Of course,' he agreed with mocking compliance.

The arm at the back of her legs relaxed its hold, letting her feet slide to the floor while his other hand retained a light, steadying grip around her waist. Having both feet on the floor didn't give Valerie any feeling of advantage. Without shoes, the top of her head barely reached past his chin. To see his face, she had to tip her head back, a much too vulnerable position. She chose instead to glare upward through the sweep of her lashes.

'I think it would be wise if you put some clothes on,' he suggested dryly as his gaze swung downward from her face, 'or at least, rearrange your sarong so that pink rose adorns a less eye-catching spot.'

His finger traced the outline of a rosebud design on the chenille bedspread. In doing so, he drew a circle around the hard button of her breast. Heat raced over her skin as Valerie jerked the bedspread higher, pulling the rose design almost to her collarbone. Judd chuckled for the second time, knowing how deeply he had disturbed her.

Spinning away from him, Valerie lifted the folds of the material up around her knees and bolted for the staircase. On the second step she stopped, remembering the predicament that waited for her upstairs. She sent an angry look over her shoulder.

'You go out there and tell that painter to get away from my window!' she ordered in an emotion-choked voice.

'I'll have him on the ground at once.' Judd grinned at her, laughter dancing wickedly in his eyes.

Valerie glanced at the boy standing beside him.

'Tadd, you come with me,' she commanded. 'It's time you were dressed, too.'

Reluctantly Tadd moved towards the stairs. As Judd started towards the door, Valerie began climbing the steps to the second floor. Clara met her at the head of the stairs, her nightgown ruffling out from beneath the hem of her quilted robe.

'What's all the commotion about?' Clara ran a frowning look over Valerie's attire. 'And what are you doing dressed like that?'

'Mr Prescott neglected to inform us that he'd hired some painters to come out to the farm,' was the short-tempered reply. 'I woke up to find one outside my window on a ladder.' Bunching the spread more tightly around her hips, Valerie started towards her bedroom.

'I've told you about going to bed like that,' Clara's reproving voice followed her. 'Haven't I warned you that some day there would be a fire or something and you'd be caught!'

Valerie stopped abruptly to make a sharp retort and Tadd, who was following close behind her, bumped into her. Her hand gripped his shoulder to steady him and remained there as she sent Clara a look that would have withered the leaves from a mighty oak, but Clara was made of stronger stuff.

Swallowing the remark she had intended to make, Valerie muttered, 'You're a lot of comfort, Clara,' and glanced at the small boy. 'Come on, Tadd. Let's get you dressed first.'

Altering her course, she pushed Tadd ahead of her to her old bedroom that Tadd now occupied.

While she went to the dresser to get his clean clothes, Tadd padded to the window and peered out.

'I don't see those men any more, Mommy. Judd made them go away,' he told her.

'Good. Now off with those pyjamas and into these clothes,' she ordered curtly.

When Tadd was dressed, Valerie sent him downstairs and went to her own room. She made certain there wasn't a painter anywhere near the vicinity of her window before getting dressed herself. When she came downstairs she walked to the kitchen where the aroma of fresh-perked coffee wafted invitingly in the air.

Tadd was sitting at the breakfast table. An elbow was resting on the top, a small hand supported his forehead, pushing his brown hair on end. A petulant scowl marked his expression.

'Mom, Clara says I have to drink some of my milk before I have another pancake.' He glared at the stout woman standing at the stove. 'Do I have to? Can't I drink it afterwards, Mom? Please?'

Valerie glanced at the glass of white liquid that hadn't been touched. 'Drink your milk, Tadd.'

'Aw, Mom!' he grumbled, and reached for the glass.

'Don't fix any pancakes for me, Clara.' Ignoring her son, Valerie walked to the counter and poured a cup of coffee. 'I'm not hungry.'

'You'd better eat something,' the woman insisted.

Before Valerie could argue the point, there was a knock on the back door and a taunting voice asked, 'Are you decent in there?'

'Yes!' Valerie shot the sharply affirmative retort

at the wire mesh where Judd's dark figure was outlined, and carried her cup to the table.

The hinges creaked as the screen door opened and
Judd walked in. 'The coffee smells good,' he remarked. After one dancing look at Valerie's still
simmering expression, he addressed his next words
to Clara. 'Do you mind if I have a cup?'

'Help yourself,' the woman shrugged indiffer-
ently.

As he walked to the counter where the coffee pot
sat, Valerie watched the easy way he moved. The
broadness of his shoulders and chest, the narrowing
to male hips, and the muscled columns of his long
legs moved in perfect harmony. His body was pro-
grammed and conditioned to perform every task
well. An ache quivered through her as Valerie remembered how well.

Pausing at the stove, Judd observed, 'Pancakes
for breakfast. Buckwheat?'

'Yes.' Clara expertly flipped one from the griddle.

'Help yourself, Judd.' Valerie heard herself offering in a caustic tone born out of a sense of inevita-
bility. In an agitated desire for movement she rose
from her chair to add more coffee to her steaming
cup. 'Orange juice. Bacon. Toast.' She listed the
choices. 'Just help yourself to anything.'

'Anything?' The soft, lilting word crossed the
room to taunt her. She pivoted and caught her
breath as his gaze leisurely roamed over her shape
to let her know his choice.

She felt as if her toes were curling from the
heat spreading through her. She turned away from
his disturbing look and breathed an emotionally-

charged, 'You know very well what I meant.' Adding a drop more coffee to her cup, Valerie silently acknowledged that she didn't have many defences against him left, certainly none when the topic became intimate. She attempted to change it. 'Did you straighten those painters out about starting work at such an hour?' she demanded.

'In a manner of speaking,' Judd replied, casually accepting the change in subject matter. 'They started early to avoid working in the heat of the day. Unfortunately, they were under the impression that all the buildings were vacant, including the house. They know better now,' he added with faint suggestiveness.

Valerie didn't need to be reminded of the early morning episode. The absence of a direct answer to her first question prompted her to ask, 'You did arrange for them to begin work at a more respectable hour, didn't you?'

'No,' he denied. 'There isn't any reason to change their working hours——'

'No reason?' she began indignantly.

But Judd continued, 'However, from now on they'll be working on the barns and stables in the mornings.'

'I should hope so,' Valerie retorted tightly.

'I drank some of my milk,' Tadd piped up, a white moustache above his upper lip. 'Can I have another pancake now?' Clara set another one in front of him. As Tadd reached for the syrup, he glanced at Judd. 'They're very good. Do you want one?'

'No, thank you. I've already had my breakfast.'

Judd drained the last of the coffee from his cup. 'It's time I was leaving. If the painters give you any trouble, Valerie, call me.'

'I will,' she agreed, but she could have told him that the only one who gave her trouble was himself. He troubled her mentally and emotionally, and there didn't seem to be any relief in sight.

CHAPTER SIX

A RESTLESSNESS raced through Valerie. She tried to contain it as she had for the last several days, but it wouldn't be suppressed. There had been too much time on her hands lately, she used as a cause. She was accustomed to working eight hours, coming home and working eight hours more with meals, housework, and wash. But here the workload of the house was shared with Clara and she had no job except to play with Tadd.

One of the painters had a radio blaring a raucous brand of music that scraped at her nerves. Of the half a dozen men painting the barns and stables, there always seemed to be one walking around, getting paint, moving ladders, doing something, which was more than Valere could say for herself.

Sighing, she left the porch and entered the house. Clara was in the living room, watching her favourite soap opera on television. Her gaze was glued to the screen and she didn't even glance up when Valerie entered the room.

'Clara,' Valerie began, only to be silenced by an upraised hand. A couple of minutes later a commercial came on and she was allowed to finish what she had started to say. 'I'm going to take Ginger out for a ride. Tadd is upstairs having a nap. Will you keep an eye on him while I'm gone?'

'Sure. Go ahead,' her friend agreed readily.

Outside, Valerie dodged the gauntlet of ladders and paint cans to retrieve the bridle and saddle from the tack room. Several people had been out to look at the bay mare Micky Flanners had suggested she sell privately, but so far no one had bought her. Valerie didn't mind. One horse wasn't that difficult to take care of and Tadd enjoyed the rides she took him on.

The bay mare trotted eagerly to the pasture fence when she approached. Lonely without her former equine companionship, the mare readily sought human company. There was never any difficulty catching her and she accepted the bit between her teeth like it was sugar.

Astride the animal, Valerie turned the brown head towards the rolling land of the empty pasture. The mare stepped out quickly, moving into a brisk canter at a slight touch from Valerie's heel. She had no destination in mind. Her only intention was to try to run off this restlessness that plagued her.

The long-legged thoroughbred mare seemed prepared to run for ever, clearing pasture fences like the born jumper Mickey had claimed she was. Valerie rode without concentrating on anything but the rhythmic stride of the animal beneath her and the pointed ears of its bobbing head.

When the bay horse slowed to a walk, Valerie wasn't aware that it was responding to her pressure on the reins. They entered a stand of trees and she ducked her head to avoid a low-hanging branch. When she straightened, it was in a clearing. Her fingers tightened on the reins, stopping the bay, as the blood drained from her face.

Unconsciously she had guided the mare to the place where she and Judd had met. From a long-ago habit, she dismounted and wound the reins around the broken branch of a tree. The mare lowered her head, blew at the grass and began to graze.

Almost in a trance, Valerie looked around her. The place hadn't seemed to change very much. The grass looked taller and thicker, promising a softer bed. She tore her gaze from it and noticed that lightning had taken a large limb from the oak tree some time ago.

Wrapping her arms tightly around her stomach, she tried to assuage the hollow ache. There was a longing for Judd so intense that it seemed to eat away at her insides. She wanted to cry from the joy she had once known here and the heartache that had followed, but no tears came.

It was crazy—it was foolish—it was destroying to want him. She was so successful at stimulating his lusty appetite, why hadn't she ever been able to arouse his love? she wondered. She was so filled with love that she thought she would explode.

The bay mare lifted her head, her ears pricking. Her sides heaved with a long, questioning whicker. Then the soft swish of grass behind her made Valerie turn as a big grey horse stopped at the edge of the clearing and Judd dismounted. He walked towards her with smooth, unhurried strides like a page from the past. Her heart lodged somewhere in the vicinity of her throat. She was unable to speak, half afraid that she might discover she was dreaming.

But his voice was no dream: 'I knew you'd come

here sooner or later.' Neither was the smouldering light in his green eyes as he came closer.

The instant he touched her, Valerie was convinced it wasn't a dream and she knew she didn't dare stay. 'It was an accident,' she insisted, her breath quickening. 'I didn't mean to come here.'

She tried to push out of his arms and make her way past him, but a sinewed arm hooked her waist and pulled her against his side. A muscled thigh brushed her legs apart to rub against her, while the hand at the small of her back pressed her close to him. His fingers cupped the side of her face and lifted it for inspection.

'Ever since the day you returned, I knew you would eventually come here.' His gaze roamed possessively over her features. 'You can't fight it any more than I can. It's always been that way with us.'

'Yes.' Her whispered agreement carried the throb of admission.

As his mouth descended on to hers, Valerie realised his persistence had finally eroded her resolve. The surroundings, her love, the feel of him were more than she could withstand and she surrendered to the pulsing fire of his embrace.

Her lips parted under the insistence of his. His practised hands moulded her more fully against his length, but it only heightened their mutual dissatisfaction with their upright position.

Burying his face in the curve of her neck, Judd swept her into his arms and carried her the few feet to the grassy nest. Kneeling, he laid her upon it, lifting the heavy mass of tawny hair and fanning it above her head. Her hands were around his neck to pull him down beside her, part of his weight crushing on to her.

'I've waited a long time to see that honey-cloud of hair on that green pillow.' His husky voice vibrated with passion. 'And to see that love-drugged look in your cat-eyes.'

His mouth kissed the hollow of her throat as his skilled fingers unbuttoned her blouse. His hand wandered over the bareness of her waist and taut stomach. It's leisurely pace sent a languorous feeling floating through her limbs. His mouth trailed a fiery path to intimately explore the rounded softness of her breast. Her nails dug into the rippling muscles of his back and Judd brought his hard lips back to hers. More of his weight moved on to her.

He rubbed his mouth against the outline of her lips. 'There were times when I wondered whether I had the control or the patience to wait for you to come here,' he admitted. 'I knew you'd been hurt and used badly. But I was also positive that I could make you forget the man who got you pregnant and ran off.'

'Forget?' Her breathless laugh was painful and bitter, because he had made her forget. With a twist, she rolled from beneath him and staggered to her feet, shakily buttoning her blouse. 'How could I forget?' The questioning statement was issued to herself. 'You are that man, Judd.'

Stunned silence greeted her tautly spoken announcement. Then Valerie heard him rise and a steel claw hooked her elbow to spin her around. A pair of blazing green eyes burned into her face.

'What are you saying?' Judd ground out savagely.

'You're Tadd's father,' she informed him with flashing defiance. 'I was almost three months pregnant when I left here seven years ago. Granddad threw me out because I wouldn't tell him who the father was. It was you ... you and your damned virility!'

'If it's true, why didn't you come to me seven years ago and tell me you were pregnant?' Judd demanded.

'If it's true?' Valerie repeated with a taunting laugh. 'You just answered your own question, Judd. You're the one and only man who has ever made love to me. But to you, I was just a cheap little tramp.'

'That isn't true,' he denied.

'Isn't it?' she mocked. 'Why should I have endured the humiliation of telling you and have you question whether you were responsible?'

'I would have helped you,' Judd replied grimly.

'What would you have done?' Valerie challenged. 'Given me money for an abortion? Or paid me hush money to keep quiet about your part in it? You made me feel small enough without taking money from you.'

'I never guessed you felt that way.' A muscle in his jaw was flexing.

'I don't think you ever considered the possibility that I had feelings,' she retorted. 'I'm a human being with feelings and a heart, Judd. I'm not made of stone like you. Look—I even bleed.' She scratched her nails across the inside of her arm, tiny drops of red appearing in the welts.

He caught at the hand that had marked her. 'You

crazy little fool!' he growled, and yanked her into his arms, crushing her tightly against him, the point of his chin rubbing the top of her head.

For an instant Valerie let herself enjoy the hard comfort of his arms before she rebelled. 'Let me go, Judd.' She strained against his hold. 'Haven't you done enough?'

He partially released her, keeping one arm firmly around her shoulders as he drew her along with him. 'Come on.'

'No!' She didn't know where he was taking her.

Stopping in front of the bay mare, Judd lifted her into the saddle. 'I'm taking you back,' he said, and handed her the reins.

'I can find my own way,' she retorted. 'I always did before.'

His hand held the mare's bridle, preventing Valerie from reining her away. 'This time I'm going with you,' he stated.

'Why?' Valerie watched him with a wary eye when he walked to the big grey.

Judd didn't respond until he had mounted and ridden the high-stepping grey over beside her. 'I'd like to have another look at my son.'

Her fingers tightened on the reins and the mare tossed her head in protest. 'Tadd is mine. You merely fathered him. He's mine, Judd,' she warned.

He didn't argue the point and instead gestured for her to lead the way to her grandfather's farm, one that Judd now owned. They cantered in silence, their horses skittish and nervous, picking up the tenseness of their riders.

Tadd had awakened from his nap when they arrived. He didn't rush out to greet Valerie, but remained sitting on the porch step, sulking because she had gone riding without him. Valerie was nervous as she walked to the house with Judd. Tadd was no longer just another little boy to him. He was his son and his green eyes were studying, inspecting and appraising the small boy.

'Did you have a good nap, Tadd?' Valerie asked with forced brightness.

'Why didn't you wait until I was up and take me for a ride?' he pouted.

'Because I wanted to go by myself,' she answered, and promised, 'You and I can go later this afternoon.'

'Okay,' Tadd sighed, accepting the alternative, and glanced at Judd. 'Hello. How come you were riding if Mom wanted to be by herself?'

'We happened to meet each other while I was on my way here,' Judd explained easily, his attention not wavering from Tadd's face.

'Were you coming over here to tell those men to go away?' Tadd wondered. 'There hasn't been any man outside Mommy's window since that other day. But one of them gave me a brush—I'll show you.' In a flash, he was on his feet and darting to the far end of the porch.

Judd slid a brief glance in Valerie's direction. 'Have you told him anything about ... his father?' he asked quietly.

'No.' She shook her head.

But his voice hadn't been pitched so softly that

Tadd hadn't picked up a piece of the conversation. He came back, holding up a worn-out brush that had not been used in some time. The bristles were stiff and broken.

As he showed it to Judd, he glanced up. 'I don't have a father. Do you?'

Judd's dark head lifted in faint surprise. Valerie couldn't tell whether it was from Tadd's directness or the acuteness of his hearing. Bemusement softened the corners of the hard male mouth.

'Yes, I had one, but he died a long time ago,' Judd admitted, and tipped his head to one side to study Tadd more closely as he asked, 'Did your father die?'

'No. I don't have a father,' Tadd repeated with childlike patience. 'Some kids don't you know,' he informed Judd with blinking innocence. 'Three of the kids I go to school with don't have dads. Of course, Cindy Tomkins has two.' He lost interest in that subject. 'It's a pretty neat brush, isn't it?'

'It sure is,' Judd agreed.

'I wanted to help them paint, but they said I couldn't. They said I was too little.' Tadd's mouth twisted, his expression indicating it was a statement he had heard many times before. 'I'll be seven on my next birthday. That isn't too little, is it?'

'I think you have to be ten years old before you can be a painter,' Judd told him.

Valerie's nerves were wearing thin. There wasn't much more of this conversation she could tolerate. Judd had seen Tadd again and talked to him. Surely that was enough?

'Tadd, why don't you run into the house and see if there isn't a carrot in the refrigerator for Ginger. I think she'd like one,' she suggested.

'Okay.' He started to turn and stopped. 'Can I feed it to her?'

'Of course,' she nodded, and he was off, slamming the screen door and tearing through the house to the kitchen. Feeling the scrutiny of Judd's eyes, her gaze slid in his direction and glanced away.

'He isn't too familiar with the birds and the bees, is he?' Judd commented dryly. 'Some children don't have a father,' he repeated Tadd's statement. 'Is that what you told him?'

'No, it's a conclusion he's reached all on his own. He has a general idea about the birds and the bees, but he hasn't comprehended the significance of it,' Valerie admitted, a shade defensively.

'What are you going to do when he does?' His level gaze never wavered from her. 'What will you tell him when he asks about his father?'

'When he's old enough to ask the question, he'll be old enough to understand the truth,' she retorted, knowing it was a day she didn't look forward to.

The sound of racing feet approached the porch in advance of the screen door banging open. 'I got the carrot!' Tadd held it up. 'Can I give it to Ginger now?'

At the nod from Valerie, Tadd started down the porch steps. As he went past Judd, he was cautioned, 'Remember, Tadd, walk up to the horse.'

With a carefree, 'I will!' Tadd raced full speed halfway across the yard, then stopped to walk the rest of the way to the pasture fence where the bay mare was tied. Valerie watched him slowly feed the gentle mare.

'I feel that I owe you something for these last seven years,' Judd said.

'You don't owe me anything.' She shrugged away the suggestion, the idea stinging.

'I mean it, Valerie. I want to take care of you and Tadd,' he stated in a firm tone.

The full fury of her sparkling eyes was directed at him. 'I wouldn't take your money then, Judd, and I won't take it now.'

Instead of being angry, Judd looked amused by her fiery display. His gaze ran over her upturned face, alight with temper and pride.

'Tigress,' he murmured. 'All this doesn't change anything.'

Unable to hold that look, Valerie glanced away. She seemed incapable of resisting him, but she tried anyway. 'Yes, it does.'

'Valerie.' His voice commanded her attention. When she didn't obey, his fingers caught her chin and turned her to face him. 'It isn't any use fighting it.'

'I've made up my mind, Judd,' she insisted stiffly. 'I won't be your lover. Please! Just leave me alone.'

His mouth slanted in amusement. 'Do you think I haven't tried?' he mocked, and kissed her hard. When he straightened, he murmured, 'And tell that battleaxe that it's impolite to eavesdrop.' With that, he turned and walked across the yard to where the grey hunter was next to Valerie's mare.

The screen door opened and Clara stepped out.

'Humphh!' she snorted. 'So it's impolite to eaves-drop, is it? What do you suppose they call what he was proposing?'

'You shouldn't have been listening,' Valerie said, and continued to watch Judd who had stopped to say goodbye to Tadd.

'You shouldn't carry on private conversations where people can overhear,' Clara retorted. 'So you decided to tell him he was the boy's father, did you?'

'Yes,' Valerie admitted.

'What do you suppose he's going to do about it?'

'There isn't anything he can do. Tadd is mine. Judd knows that,' Valerie insisted.

'Mark my words, he'll figure out a way to use it to his advantage. Judd Prescott is a tenacious man.' There was a hint of admiration in her voice as Clara watched him ride away.

CHAPTER SEVEN

TWICE more that week Judd called ostensibly to check on the progress of the painting crew, but that possessive light was in his eyes whenever his gaze met Valerie's. It held a warning or a promise, depending on her mood at the time. His attitude towards Tadd remained relatively casual, a little more interested and occasionally warmer at different moments.

Valerie was in the kitchen helping Clara wash the breakfast dishes when a car drove into the yard. The painting crew had finished the day before, so she knew it wasn't one of them. As she walked to the front door, she wiped her hands dry on the towel and wondered if the lawyer, Jefferson Burrows, had more papers for her to sign.

Judd's visits had always been made on horseback. It hadn't occurred to her that the car might have been driven by him. Not until she saw him step out. Tadd was outside playing and immediately stopped what he was doing to rush forward to greet Judd.

After sending one green-eyed glance at Valerie standing on the porch, Judd directed his attention on the boy skipping along beside him. His hair gleamed jet black in the sunlight, with Tadd's a lighter hue.

'Do you have anything planned to do today?' Judd asked him.

'Mom and me are going riding later on,' Tadd answered after thinking for a minute.

'That's something you could do tomorrow if you have a place to visit today, isn't it?' Judd suggested, and Valerie felt a tiny leap of alarm.

'I guess so,' Tadd agreed, then frowned. 'But we don't have a place to visit.' The frown lifted. 'How come you drove a car? Are you going to take us some place?'

'I might,' was the smiling response.

'Tadd, come into the house and wash your hands!' Valerie called sharply.

With a gleeful expression, Tadd came bounding to the porch hopping excitedly from one foot to the other. 'Mom, did you hear? Judd said he might take us some place.'

'Yes, I heard what he said.' She sent Judd an angry look and attempted to smile at her son. 'Go into the house and wash your hands like you were told.'

'Find out where we're going?' Tadd asked over his shoulder, and hurried into the house.

Descending the porch steps, Valerie walked out to confront Judd. 'Why did you tell Tadd we might be going some place with you?' she demanded angrily. 'It isn't fair to raise a little boy's hopes up like that.'

'Why?' He returned her look with feigned innocence. 'I came over to ask you and Tadd to spend the day with me. There's a tobacco auction over by Lothian, probably one of the last of the season. I thought Tadd might find it interesting.'

'I'm sure he would find it very interesting, but we

aren't going,' she stated flatly. 'And you shouldn't have let Tadd think we would.'

'How did I know you'd refuse?' he smiled lazily. 'I hadn't even asked you yet when I mentioned it to him.'

'You knew very well I'd refuse!' she snapped.

'Temper, temper, little spitfire,' Judd taunted.

'Of course I'm angry,' Valerie defended. 'You've made me the villain as far as Tadd is concerned.'

'You could always change your mind and agree to come with me,' he reminded her.

'You know I won't.'

'Yes you will.' His level gaze became deadly serious. 'Otherwise I'll have to have a talk with Tadd and tell him who his father is.'

Valerie paled. 'You wouldn't do that?' she protested. 'He wouldn't understand. He'd be hurt and confused. You wouldn't be that ruthless!'

'I'll have my way, Valerie.' It wasn't an idle warning. 'Will you come or shall I have a talk with Tadd?'

Tears burned the back of her eyes and she bit the inside of her lip to keep it from quivering. She had known he was hard, and not above using people to get what he wanted, and he'd already made it plain that he wanted her.

'If I agree to come, will you give me your word to say nothing to Tadd about being his father?' she demanded tightly.

'You have my word,' Judd agreed, 'if you come.'

'I ... I'll need a few minutes to change my clothes,' Valerie requested.

His skimming gaze conveyed the message that he

prefered her without any, but he said, 'Take all the time you need. I'll be waiting.'

Frustrated, Valerie ground out, 'You can wait until hell freezes over and it still won't do any good!' Pivoting on her heel, she rushed into the house.

Fifteen minutes later she emerged cool and composed in a yellow-flowered cotton sundress. Tadd's face and hands had been scrubbed and inspected by Clara, his shirt and pants changed to a clean set. Valerie couldn't help thinking that the three of them probably looked like your ideal American family, leaving on a day's outing to a tobacco auction in Lothian, Maryland. It hurt to know that they would never be a family in the legal sense, but Tadd's steady stream of chatter didn't give Valerie any time to dwell on that.

The sights, sounds, and smells of the tobacco auction proved to be as fascinating to Valerie as they were to Tadd. Various grades of Maryland tobacco were sold off in lots. The rhythmic cadence of the auctioneer's voice rang through the area, the slurring words, punctuated by a clear 'Sold!' at the end. The summer air was aromatically pungent with the smell of stacks of drying tobacco leaves. Colours varied from dark gold to brown.

They wandered around the auction area and strolled through the warehouse. Tadd saw most of the scene from Judd's shoulders. They had a cold drink beneath a shade tree.

Later, Judd drove to a park and they picnicked from a basket his mother had packed. Through it all, Judd was at his charming best and Valerie found herself succumbing to his spell as if she didn't have better sense.

She took his hand, accepted the arm that occasionally encircled her shoulders, smiled into the green eyes that glinted at her, and warmed under the feather kisses Judd would bestow on the inside of her wrist or her hair. In spite of her better judgment, she relaxed and enjoyed his company, flirting with him and feeling carelessly happy all the while.

As they lingered at the picnic area, Judd peeled an orange and began feeding her sections while Tadd played on the swings. Each time a bead of juice formed on her lips he kissed it away until Tadd demanded his share of the attention by handing Judd an orange to peel for him.

When they started back in the early afternoon, Valerie was too content to care that it would soon be over. She closed her eyes and listened to the mostly one-sided conversation between Tadd and Judd. A faint smile tugged at the corners of her mouth at Tadd's domination.

The miles sped away beneath the swiftly turning tyres. Valerie guessed that they were almost home, but she didn't want to open her eyes to see how close they were. A large male hand took hold of one of hers. Her lashes slowly lifted to watch Judd carry it to his mouth, kissing the sensitive palm. His gaze left the road in front of him long enough to send one lazy, sweeping glance at her.

'Did you enjoy yourself today?' he asked softly.

'Yes, very much,' she admitted.

Tadd, who couldn't be silent for long cried, 'Look at all the horses, Mommy!'

Dragging her gaze from Judd's compelling profile, she glanced out of the window. The familiar black fences of Meadow Farms were on either side of the car. She sat up straighter, realising Judd had turned off the road that would have taken them to her grandfather's farm.

'Where are we going?' she asked. There was only one destination possible at the end of this lane, the headquarters of Meadow Farms.

'Are we going to see the horses?' Tadd asked, leaning over the seat.

'There's someone who wants to see you,' Judd answered, glancing in Tadd's direction.

'See me?' His voice almost squeaked in disbelief. 'Who?'

'Who?' Valerie echoed the demand, a quiver of uncertainty racing through her.

'Mickey Flanners,' Judd answered. 'When I mentioned I'd be seeing you today, he asked me to bring you over if we had time.'

'I haven't seen Mickey in a long time,' Tadd declared in a tone that exaggerated the time span.

'That's what he said.' Judd slowed the car as the lane split ahead of them.

In one direction were the stables and barns of the thoroughbred breeding farm; in the other direction was the main house where the Prescotts lived. Judd made the turn in the latter direction. Valerie, who had relaxed upon learning it was Mickey Flanners they were going to see, felt her nerves stretching tense.

The lane curled into a circular driveway in front of a large pillared house, glistening white in the bright afternoon sunlight. To Valerie, it appeared the embodiment of gracious living, a sharp contrast to the simple farmhouse where she was raised.

'Is *this* where Mickey lives?' Tadd asked in an awed voice.

'No, this is where I live,' Judd explained, stopping the car in front of the main entrance to the house. He glanced at Valerie and saw the hesitation in her gold-flecked eyes. 'I'd be on my mother's black list if I don't stop at the house first so she can say hello to you and Tadd.'

'Judd, really——' Valerie started to protest, but it was too late.

The front door of the house had opened and Judd's mother was coming out to greet them, petite and striking with those angel wings of silver in her dark hair. The white pleated skirt and the blue and white polka-dot top with a matching short-sleeved jacket in blue that Maureen Prescott wore was so casually elegant that Valerie felt self-conscious about her becoming but simple cotton sundress.

'Here's Mother now.' Judd opened his door and stepped out.

It wasn't manners that kept Valerie inside the car. The magnificent house, the beautifully landscaped grounds, the status attached to the Prescott name, and the woman waiting on the portico warned her that she was out of her league.

Her door was opened and Judd stood waiting, a hand extended to help her out of the car. She turned her troubled and uncertain gaze to him. He seemed to study it with a trace of amusement that didn't make her feel any more comfortable.

'What happened to my tigress?' he chided softly. 'You look like a shy little kitten. Come on.' He reached in and took her hand to draw her out of the car.

Once she was standing beside him, Judd retained his hold of her hand. Valerie absorbed strength from his touch, but the twinges of unease didn't completely go away. It seemed a very long way from the car up the walk to the steps leading to the columned portico. To cover her nervousness, Valerie held herself more stiffly erect, her chin lifted a fraction of an inch higher than normal, her almond gold eyes wide and proud.

Tadd didn't appear to suffer from any of Valerie's pangs of self-consciousness. He skipped and hopped, turned and looked, and generally let his curious eyes take in everything there was to see. He exhibited no shyness at all when the unknown woman walked forward to meet them.

'Hello, Valerie. I'm so glad you were able to call in,' Judd's mother greeted her warmly, a smile of welcome curving her mouth.

'Thank you, Mrs Prescott,' Valerie answered, and suddenly wished that Judd would let go of her hand, but he didn't.

'Please, call me Maureen,' the other woman insisted with such friendliness that Valerie was reminded her reputation as hostess was without equal.

This open acceptance of her only made Valerie more uneasy. 'That's very kind of you ... Maureen.' She faltered stiffly over the name.

Maureen Prescott either didn't notice or overlooked Valerie's stilted tones as she turned to Tadd, bending slightly at the waist. 'And you must be Tadd.'

After an admitting bob of his head, he asked, 'How did you know me?'

The woman's smile widened. 'I've heard a lot about you.'

'Who are you?' Tadd wanted to know.

'I'm ... Judd's mother.'

Did Valerie imagine it or had there been a pulse-beat of hesitation before Maureen Prescott had explained her relationship? Then Valerie realised she was being ridiculously over-sensitive to the situation.

'Say hello to Mrs Prescott, Tadd,' Valerie prompted her son.

Dutifully he extended a hand to the woman facing him and recited politely, 'Hello, Mrs Prescott.'

'Mrs Prescott is quite a mouthful, isn't it?' The teasing smile on Maureen's lips was warm with understanding. 'Why don't you call me Reeny, Tadd?' she suggested.

'Reeny is what my nieces and nephews call her,' Judd explained quietly to Valerie. 'When they were little, they couldn't pronounce her given name, so they shortened.'

Valerie was uncomfortably aware that Tadd had been given permission to use the same name that the other grandchildren called their grandmother. She felt the creeping warmth of embarrassment in her cheeks. Did Maureen Prescott know Tadd was her grandchild? Had Judd told her?

Almost in panic, she searched the woman's face

for any indication of hidden knowledge. But the turquoise eyes were clear without a trace of cognisance. A tremor of relief quaked through Valerie. She wasn't sure she could have handled it if this genteel woman had known the truth.

'Reeny is nice,' Tadd agreed to the name.

'I'm glad you like it, Tadd.' Maureen Prescott straightened and cast an apologetic smile at Judd. 'Frank Andrews called and left a mesage for you to phone him the instant you came back.' With a glance at Valerie, she added, 'It seems every time a person tries to set aside a day strictly for pleasure, something urgent like this crops up.'

Valerie's head moved in a rigid nod of understanding before a slight movement from Judd drew her attention. A look of grim resignation had thinned his mouth and added a glitter of impatience to his eyes.

'I'm sorry, Valerie,' he apologised for the intrusion of business. 'But it'll only take a few minutes to phone him.'

'That's all right. Go ahead,' she insisted, and untangled her fingers from the grip of his to clasp her hands nervously in front of her.

'While Judd is making his phone call, you and Tadd can come with me. After that long drive, I'm sure you're thirsty and I have a big pitcher of lemonade all made, as well as some cookies,' Judd's mother invited.

'No, thank you, Mrs Prescott ... Maureen,' Valerie refused quickly, and reached for Tadd's hand. 'It's very kind of you, but Tadd and I will walk down to the stables and find Mickey.'

'You'll do no such thing, Valerie.' Judd's low voice rumbled through the air with ominous softness. Her sideways glance saw the hardened jaw and angry fire in his eyes. His look held a silent warning not to persist in her refusal of the invitation. 'I'll be through in a few minutes to take you myself. In the meantime I'm sure Tadd,' his gaze flicked to the boy, 'would like to have some cookies and lemonade. Wouldn't you, Tadd?'

'Yes.' The response was quick and without hesitation, followed by an uncertain glance at Valerie. 'Please,' Tadd added.

'Very well,' Valerie agreed, smiling stiffly, and added a defensive, 'If you are sure we aren't putting you to any trouble?'

'None at all,' Judd's mother assured her, and turned to walk towards the front door.

Judd's fingers dug into the flesh of Valerie's arm in a punishing grip as he escorted her up the steps to the portico. At the double wide entrance to the house, he let her go to open the door for his mother, then waited for her and Tadd to precede him inside.

'Excuse me.' Almost immediately upon entering, Judd took his leave from them. 'I won't be long.' His look warned Valerie that he expected to find her in the house when he was finished.

'We'll be on the veranda, Judd,' his mother told him.

As Valerie watched him walk away, she suddenly became conscious of the expansive foyer dominated by a grand staircase rising to the second floor. The foyer was actually an enormously wide hallway splitting the house down the centre with rooms branching off from it.

Furniture gleamed with the rich-grained lustre of hardwood. Vases of flowers and art objects adorned their tops. Valerie took a tighter grip on Tadd's hand, knowing she couldn't afford to replace anything he might accidentally break. It was a stunning, artfully decorated home, elegance and beauty blended to comfort, like something out of the pages of a magazine.

'We'll go this way.' Maureen Prescott started forward to lead the way, the clicking sound of her heels on the white-tiled floor echoing through the massive house.

'You have a lovely home.' Valerie felt obligated to make some comment, but her tone made the compliment sound uncertain.

'It's a bit intimidating, isn't it?' the woman laughed in gentle understanding. 'I remember the first time Blane, Judd's father, brought me here to meet his parents. It was shortly after we'd become engaged and the place terrified me. It was much more formal then. When Blane told me that we would live here after we were married, I wanted to break the engagement, but fortunately he talked me out of that.'

Maureen Prescott's instinctive knowledge of Valerie's reaction allowed her to relax a little. It was comforting to know that someone else had been awed by this impressive home.

'The house is at its best when it's filled with people, especially children,' Maureen continued in an affectionate voice. 'It seems to come to life then. When my five were growing up, the house never seemed big enough—which sounds hard to believe, doesn't it?'

'A little,' Valerie admitted.

'They seemed to fill every corner of it with their projects and pets and friends. That reminds me,' she glanced down at the brown-haired boy trotting along beside Valerie, 'there's something outside that I want to show you.'

'What is it?' Tadd asked, his olive-brown eyes rounding.

'You'll see,' Maureen promised mysteriously, and paused to open a set of French doors on to the veranda. As she stepped outside, she called, 'Here, Sable!'

A female German Shepherd with a coat as black and sleek as its name came loping across the yard, panting a happy grin, tail wagging. Ten roly-poly miniatures tumbled over themselves in an effort to match their mother's gait.

'Puppies!' Tadd squealed in delight and followed Maureen Prescott to the edge of the veranda. The female Shepherd washed his face with a single lick before greeting its mistress. Tadd's interest was in the ten little puppies bringing up the rear. 'Can I play with them?'

'Of course you may.' The instant she gave permission he was racing out to meet the pups. When he knelt on the ground, he was immediately under siege. Valerie joined in with the older woman's laughter as Tadd began giggling in his attempts to elude ten licking tongues. 'Puppies and children are made for each other,' Maureen declared in a voice breathless from laughter. 'Come on, let's sit down and have that drink I promised you. I don't believe Tadd will be interested in lemonade and cookies for a while.'

'I'm sure he's forgotten all about it,' Valerie agreed, and followed the woman to a white grille-work table with a glass top.

A pitcher of lemonade sat in the centre, condensation beading moisture on the outside. Four glasses filled with ice surrounded it as well as a plate of chocolate drop cookies with frosting on the top. Valerie sat down in one of the white iron lace chairs around the table, plump cushions of green softening the hard seats.

'Tadd is really enjoying himself. The apartment where we live in Cincinnati doesn't permit pets, so this is really a treat for him,' Valerie explained, taking the glass of lemonade she was handed and thanking her.

'Misty, my second daughter, lives in a complex that doesn't allow animals either, and her children are at an age when they want to bring home every stray cat and dog they find. She and her husband have had a time keeping them from sneaking one in. I think their love of animals is part of the reason they come home to Meadow Farms so often. There's Sable and her puppies, the horses, and cats at the barns. But I don't mind what their reason is,' Maureen insisted. 'I just enjoy having them come. Although it's quite a houseful when they're all here at once.'

'Are all your children married?' Valerie asked politely.

'Yes, with the exception of Judd, of course,' Maureen answered with a smiling sigh. 'There have been times when I've wondered if my first-born was ever going to get married, but I've never said anything to him.'

'I'm sure there are any number of women who would like to be the one to put an end to your wondering.' Valerie was careful not to make it sound as if she was one of them.

'That's the problem—there've been too many women,' Maureen Prescott observed with a trace of sad resignment. 'The Prescott name, the wealth and his own singular attractiveness—Judd has been the object of many a woman's matrimonial eye. I'm afraid it's made him feel very cynical towards sex.'

'I can imagine,' Valerie agreed and sipped at the tart, cold liquid in her glass.

'Yes, I've often teased him that I don't know if he's more particular about matching the blood-lines of his thoroughbreds or finding a compatible blood-line for a wife. He always answers that if he ever finds a woman with breeding, spirit and staying power, he'll marry her. Of course, we're only joking,' his mother qualified it with a dismissing laugh.

Perhaps she had been teasing, but Valerie wouldn't be surprised to discover that Judd wasn't. She knew how cold-blooded he could be about some things . . . and so hot-blooded towards others.

Maureen's comment made her wonder whether Judd's mother was subtly trying to warn her that she wasn't good enough for her son. Not that it was needed. Valerie had long been aware of Judd's low opinion of her, an opinion she sometimes forgot, like earlier today. That feeling of unease and a panic to get away came over her again. She had to change the subject away from the discussion of Judd.

Her glance swung over the lawn, including a glimpse of a swiming pool behind some concealing shrubbery. 'You must enjoy living here, Mrs Prescott. It's peaceful, yet with all the conveniences.'

'Yes, I love it here,' Maureen agreed. 'But you must call me Maureen. I learned that there were two requirements that were needed to enjoy living here the first year I was married. You have to like country life and you have to *love* horses. Fortunately I managed to fulfil both. The only objection I have is at weaning time when the mares and foals are separated. It tears at my heart to hear them calling back and forth from the pastures to each other. I usually arrange to visit my youngest son, Randall, and his family in Baltimore then. Judd insists that it's silly and impractical to be upset by it, but then he isn't a mother.'

The veranda door behind Valerie opened. She glanced over her shoulder, her heart skipping madly against her ribs as Judd's gaze slid warmly over her. Damn, but she couldn't stop loving him, even when she had admitted to herself only a moment ago that it was no good.

Smiling crookedly, he walked to the table. 'I told you I wouldn't be long.' He glanced to the lawn where Tadd was still playing with the puppies, the black Shepherd lying in the grass and looking on. 'Tadd is enjoying himself. What have you two been doing?'

'Gossiping about you, of course,' his mother replied.

'I didn't realise you gossiped, Mother.' His comment held a touch of dry mockery.

'I'm a woman,' she said in explanation. 'Would you like some lemonade?'

'Yes, I'll have a glass, Mother. Thank you.' Judd pulled one of the chairs closer to Valerie and sat down. His hand rested on the back of her chair, a finger absently stroking the bare skin of her shoulder. She felt that quivering ache to know the fullness of his caresses and had to move or betray that need.

'Tadd's been so busy playing with the puppies he hasn't had time for lemonade,' said Valerie, rising from her chair. 'I think I'll see if he wants some now.'

Avoiding the glitter of Judd's green eyes, she walked to the edge of the veranda. All but one of the puppies had grown tired of Tadd's games and had rolled into sleepy balls on the lawn.

'Let the puppies rest for a while, Tadd,' she called. 'Come and have some lemonade and cookies.'

'Okay,' he agreed, and stood up, hugging the last puppy in his arms as he started towards the veranda. The mother Shepherd rose, made a counting glance at the sleeping litter, and pricked her ears towards Tadd.

'Leave the puppy there, Tadd,' Valerie told him. 'It's mother wants to keep them all together so they won't accidentally become lost.'

Glancing over his shoulder, Tadd saw the anxious black dog looking at him and reluctantly put the puppy on to the grass. The puppy didn't seem sure what it was supposed to do, but its mother trotted over, washed its face, and directed it towards the others. Tadd, who seemed to know only one speed, ran to the veranda. He stopped when he reached Valerie, his face aglow, happiness beaming from his expressive hazel-green eyes.

'Did you see the puppy? He likes me, Mom,' he informed her with an eager smile.

'I'm sure he does.' She tucked his shirt inside his pants and brushed at the grass stains on his clothes. Finished, she poked a playful finger at his stomach. 'How about some cookies and lemonade for that hole in your tummy?'

'Okay.' Tadd skipped alongside of her to the table, hopping on to one of the chairs and resting his elbows on the glass-topped table. Maureen Prescott gave him a glass of lemonade and offered him a cookie. He took one from the plate. 'Are all those puppies yours, Reeny?' He used the nickname without hesitation.

'I guess they are,' she smiled.

'You're lucky.' Tadd took a swallow from the glass as Valerie sat down in her chair, scooting it closer to the table to be out of Judd's reach, a fact he noted with a bemused twitch of his mouth. 'I wish I could have one puppy,' Tadd sighed, and licked at the frosting on the cookie.

'I'm afraid they aren't old enough to leave their mother yet,' Maureen Prescott explained.

'Are you going to keep all of them?' His look said that would be greedy.

'No, we'll keep one or two and find good homes

for the others,' the woman admitted. 'But not for another two or three weeks.'

'We have a good home, don't we, Mom?' Tadd seized on the phrase.

'No, we don't, Tadd,' Valerie denied. 'Those puppies are going to grow into big dogs like their mother. They need lots of room. Besides, you know that pets aren't allowed where we live.'

'Your mother is right,' Judd inserted as Tadd twisted his mouth into a grimace. 'A puppy like these needs room to run. You really should live in the country to have a dog like Sable, somewhere like your grandfather's farm. Maybe then your mother would let you have one of the puppies.'

Valerie shot him an angry look. She recognised Judd's ploy and resented him for using Tadd's desire for a puppy as a wedge to get what he wanted. Tadd latched on to the idea as Judd had known he would.

'But we already live there.' He turned an earnest, beseeching look on Valerie.

'Only until the end of the summer,' she reminded him.

'Why can't we stay there for ever and I could have my puppy,' Tadd argued, forgetting the cookie he held.

'But we don't own it.' She felt the lazy regard of Judd's green eyes and knew he was enjoying the awkward situation she was in. 'Eat your cookie before you make a mess.'

'We don't own the apartment in Cincinnati either,' Tadd argued. 'So why can't we stay here?'

'Because I have to work. I have a job, remem-

ber?' Valerie tried to be patient and reasonable
with his demands, knowing she shouldn't release
her shortening temper on him.

'No, you don't. You got fired—I heard you tell
Clara,' he retorted.

'We'll discuss this later, Tadd,' she said firmly.
'Finish your cookie.'

For a minute, he opened his mouth to continue
his stubborn argument, but the warning look
Valerie gave him made him take a bite of the cookie.
Tadd was wise enough to know that arousing her
temper would accomplish nothing.

'I'm sorry, Valerie,' Maureen Prescott sympa-
thised with her dilemma. 'It isn't easy to say "no" to
him.'

'It isn't,' she agreed, and flashed a look at Judd.
'But it's a word you learn when you become an
adult, sometimes the hard way.'

A dark brow flickered upward in a faintly challenging gesture, but Judd gave no other sign that
he had received her veiled message. Tadd washed
his cookie down with lemonade and turned to Judd.

'Are we going to see Mickey?' he asked.

'Whenever you're ready,' Judd conceded.

Tadd hopped off the chair, not even cookies and
lemonade keeping him seated for long. 'Maybe we
can look at the horses, too?' he suggested.

'I think Mickey's planned to show you around
and meet the new horses he's looking after.' Judd
rose from his chair when Valerie did. She avoided
the hand that would have taken possession of her
arm and walked to Tadd.

'Thank you for the lemonade and cookies,

Mrs ... Maureen,' she said.

'Yes, thank you,' Tadd piped his agreement.

'You're very welcome. And please, come any time,' the other woman insisted generously.

'Maybe I could play with the puppies again,' Tadd suggested, looking up at Valerie.

'We'll see,' she responded stiffly and pushed him forward.

'It's shorter to cut across the lawn,' said Judd with a gesture of his hand to indicate the direction they would take.

Despite Valerie's efforts to keep Tadd at her side, he skipped into the lead and she was forced to walk with Judd. She was aware of the way he shortened his long strides to match hers. He made no attempt at conversation, letting his nearness wreak havoc on her senses.

At the barns, they had no trouble finding Mickey. He appeared from one of them as they arrived. He hurried towards them, his bowed legs giving a slight waddle to his walk. Tadd ran forward to meet him.

'Hello, Valerie. How have you been?' Mickey greeted her with his usual face-splitting grin.

'Fine,' she responded, a little of her tension easing. 'Tadd has missed you.'

'I've missed him, too.' Mickey glanced down at the boy holding his hand. 'Come on, lad. I want you to see some of the finest looking horseflesh there is in this part of the world. You've got to learn to know a great horse when you see one if you want to work with horses when you grow up.'

'I do.' Tadd trotted eagerly beside him as Mickey

turned to retrace his path to the stable. 'I'm going to have a lot of animals when I grow up—horses and dogs and everything.'

Valerie followed them with Judd remaining at her side. She glanced at his jutting profile through the sweep of her gold-tipped lashes. The hard sensuality of his features attracted her despite her anger.

'It wasn't fair of you to tempt Tadd with the prospect of a puppy,' she protested in a low, agitated breath.

Judd's gaze slid lazily down to her face. 'All's fair,' he countered smoothly.

In the shade of the stable overhang, Valerie stopped. 'The end does not justify the means,' she said sharply.

Judd stopped, looking down at her in a way that heated her flesh. 'You can justify any means if you want something badly enough—and you know what I want.'

The message in his eyes seemed to cut off her breath. She could feel the powerful undertow of desire tugging at her, threatening to drag her under the control of his will. She seemed powerless to resist.

Farther down the stable row, Tadd glanced over his shoulder at the couple lagging behind. 'Mom, are you coming?' he called.

Her breath came back in a rush of self-consciousness. 'Yes, Tadd,' she answered, and turned to catch up with them.

'You can't run away from it,' Judd's low voice mocked her disguised flight. He lingered for an instant, then leisurely moved to follow her.

CHAPTER EIGHT

THE quartet led by Mickey Flanders had made almost a full tour of the brood-farm buildings, impressive in its efficiency. Nothing had been overlooked, especially in the foaling barn, a facility that Valerie was sure had no equal.

The tour had paused at a paddock fence where Tadd had climbed to the top rail to watch a pair of galloping yearlings cavorting and kicking up their heels. From the stud barns came the piercing squeal of a stallion answered by the challenging scream of a second. Valerie glanced towards the sound, noticing Judd had done the same.

A frown flickered across his face, followed by a crooked smile of dismissal. 'It sounds as if Battleground and Kings Ruler are at it again. They're always feuding with each other across the way.'

Valerie nodded in silent understanding. Stallions were often jealously competitive. The instinct within them was strong to fight to protect their territory, which was why they had to be kept separated by the strongest of fences. With Judd's explanation echoing in her mind, she ignored the angry exchange of whistles that had resumed.

A muffled shout of alarm pivoted Judd around. More shouts were followed by a flurry of activity around the stud barn. A grimness claimed his expression.

'I'll be back,' he said without glancing at her.

His long, ground-eating strides were already covering the distance to the stallion pens before either Valerie or Mickey thought to move. Tadd followed curiously after them, sensing something different in the air.

When Valerie reached the barrier of the first stud pen, she felt the first sickening jolt of danger. The two stallions were locked in combat, rearing, jaws open and heads snaking for each other's jugular vein. The clang of pawing, steel hooves striking against each other vibrated in the air amidst the blowing snorts and rumbling neighs. Stablehands were warily trying to separate the pair. The blood drained from her face as she saw Judd wading into the thick of it.

'Stop him, Mickey!' she breathed to the ex-jockey beside her.

'Are you crazy?' he asked in disbelief. 'Judd isn't going to stand by and watch his two prize stallions kill each other.'

She could hear him snapping orders to co-ordinate the efforts. Fear for his safety overpowered her and she turned away. 'I can't watch.' Valerie knew what those murderous hooves could do. They were capable of tearing away hunks of human flesh, exposing the bones. 'Tell me what happens, Mickey.' She closed her eyes, but she couldn't shut her ears to the sounds. 'No, I don't want to know,' she groaned, and remembered Tadd.

She reached for him, trying to hide his face from the sight, but he tore out of her arms. 'I want to see,

Mommy!' he cried fearlessly, and raced to Mickey's side.

Valerie felt sick with fear. The turmoil from the stud pen seemed to go on without end. Her eyes were tightly closed, her back to the scene as she prayed desperately that Judd would be unharmed. She hadn't the strength for anything else. Fear had turned her into jelly.

'Hot damn! He did it!' Mickey shouted, and danced a little jig, stopping at the sight of Valerie's ashen face as she collapsed weakly against a fence post. 'Hey, Valerie,' his voice was anxious with concern. 'It's over.'

'Judd——?' was all she could manage as a violent trembling seized her.

'He's fine.' Mickey said it as though she shouldn't have thought otherwise. Tipping his head to one side, he looked up at her, smiling in gentle understanding. 'You're still in love with him, aren't you?' he commented.

She nodded her head in a numbed, affirmative gesture before catching the phrasing of his question. 'How——' she began, but her choked voice didn't seem to want to work.

'I noticed all those rides you were taking seven years ago and the look that was in your eyes when you came back. I knew a man put it there,' Mickey explained softly. 'And I happened to notice that Judd was taking rides the same time you were. I just put two and two together.' At the apprehensive light in her eyes, he answered her unspoken question. 'You're grandad didn't know and I didn't see where it was my place to enlighten him. There

was enough grief around the place after you left
without adding to it.'

A shuddering sigh of gratitude rippled her and
she smiled weakly. Her stomach had finally begun
to stop its nauseous churning, but her legs were
still treacherously weak. She gripped the fence
tightly for support as Mickey turned away. She
didn't guess why until she heard Judd's grim voice
speaking as he approached them.

'I've fired that new man, Rathburn. The stupid
fool had to clean King's paddock, so he put the
stallion in the one next to Battleground and didn't
check the gates,' Judd said with ruthless scorn for
the guilty man's incompetence. 'Battleground has
some wicked-looking cuts. The vet is on his way, but
you'd better see if you can't give Jim a hand, Mick.'

'Right away.' The ex-jockey moved off at a shuff-
ling trot.

'That was really something!' Tadd breathed his
excitement.

'Is that right?' Judd's mocking voice sounded
tolerantly amused.

Valerie didn't find anything humorous about the
near-disaster that could have ultimately crippled
horse and man. Glancing over her shoulder, she cast
Judd an accusing look, her face still white as a sheet.
His white shirt was stained with dirt and sweat, and
a telltale scattering of animal hairs to show he had
put himself in equal danger as his stablehands.

'You could have been killed or maimed!' A thin
thread of her previous fear ran through her hoarse
voice.

His gaze narrowed on her in sharp concern. 'You

look like a ghost, Valerie,' Judd concluded in his own accusation. 'Quick, Tadd, run and get your mother some water.'

His hand gripped the boy's shoulder and sent him speeding on his way. Then he was walking to her. Valerie turned towards the fence, relieved that he had come away unscathed, frightened by what might have happened, and weak with her love for him. His hands spanned her waist to turn her from the fence and receive the complacent study of his gaze.

'As many times as you've wished me to hell, I would have thought you would relish the prospect of my death,' Judd taunted her.

'No,' Valerie denied, and protested painfully, 'That's a cruel thing to say!'

'Why? Do you really care what happens to me?' His voice was dry and baiting.

'I do.' What was the use in denying it? Her down-cast gaze noticed the smear of red blood on the sleeve of his shirt. It was horse blood. At the sight of it, her hands spread across his chest to feel the steady beat of his heart. She swayed against him, the side of her cheek brushing against the hair-roughened chest where his shirt was unbuttoned. She wished she could absorb some of his indomitable strength. 'I don't want to care, but I do,' Valerie admitted in an aching breath.

His arms tightened around her in a crushing circle. The force of it tipped her head back and his mouth bruised her cheekbone. 'You're mine, Valerie,' he growled in possession. 'You belong to me.'

'Yes,' she agreed to the inevitable.

'There'll be no more talk about you leaving in September,' Judd warned.

'No,' Valerie surrendered to his demand.

With that final acquiescence, his mouth sought and found her parted lips. He kissed her deeply, savouring this moment when she had yielded to his will and admitted what she couldn't hide. He stirred her to passion, creating a languorous flame that ravished her. She moulded herself to his length, to fire his blood as he had hers. The sudden bruising demand of his mouth consoled her that he couldn't resist her either.

'Mommy?' Tadd's anxious voice tore her lips from the satisfaction of Judd's kiss. Her dazed eyes focused slowly on the small boy running towards them. 'Reeny's bringing the water. Is Mommy all right?'

Judd's bulk was shielding Valerie from the view of both the boy and the woman hurrying behind him. With shuddering reluctance Judd relaxed his hold to let her feet rest firmly on the ground, instead of just her toes. His green eyes blazed over her face in promise and possession, letting her see he didn't welcome the interruption before he turned to meet it. A supporting arm remained curved across her back and waist, keeping her body in contact with his side.

'What's happened, Judd?' His mother hurried forward, a glass of water in her hand. Her gaze flicked from her son to Valerie, and Valerie guessed that Maureen Prescott had recognised that embrace for what it had been. She flushed self-consciously.

'I heard an uproar down around the stallion barns, then Tadd came running to the house talking about horses fighting and Valerie needing water. I didn't know whether to listen to him or call an ambulance.'

Judd explained briefly about the stallion fight, glossing over his part in it, and concluded, 'It left Valerie a little shaken, so I sent Tadd to the house as an excuse to get him away. I thought she was going to faint and I didn't want that scaring him.' He took the glass from his mother's hand and offered it to Valerie. 'You might want that drink now, though.'

'Thank you.' Nervously she took the glass and sipped from it, too self-conscious about the scene his mother had witnessed to draw attention to herself by refusing his suggestion.

'Do you feel all right now, Valerie?' Maureen asked with concern.

'Yes, I'm fine.' But her voice sounded breathless and not altogether sure.

'You look a little pale,' the other woman observed, frowning anxiously. 'You'd better come up to the house and rest for a few minutes.'

'No, really I——' Valerie tried to protest.

But Judd interrupted, 'Do you want me to carry you?'

'No, I ... I can walk,' she stammered, and flashed a nervous glance at his mother.

Incapable of conversation, Valerie was relieved that no one seemed to expect any from her as they walked to the house. Judd's arm remained around her, his thigh brushing against hers. She kept wondering what his mother was thinking and whether she objected to what was apparently going on. But she guessed that Maureen Prescott was too polite and well-bred to let her feelings show.

As they crossed the lawn to the veranda, Tadd began his own description of the scene at the stud-pens. 'Mickey and I was watching it all, Reeny. You should have seen Judd when he——'

Judd must have felt the slight tremor that vibrated through her. 'I think that's enough about that, Tadd,' he silenced the boy. ''We don't want to upset your mother again, do we?'

'No,' Tadd agreed, darting an anxious look at Valerie.

'Why don't you play with the puppies, Tadd?' Maureen suggested, and he wandered towards the sleeping pile of black fur, but with some reluctance.

'I'm sorry.' Valerie felt obliged to apologise for her behaviour after she came under the scrutiny of Judd's mother as well. 'I'm not usually a 'fraidy-cat about such things.'

'No, you're not,' Judd agreed with a gently taunting smile, and escorted her to a cushioned lounge chair. 'A spitting feline, maybe,' he qualified.

'There's no need to apologise, Valerie,' his mother inserted. 'I saw a stallion fight once. It was a vicious thing, so I quite understand your reaction.'

'Comfortable?' Judd enquired after seating her in the chair.

'Yes.' But she was beginning to feel like a fraud.

'You relax for a little while,' he ordered. 'I'm going to wash up and change my shirt,' he said, glancing down at his soiled front. 'I won't be long.'

When he had disappeared into the house via the veranda doors, his mother suggested, 'There's some lemonade left if you'd like some.'

'No, thank you,' Valerie refused.

Tadd came wandering back on to the veranda, a sleepy-eyed puppy in his arms. He stopped at the lounge chair, studying Valerie with a troubled light in his eyes.

'Are you all right, Mommy?'

His appealing concern drew a faint smile. 'Yes, Tadd, I'm fine,' she assured him.

'Maybe you'd feel better if you held the puppy.' He offered her the soft ball of fur with enormous feet.

'Thanks, Tadd, but I think the puppy would like it better if you held it,' Valerie refused, her heart warming at his touching gesture.

'It's sleepy anyway,' he shrugged, and walked over to the grass to let it go. 'Would you want to play a game, Mom?'

'No, thanks.'

He came back over to her chair. 'What am I going to do while you're resting?' he wanted to know.

'Would you like some more cookies and lemonade?' Maureen Prescott suggested.

'No, thank you.' He half-turned to look at her. 'Have you got any more animals for me to play with?'

'No, I don't believe so,' the woman tried not to smile at the question. 'But there's a sandbox over by those trees. If I'm not mistaken, there's a toy truck in that chest over there. You can take the truck and play with it in the sandbox.'

'Great!' Tadd dashed to the toy chest she had indicated, retrieved the truck and headed for the sandbox.

'Tadd isn't used to entertaining himself,' Valerie explained. 'There are a lot of children his age in the apartment building where we live, so he's used to playing with them.'

'It's good that he has children to play with,' Maureen commented.

'Yes,' Valerie agreed. 'I think that's the only thing he's missed this summer. Mickey played with him at the farm a lot. Now that he's gone, Tadd gets lonely once in a while.'

'Ellie, my oldest daughter, is coming this weekend with her husband and their six-year-old daughter. Meg is a regular tomboy. Why don't you bring Tadd over Sunday afternoon?' Maureen suggested. 'They'll have fun playing together.'

'I ... I don't believe so.' Valerie hesitated before rejecting the invitation.

'Please try,' the woman urged.

'Try what?' Judd appeared, catching the tail end of their conversation.

'I suggested to Valerie that she bring Tadd over on Sunday to play with Meg, but she doesn't think she'll be able to,' his mother explained.

'Oh?' His gaze flicked curiously to Valerie. 'Why?'

'I'm not sure it will be possible yet. I'll have to speak to Clara.' Valerie couldn't explain the reason for her hesitation. She had the feeling it wouldn't be wise to become too closely involved with any more members of the Prescott family.

'Don't worry, Mother,' said Judd. 'I can almost guarantee you that Tadd will be here. Valerie and I are having dinner together on Saturday night. I'll persuade her to change her mind.'

Dinner together? It was the first she knew about it, but she tried not to let on. Things were happening at such a rapid pace that she couldn't keep up with them. She needed time to take stock of things and understand what was going on.

'I hope you will,' his mother said, 'Tadd is a wonderful boy. You must be very proud of him, Valerie.'

'I am,' Valerie admitted, feeling vaguely uncomfortable again.

'He has such an appealing face.' Maureen was looking towards the sandbox where Tadd was playing with the truck. 'And those eyes of his are so expressive. There's something about him that makes him so very special, but those children generally are,' she concluded.

'Those children?' Valerie stiffened.

A pair of turquoise eyes rounded in dismay as Maureen realised what she had said. She glanced quickly at Judd, an apology in her look. Valerie's questioning eyes were directed at him as well.

Undaunted by either of them, he replied smoothly, 'I believe Mother means "those children" who are born out of wedlock.'

'I'm sorry, Valerie,' Maureen apologised. 'I didn't mean to offend you by that remark—truly I didn't.'

'It's quite all right.' Valerie hid her embarrassment behind a proud look. 'I've never attempted to hide the fact that Tadd is illegitimate. And I have heard it said that "those children" tend to be more precious and appealing as a result. Tadd seems to be an example of that, but I doubt if it's always the case.'

'I certainly didn't mean to hurt your feelings,' Maureen insisted again. 'It's just that I've been watching Tadd,' she rushed her explanation, 'and he's so like Judd in many ways that—— Oh, dear, I've made it worse!' she exclaimed as she looked into Valerie's whitened face.

'No, no,' Valerie denied with a tight, strained smile. 'I understand perfectly.'

A nauseous lump was rising in her throat as she truly began to understand. Maureen Prescott had known all along that her son was Tadd's father. Judd had obviously told his mother, but hadn't bothered to tell her that he had. She hadn't thought it was possible to feel cheap and humiliated again, but she did.

'I didn't see any reason not to tell her,' Judd explained, watching Valerie through narrowed eyes.

'Of course there isn't,' she agreed, feeling her poise cracking and struggling inwardly to keep it from falling apart.

'I'm relieved,' his mother smiled, somewhat nervously. 'And I do hope it won't influence your decision about bringing Tadd here on Sunday. I would sincerely enjoy having him come.'

'Don't worry about that, Mother,' Judd inserted.
'I'm sure Valerie will agree.'

'Your son can be very persuasive,' Valerie commented, and felt a rising well of panic. 'I don't mean to be rude, Mrs Prescott,' she rose from the lounge chair, 'but I'm really not feeling all that well. Would you mind if Judd took us home now? You've been very gracious to Tadd and me and I want to thank you for that.'

'You're very welcome, of course,' Maureen returned, hiding her confusion with a smile. 'I'll call Tadd for you.'

'Thank you.' Valerie was aware of Judd standing beside her, examining the pallor in her face.

'What's wrong, Valerie?' he asked quietly.

'A headache—a nervous reaction, I suppose.' Her temples were throbbing, so her excuse wasn't totally false.

He seemed to accept her surface explanation without delving further. When Tadd came racing to the veranda, Maureen Prescott walked them through the house to the front door and bid them goodbye. As they drove away, Tadd's face was pressed to the window glass to watch the horses in the pasture.

Valerie sat silently in the front seat. Judd slid her a questioning look. 'Does it bother you that Mother knows?' he asked, phrasing it so Tadd wouldn't attach any significance to it.

'No.' She leaned her head against the seat rest. 'Why should it?' she countered with forced nonchalance.

But it beat at her like a hammer. To realise that

her relationship with Judd was out in the open
was worse than if it had been a secret, clandestine
affair. Kept woman, mistress, consort, all were terms
for the same thing. She had agreed to it—in the
stableyard in Judd's arms. There was no doubt
over how deeply she loved him.

But she had more to think of than just herself.
There was Tadd. Valerie closed her eyes in pain.
Maureen Prescott was eager for him to visit on
Sunday, but the invitation naturally hadn't included her. Was Tadd going to grow up on the fringes
of the Prescott family, invited into the circle on
their whim? He would be a Prescott without a right
to the name. How would he feel when he discovered
the truth? Would he become bitter and resentful
that his mother was the mistress to the man who
was his father?

Valerie was tormented by the love she felt for
Judd and the life with him that she never could
know. It gnawed at her until she thought she would
be torn in two. It was a searing, raw ache that made
her heart bleed.

'Valerie?' Judd's hand touched her shoulder.

She opened her eyes to discover the car was parked
in front of the farmhouse. The screen door was
already slamming behind Tadd, who was racing
into the house to be the first to tell Clara of all that
had happened today.

'I ... I didn't realise we were here already,'
Valerie began in painful confusion.

'I noticed,' he responded dryly. His hand slid
under her hair, discovering the tense muscles in her
neck and massaging them. 'You do know you're

having dinner with me on Saturday night, tomorrow night,' he told her.

'So you told me.' She couldn't relax under his touch, if anything she became stiffer.

'You're going.' It was a statement that demanded her agreement.

'Yes,' Valerie lied because it was easier.

Judd leaned over and rubbed his mouth against the corner of her lips. She breathed in sharply, filling her lungs with the scent of him. It was like a heady wine. Judd began nibbling the curve of her lip, teasing and tantalising her with his kiss.

'Please, Judd, don't!' She turned her head away from his tempting mouth because she knew the power of his kiss could make her forget everything.

He hooked a hard finger around her chin and turned her to face him. His sharp gaze inspected her pale face and the carefully lowered lashes.

'What is it?' He sensed something was wrong and demanded to know the cause.

'I really do have a headache,' Valerie insisted with a nervous smile. 'It'll go away, but I need to lie down for a while.'

'Alone?' His brow quirked suggestively, then he sighed, 'Never mind. Forget I said that. I'll call you later to be sure you're all right.'

'Make it this evening,' Valerie asked quickly, and hurried to answer the question in his eyes. 'By the time I rest for an hour or two, it'll be time to eat. Then there's the dishes to be done, and Tadd won't take a bath unless someone is standing over him. So I'll be busy until——' His fingers touched her lips to silence them.

'I'll phone you later this evening,' he agreed. 'Or I'll come over if you can think of a way to get that battleaxe out of the house.'

It was starting already, she thought in panic. 'You'd better call first,' she said.

'Very well, I will.' He kissed her lightly.

CHAPTER NINE

VALERIE paused on the porch to wave to Judd and stayed until he had driven out of sight down the lane. She felt the beginning of a sob in her throat and knew she didn't have time for tears. Lifting her chin, she turned and walked into the house.

'My gracious, it certainly sounds as if you've had a full day,' Clara commented. 'Tadd has been running non-stop for the last five minutes and doesn't give any indication of wearing down. What's all this about horses and puppies? I thought you were going to a tobacco auction. That's what you told me.'

'We did go,' Valerie admitted, 'but that was earlier today. Then we went over to the Prescott place to see Mickey.' She glanced down at her son. 'Tadd, why don't you go outside and play for a while?'

'Aw, Mom,' he protested, 'I wanted to tell Clara about the puppies.'

'Later,' she insisted. Reluctantly Tadd walked to the door, his feet dragging, and slammed the screen shut. Valerie turned o Clara. 'How much gas is in the car?'

'I filled it up the other day when I was in town. Why?' Clara was startled by the question.

Valerie was already hurrying through the living room, picking up the odds and ends of personal items that had managed to become scattered around. She began stuffing them in a paper sack.

'What about the oil? Did you have it checked?' she asked.

'As a matter of fact, I did.' A pair of hands moved to rest on broad hips. 'Would you mind telling me why you're asking these questions?'

Valerie stopped in the centre of the room, pressing a hand against her forehead. 'I can't remember. Did we put the suitcases in the empty bedroom upstairs or down in the basement?'

'Upstairs. And what do we need the suitcases for?' Clara followed as Valerie headed for the staircase.

'Because we're leaving. What other reason would I have for asking about the car and suitcases?' Valerie retorted sharply.

'Would you like to run that by me once more? Did I hear you say we were leaving?' repeated Clara.

'That's exactly what I said.' Valerie opened the door to the empty bedroom, grabbed two of the suitcases in the corner, and walked to Tadd's room.

'I thought we were staying here until summer was over,' her friend reminded her.

'I've changed my mind. Isn't it obvious?' Valerie opened drawers, taking out whole stacks of clothes regardless of their order or neatness, and jamming them into the opened suitcase.

'Suppose you give me three guesses as to why?' Clara challenged. 'Judd Prescott, Judd Prescott, and Judd Prescott. What happened today?'

'I don't have time to go into it right now,' Valerie stalled. 'Would you mind helping me pack?' she demanded. 'I don't want to take all night.'

'I'll help,' Clara replied, walking to the closet without any degree of haste. 'But I doubt if what you're doing could be called packing. What's the big rush anyway? You surely aren't planning to leave onight?' Shrewd blue eyes swept piercingly to Valerie.

'We're leaving tonight.' The first suitcase was filled to the point of overflowing. Valerie had to sit on it to get it latched. 'We'll never be able to put everything in these suitcases. Where are the boxes your sister used to send our things? We didn't throw them away, did we?'

But her friend was still concentrating on her first statement. 'Tonight? You can't mean to leave tonight?' she frowned. 'There's only a few hours of daylight left. The sensible thing is to leave first thing in the morning.'

'No, it isn't,' Valerie denied. 'We're leaving tonight. Now where are the boxes?'

'Forget the boxes. I want to know why we have to leave tonight. And I'm not answering another question or lifting a hand until you tell me.' Clara dropped the clothes in her hand on a chair.

'Clara, for heaven's sake, I don't have time for all this.' Valerie hurried to the chair and grabbed the clothes to stuff them in the second suitcase. 'Judd will be calling later on and I want to be gone before he does.'

'And that's your reason?' her friend sniffed in scoffing challenge. 'It seems mighty ridiculous to me!'

'Don't you understand?' Valerie whirled to face

her. The conflicting emotions and raw pain that she had pushed aside, threatened to surface. Her chin quivered as she fought to hold them back. 'If I don't leave tonight, I never will!'

'I think you'd better sit down and tell me what's happened,' said Clara in a voice that would stand for no argument.

'No, I won't sit down.' Valerie sniffed away a tear and shook back her caramel hair. 'There's too much to do and not enough time.' She walked to the chest of drawers and opened the last one to take out the balance of clothes.

'Well, you're going to tell me what happened,' Clara insisted.

Another tear was forming in the corner of her eye and Valerie wiped it quickly away with a forefinger. 'Judd's mother, Mrs Prescott, knows about Tadd, that Judd is his father. She wants Tadd to come over on Sunday to play with another one of her grandchildren. It's all out in the open, and I can't handle it.'

'What is Judd's reaction to this?' Clara gathered up Tadd's few toys and put them in a sack.

'He told his mother he would persuade me to bring Tadd.'

'So? Don't let him persuade you?' her friend shrugged.

Valerie's laugh held no humour. 'All he has to do is hold me in his arms and I'll agree to anything. I did today. I promised I wouldn't leave here. I'm so in love with him I'm losing my pride and my self-respect.'

'It isn't one-sided. Judd is absolutely besotted

with you,' Clara said. 'I've seen the way he watches you. He never takes his eyes off you. He knows when you blink or take a breath.'

'I know and it doesn't make it any easier. Clara, he wants me to become his——' She broke off the sentence with a hurtful sigh. 'I can't even say the word without thinking what it would ultimately do to Tadd.'

'Maybe he'll marry you,' Clara suggested in an effort to comfort.

Valerie shook her head, pressing her lips tightly together for an instant. 'I'm not good enough for a Prescott to marry. I lack breeding,' she said bitterly. 'I can't stay, Clara.' Her hands absently wadded the bundle of clothes in her hand, her fingers digging into the material. 'I can't stay.'

There was silence. Then a detergent-rough hand gently touched her shoulder. 'The boxes are in my bedroom closet. I'll get them.'

'Thank you, Clara,' Valerie muttered in a voice tight and choked with emotion.

When the two suitcases were packed, she set them at the head of the stairs and took two more to her bedroom. With Clara's help, all her personal belongings were packed in either the luggage or the cardboard shipping crates. As soon as that room was cleared of their possessions they started on Clara's. No time was wasted on neatness or order.

'All that's left is to lug all this downstairs and out to the car,' said Clara, taking a deep breath as she studied the pile of luggage and boxes in front of the staircase.

'And to check downstairs,' Valerie added, picking

up one case and juggling another under the same arm. 'We'd better be sure to get everything because I'm not coming back no matter what we leave behind,' she declared grimly, and reached for the third.

Leading the way, Valerie descended the stairs. Clara followed with one of the boxes. Tadd came bounding on to the porch as Valerie approached the door.

'Open the door for me, Tadd,' she called through the wire mesh.

'I'm tired of playing, Mom.' He held the door open for her and stared curiously at the suitcase she carried. 'What are you doing? Are you going somewhere?'

'Yes. Don't let go of the door. Clara is right behind me.' Valerie rushed when she saw him take a step to follow her.

'Hurry up, Clara.' Tadd waited impatiently for the stout woman to manoeuvre the box through the opening, then let the door slam and raced to catch up to Valerie. 'Is Clara going too?'

'We're all going,' Valerie answered, and set the cases on the ground next to the car. 'Where are the keys for the trunk, Clara? Are they in the ignition?'

'I'll bet they're in the house in my handbag,' the woman grumbled, and set the box beside the luggage. 'Stay here. I'll go and get them.'

'Where are we going, Mom?' Tadd wanted to know, tugging at her skirt to get her attention.

'We're going home,' she told him, only Cincinnati didn't seem like home any more. This place was home.

'Home? To Cincinnati?' Tadd frowned.

'Yes. Back to our apartment,' Valerie answered sharply.

'Is summer over already?' His expression was both puzzled and crestfallen, a sad light in his eyes.

'No, not quite,' she admitted, and glanced to the house. What was keeping Clara? She could have been bringing out more of the boxes instead of standing here.

'But I thought we were going to stay here until summer was over,' Tadd reminded her. 'That's what you said.'

'I changed my mind.' Please, Valerie thought desperately, I don't want to argue with you.

'Why are we leaving?' he asked. 'If summer isn't over, why do we have to go back?'

'Because I said we are.' She wasn't about to explain the reasons to him. In the first place, he wouldn't understand. And in the second, it would be too painful. The breeze whipped a strand of hair across her cheek and she pushed it away with an impatient gesture.

'But I don't want to go back,' Tadd protested in a petulant tone.

'Yes, you do,' Valerie insisted.

'No, I don't.' His mouth was pulled into a mutinous pout.

'What about all your friends?' Valerie attempted to reason with him. 'Wouldn't you like to go back and play with them? It's been quite a while since you've ridden on Mike's Big Wheels. That was a lot of fun, remember?'

'I don't care about Mike's dumb ole Big Wheels,'

Tadd grumbled, the pouting mouth growing more pronounced. 'It's not nearly as much fun as riding Ginger anyway. I want to stay here.'

'We're not going to stay here. We're leaving. We're going back to Cincinnati.' Valerie stressed each sentence with decisive emphasis. 'So you might as well get that straight right now.'

'I don't want to go,' he repeated, his voice raising in rebellious protest. 'Judd said if we lived here, maybe I could have a puppy.'

'I'm not going to listen to any more talk about puppies!' Valerie retorted, her nerves snapping under the strain of his persistent arguing. 'We're leaving, and that's final!'

'Well, I'm not going!' Tadd shouted, backing away and breaking into angry tears.

'Tadd.' Valerie immediately regretted her sharpness, but he was already turning away and running towards the pasture. She could hear his sobbing. 'Tadd, come back here!'

But he ignored the command, his little legs churning faster. He was running into the lowering sun. Valerie shaded her eyes with her hand to shield out the glaring light. She waited for him to stop at the paddock fence, but instead he scooted under it and kept running.

'Tadd, come back here!' she called anxiously.

'I've got the keys.' Clara came out of the house, dangling the car keys in front of her. 'I couldn't remember where I left my handbag. I finally found it underneath the kitchen table. If it was a snake, it would have bit me.'

'Would you pack all this in the trunk?' Valerie motioned to the luggage as she started towards the pasture. 'I'd better get Tadd.'

'Where's he gone?' Frowning, Clara glanced around the yard, missing the small figure racing across the pasture.

'I lost my temper with him because he said he didn't want to go,' Valerie explained. 'Now he's run off.'

'Let him be.' Clara dismissed any urgency to the situation with a wave of her hand. 'He's just going to sulk for a while. He'll be back. Meanwhile he won't be underfoot.'

'I don't know.' Valerie hesitated.

'He won't go far,' the other woman assured her as she walked to the car to unlock the boot and begin arranging the luggage and boxes inside.

'He was very upset.' Gazing across, she could see Tadd had stopped running and was leaning against a tree to cry.

'Of course he was upset,' Clara agreed in a voice that disdainfully dismissed any other thought. 'Any child gets upset when it doesn't get its way. You go right ahead and handle the situation any way you want. I don't want to be telling you how you should raise your kid.'

Valerie received her friend's subtle message that she was making a mountain out of a molehill and sighed, 'You may be right.'

'If you ain't going after him, you could give me a hand with some of this stuff. You're the one who was in such an all-fired hurry to leave,' came the gruff reminder. Then Clara muttered to herself, 'I get the feeling we're making our getaway after robbing a bank.'

When another glance at the pasture showed that Tadd was in the same place, Valerie hesitated an instant longer, then turned to help Clara with the luggage. A second trip into the house brought everything down from upstairs.

A search of the ground floor added a box of belongings. Valerie carried it to the car. Her gaze swung automatically to the paddock, but this time there was no sign of Tadd. She walked to the fence and called him. The bay mare lifted her head in answer, then went back to grazing.

What had merely been concern changed to worry as Valerie hesitantly retraced her steps to the house. The sounds coming from the kitchen located Clara for her. She walked quickly to the room.

'You haven't seen Tadd, have you?' she asked hopefully. 'He isn't in the pasture any more and I thought he might have slipped into the house.'

'I haven't seen hide nor hair of him.' Clara shook her wiry, frosted-grey hair. 'Would you look at all this food? It seems a shame to leave it.'

'We don't have much choice. It would spoil if we tried to take it with us.' Valerie's response was automatic. 'Where do you suppose Tadd is?'

'Probably somewhere around the barns.' The dismissing lift of Clara's wide shoulders indicated that she still believed he wasn't far away. 'Since we haven't had any supper, I'll fix some sandwiches and snacks to take along with us. That way we'll get to use up some of this food and not leave so much behind.'

'I'm going to check the barns to see if Tadd is there,' Valerie said with an uneasy feeling growing inside her.

A walk through the barns proved fruitless and her calls went unanswered. She hurried back to the house to tell Clara.

'He wasn't there,' she said with a trace of breathless panic.

'The little imp!' Clara wiped her hands on a towel. 'He's probably off hiding somewhere.'

'Well, we can't leave without him,' Valerie said as if Clara had foolishly implied that they would. 'I'm going to walk out to the pasture where I saw him last.'

'I'l check through the house to make sure he didn't sneak in here when we weren't looking.' Clara put aside the food she was preparing for the trip and started towards the other rooms.

While Clara began a search of the house, Valerie hurried to the paddock. She ducked between the fence rails and walked swiftly through the tall grass to the tree on the far side of the pasture where she had last seen Tadd.

'Tadd!' She stopped when she reached the tree and used it as a pivot point to make a sweeping arc of the surrounding country. 'Tadd, where are you?' A bird chattered loudly in the only response she received. 'Tadd, answer me!' Her voice rose on a desperate note.

From the point of the tree there was a faint trail angling away from it, barely discernible by the tall, thick grass that had been pushed down by running feet. The vague path seemed to be heading in the opposite direction of the house. It was the only clue Valerie had and she followed it.

It lead her to the boundary fence with Meadow Farms and beyond. Halfway across the adjoining pasture, the grass thinned. Grazing horses had cropped the blades too close to the ground. She lost the trail that had taken her this far, and stopped, looking around for any hint that would tell her which direction Tad had gone.

'Tadd, where are you going?' she muttered, wishing she could crawl inside her young son's mind and discover his intention.

Did he know he had crossed on to the home farm of the Prescotts? It didn't seem likely. Despite the time they had spent there, Tadd wasn't familiar with the area beyond the farm and its immediate pastures. Yet it was possible that he knew the general direction of Meadow Farms' main quarters.

But why would he go there? To see Judd and enlist his support to persuade her to stay? No, Valerie dismissed that. Tadd was too young to think in such terms. The idea of finding Judd wouldn't lead him to the Prescott house, but the puppies might.

Hoping that she was reading his mind, she set off in the general direction of the Meadow Farms' buildings. Her pace quickened with her growing desire to find Tadd before he reached his destination. The last thing her panicking heart wanted was a confrontation with Judd. She had to find Tadd before he found the puppies and Judd.

As she crossed the meadow, Valerie caught herself biting her lip. There was painful constriction in her chest and her breath was coming in half-sobs. It did no good to try to calm her trembling nerves.

The ground rumbled with the pounding of galloping hooves and she glanced up to see Judd on the grey hunter riding towards her. She looked around for somewhere to hide, but it was too late. He had already seen her. Besides, she had to know if he had found Tadd, regardless of whether Judd had learned of her intention to leave. At the moment, finding Tadd was more important.

Judd didn't slow his horse until he was almost up to her. He dismounted before it came to a full stop. Then his long strides carried him swiftly towards her, holding the reins in his hand and leading the horse to her.

'Have you seen Tadd?' Her worried gaze searched his grimly set features. 'He ran off and I can't find him.'

'I know,' said Judd, and explained tersely, 'I phoned the house a few minutes ago to find out how you were feeling and Clara told me Tadd was missing.' His large hand took hold of her arm and started to pull her towards the horse. 'Come on.'

'No!' Valerie struggled in panic. 'You don't understand. I have to find Tadd,' she protested frantically.

If Judd hadn't seen Tadd, it meant he was still out there somewhere, possibly lost. The shadows cast by the sun were already long. Soon it would be dusk. She had to find him before darkness came and there was a lot of ground yet to be covered. That knowledge made her resist Judd's attempt to take her with him all the more wildly.

'Dammit, Valerie. Stop it! You're coming with me,' Judd snapped with savage insistence. Her arms became captured by the iron grip of his hands.

'No, I won't!' she denied violently. 'I won't!'

A hard shake jarred her into silence. 'Will you listen to me?' His angry face was close to hers, his eyes glittering into hers in hard demand. 'I have a feeling,' he said tightly, 'I think I know where Tadd is. Now, will you come with me or do I have to throw you over my shoulder and take you with me?'

Tears of panic had begun to scorch her eyes. She blinked at them and nodded her head mutely. But Judd didn't alter his hold. He seemed determined to hear her voice an agreement before he believed her.

'I ... I'll come with y-you.' She managed to force out a shaky agreement.

His hands shifted their grip from her arms to her waist. He lifted her up to sit sideways on the front of the saddle. Then he swung up behind her, his arms circling her to hold the reins and guide the grey.

The horse lunged into a canter, throwing Valerie against Judd's chest. An arm at her waist tightened to offer support. The solidness of his chest offered comfort and strength. Valerie let herself relax against it. She hadn't realised how heavy the weight of concern had been for Tadd's whereabouts until Judd had taken on half of the burden.

Through the cotton skirt of her sundress she could feel the hard muscles of his thighs. Her gaze swept up to study his face through the curl of her gold-tipped lashes. The jutting angle of his jaw and the line of his mouth were set with grim purpose. He slowed the horse as they entered a grouping of trees and wound their way through them.

As if feeling her look, he glanced down and the light in his green eyes became softly mocking. 'When you were spitting at me in all your fury, did you really believe I was going to try to keep you from finding our son?'

'I didn't know,' Valerie answered, uncertain now as to what she had believed his intention was.

'I guess I have given you cause in the past to question my motives,' Judd admitted.

'Sometimes,' she agreed, but she didn't question them now.

His gaze was drawn beyond her and he reined in the grey. 'Look,' he instructed quietly.

Valerie turned and saw a familiar grassy clearing. They had stopped on the edge of it. In the middle of it, a small figure lay on his stomach, a position from which Tadd had cried himself to sleep.

Her gaze lifted in stunned wonderment to Judd's face. 'How?' she whispered.

'I can't begin to explain it.' He shook his head with a similar expression of awed confusion mixed with quiet acceptance of the fact. His gaze wandered gently back to hers. 'Any more than I can explain how I knew Tadd would be here.'

Valerie remembered stories of the salmon finding their way back to their spawning grounds and wondered if Tadd possessed that same mysterious instinct in order to be led here. It was a miracle that filled her with a glowing warmth.

Judd swung off the horse and reached up to lift her down. His look, as their eyes met, mirrored her marvelling feeling. When her feet were on the ground, her hands remained on his shoulders as she stood close to him, unmoving.

'It's right, isn't it?' Judd murmured. 'It proves that what we shared here was something special.'

'Yes,' Valerie agreed, a throb of profound emotion in her answer.

His mouth came down on hers to seal the wonder of their blessing. The closeness they shared was marked by a spiritual union rather than mere physical contact. The beauty of it filled Valerie with a sublime sense of joy such as she had never experienced in his arms. It was nearly as awe-inspiring as the miracle they had witnessed.

When they parted, she was incapable of speech. Judd let her turn from his arms and followed silently as she made her way across the clearing to the place where their son lay. She knelt beside him, staring for a moment at his sleeping tear-streaked face.

'Tadd darling.' Her voice sounded husky and unbelievably loving. 'Wake up! Mommy's here.'

He struggled awake, blinking at her with the misty eyes of a child that had suffered a bad dream and still wasn't certain it had ended. She smoothed the rumpled mop of brown hair on his forehead and wiped his damp cheek with her thumb.

'Mommy?' His voice wavered.

'I'm here,' she assured him.

'I didn't mean to run away.' His lips quivered. 'I

was going to come back after I got a puppy. But I couldn't find Judd's house, and I . . . I couldn't find you.'

'It doesn't matter,' Valerie said to dismiss the remnants of his fear. 'We found you.'

She gathered him into her arms, letting his arms wind around her neck in a strangling hold as he began to cry again. Judd crouched down beside them, his hand reaching out to hold Tadd's shoulder.

'It's all right, son,' he offered in comfort. 'We're here. There's nothing to be frightened about any more.'

Tadd lifted his head to stare at Judd, sniffling back his tears. Almost immediately he turned away and buried his face against Valerie. Hurt flickered briefly in Judd's eyes at the rejection in Tadd's action.

'I think he's embarrassed to have you see him cry,' Valerie whispered the explanation.

The stiffness went out of Judd's smile. 'Everyone cries, Tadd, no matter how old they are,' he assured the small boy, and was rewarded with a peeping look. Like Tadd, Valerie had difficulty in imagining that Judd had ever cried in his life, but his quiet words of assurance had eased the damage to a small boy's pride. 'Come on,' said Judd, rising to his feet, 'It's almost dark. It's time we were getting you home.'

Tadd's arms remained firmly entwined around her neck. At Judd's questioning look, Valerie responded, 'I can carry him,' and lifted her clinging son as she rose.

Judd mounted the grey horse and reached down for Valerie to hand him Tadd. When Tadd was positioned astride the grey behind him, Judd slipped his foot from the left stirrup and helped Valerie into the saddle in front of him. The grey pranced beneath the extra weight.

'Hang on, Tadd,' Judd instructed, and a pair of small arms obediently tightened around his waist. Judd turned the grey horse towards the farmhouse.

CHAPTER TEN

Twilight was purpling the sky as they approached the house. Judd reined the grey horse towards the paddock gate and leaned sideways to unlatch it, swinging it open and riding the horse through. Stopping in front of the porch, he reached behind him and swung Tadd to the ground, then dismounted to lift Valerie down.

'Thank the Lord, you found him!' Clara came bustling on to the porch as if she had been standing at the window watching for them.

'A little frightened, but safe and sound,' said Judd, his hand rested lightly on Valerie's waist. He glanced down at her, smiling gently at the experience they had shared.

Tadd went racing on to the porch. 'I was going to Judd's house to see the puppies and I got lost,' he told Clara. Now that he was safely back, the episode had become an adventure to be recounted.

Clara's knees made a cracking sound as she bent to take hold of his shoulders and scold him. 'You should be spanked for the way you made your mother and me worry!' But already she was pulling him into her arms to hug him tightly. Tadd squirmed in embarrassment when Clara kissed his cheek and rubbed his hand over the spot when she straightened. 'If you hadn't come back before dark, I was going to call the sheriff and have them send out a search party.'

'I think we're all glad it wasn't necessary,' Judd inserted, and started towards the porch with Valerie at his side.

'Isn't that the truth!' Clara agreed emphatically.

'If it hadn't been for Judd, I wouldn't have found him,' Valerie stated, giving the credit for finding Tadd where it was due.

'Someone else had more to do with it than I did.' Judd gave the responsibility to someone higher up.

As he took the first step on to the porch, Valerie felt his gaze slide past her to the car. The moment she had been dreading ever since the house had come into sight was there. The boot of the car was opened and all of the suitcases and boxes stuffed inside were in plain sight. Judd stiffened to a halt. As his arm dropped from her waist, Valerie continued up the porch steps, a tightness gripping her throat.

'What's going on here? Is someone leaving?' His low, slicing demand was initially met with pulsing silence.

She turned to face him. Leaving after what they had just shared was going to be a hundred times more difficult, but Valerie knew it was a decision she had to stand behind. The words of response were a long time in coming.

Finally it was Tadd who answered him. 'We're going back to Cincinnati. That's why I ran away— 'cause I wanted to stay here and have a puppy and Mom said I couldn't.'

At the cold fury gathering in Judd's gaze, Valerie half turned her head, her eyes never leaving Judd's face. 'Clara, will you take Tadd in the house? He hasn't had any supper. He's probably hungry.'

'Of course,' her friend agreed in a subdued voice. 'Come with me, Tadd.' Clara ushered him towards the door and into the house.

When the screen door closed behind them, Judd slowly mounted the steps to stand before Valerie. 'Is it true what Tadd said? Are you leaving?' His voice rumbled out the questions from somewhere deep inside, like distant thunder.

She swallowed and forced out a calm answer. 'Yes, it's true.'

'You promised you'd stay,' Judd reminded her in a savage breath.

'No, I promised there'd be no more talk about me leaving,' she corrected, her jaw rigid with control.

'So you were going to leave without talking about it,' he accused. 'You knew I was going to call. You knew I wanted to see you tonight.'

'And I wanted to be gone before you did,' Valerie admitted. He grabbed her shoulders. 'Don't touch me, Judd. Please don't touch me,' she demanded in a voice that broke under the strain. If he held her, she knew she would give in, whether or not it was right or wrong.

He released her as abruptly as he had taken her. Turning away, he swung a fist at an upright post. The force of the blow shook the dust from the porch rafters.

'Why?' he demanded in a tortured voice and spun around to face her. 'Dammit to hell, Valerie! I've got a right to know why!'

For a choked moment she couldn't answer him. A welling of tears had turned his eyes into viridescent pools of anguish. She wanted to reach up and touch the sparkling drops to see if they were real or merely crocodile tears. The sight of them held her spellbound.

'When I discovered your mother knew about us ... and Tadd, I realised I couldn't stay no matter how much I wanted to,' she explained hesitantly. 'Maybe if I hadn't learned that she knew, or maybe if I'd never met her, it would have been easier to stay. Now, it's impossible.'

'Why is my mother to blame for you leaving?' Confusion and anger burned in his look as he searched her expression, trying to follow her logic that he didn't understand.

'I don't really blame her.' Valerie was having difficulty finding the right words. 'I'm sure it's only natural that she wants to become acquainted with your son.'

'You'd better explain to me what you're talking about, because you aren't making any sense,' Judd warned. 'In one breath you say you want to stay and in the next you're saying you can't because of my mother. Either you want to stay or you don't!'

'I can't,' she stated. Her chin quivered with the pain her words were causing. 'Don't you see, Judd? What will Tadd think when he learns about us? Eventually he will. We can't keep it from him for ever. I can't become your mistress. I can't put my wants above Tadd's needs.'

'Then you do love me?' His hands recaptured her

arms. 'Valerie, I have to know,' he demanded roughly.

'Yes, I love you,' she choked out the admission, and averted her gaze. 'But it doesn't change anything. Nothing at all, Judd.' Relief trembled through her when he let her go. She closed her eyes and fought the attraction that made her want to go back into his arms.

'I wanted to see you tonight to give you this.' A snapping sound opened her eyes. Judd was holding a small box. In a bed of green velvet was an engagement ring, set with an emerald flanked by diamonds. Valerie gasped at the sight of it. 'And to ask you to marry me.'

Her gaze flew to his as she took a step backwards. 'Don't joke about this,' she pleaded.

'It isn't a joke,' Judd assured her. 'As a matter of fact, I bought the ring the day after you told me about Tadd. But I didn't give it to you before now because I didn't want you marrying me because of him.'

'I don't understand,' she murmured, afraid that Judd didn't mean what he was implying.

'I didn't want you marrying me in order to have a father for your child—our child,' he corrected. 'I didn't want you marrying me for the Prescott name or wealth. I wanted your reason to be because you loved me and wanted me as much as I love and want you.'

A piercing joy flashed through her. She stared into the warm green fires of his eyes that seemed to echo the words he had just spoken. She was afraid to say anything in case she was dreaming.

'Until today I wasn't certain how much you really cared about me,' Judd continued. 'But when I saw the terror in your eyes at the thought that I might have been hurt by the stallions, I knew that what you felt for me was real. My name and position meant nothing to you, not even the fact that I'm the father of your son.'

Without waiting for an affirmative acceptance of his proposal, Judd took her left hand and slipped the ring on her finger. Valerie watched, slightly dazed, as he lifted her hand to his mouth and kissed the emerald stone that was the same vivid colour as his eyes.

'You can't really want to marry me.' She heard herself say. 'I'm not good enough for you.'

Anger flashed in his eyes. 'Don't ever say that again!'

Valerie glowed under the violent dismissal of her statement, but she persisted, 'Your mother told me you'd always said you wanted your wife to have classy breeding, spirit and staying power. My background is very common.'

Judd's mouth thinned impatiently, but he responded to her argument. 'Class has nothing to do with a person's social position. I became acquainted with your grandfather and know you come from fine stock. That untamed streak in you proves your spirit. And as for staying power, after seven years I believe that has answered itself.'

'Judd——' she began.

'No more discussion,' he interrupted. 'You're going to marry me and that's the end of it.'

'Yes!' She breathed the answer against his lips

an instant before he claimed hers.

An involuntary moan escaped her throat at the completeness of her love. His kiss was thorough, his masterful technique without fault. Beneath her hands, she could feel the thudding of his heart, racing as madly as her own. Yet her appetite seemed insatiable.

'I thought I loved you seven years ago, Judd,' she murmured as he trailed kisses down to her neck, 'but it's nothing compared to what I feel for you now.'

'I was such a fool then, darling,' he muttered against her skin. 'A blind, arrogant fool.'

'It doesn't matter that you didn't love me then,' she told him softly. 'It's enough that you love me now.'

'I was obsessed with you seven years ago,' Judd confessed, lifting his head to let his fingers stroke her cheek and trace the outline of her lips.

'I was just someone you made love to.' Valerie denied his attempt to have her believe she had been special to him. The past was behind them. The way he felt towards her at this moment was all that counted.

'For every time I made love to you, there were a hundred times that I wanted to,' Judd replied. 'It irritated me that a fiery little kitten could sink her claws into me that way. All you had to do seven years ago was crook your little finger at me and I came running. Do you have any idea how deflating it was to my masculine pride to realise that I had no control where you were concerned?'

'No, I didn't know.' She looked at him in surprise.

His green eyes were dark and smouldering. There was no mistaking that he meant every word he was saying. His caressing thumb parted her lips and probed at the white barrier of her teeth. Unconsciously Valerie nibbled at its end, the tip of her tongue tasting the saltiness of his skin.

'God, you're beautiful, Valerie,' he said it as reverently as a prayer and moved to let his mouth take the place of his thumb, letting it slide to her chin.

He fired her soul with his burning need of her. Valerie arched closer to him, pliantly moulding herself to his hard length. His hands were crushing and caressing, fanning the flames that were threatening to burn out of control. Just in time, he pulled back, shuddering against her with the force of his emotion and rubbing his forehead against hers. He breathed in deeply to regain his sanity.

'Do you see what I mean?' he asked after several seconds. The rawness in his teasing voice vibrated in the air. 'I never intended to make love to you that first time, but your kisses were like a drug that I'd become addicted to. After a while, they weren't enough. I needed something more potent. Even if you hadn't been willing, I would have taken you that first time. It isn't something I'm very proud to admit.'

'But I did want you to make love to me, Judd,' Valerie assured him, hearing the disturbed shakiness in her own voice. 'Foolishly I thought it was the only way to hold you. Also, I wasn't satisfied any more either. I wanted to be yours completely and I thought that was the way.'

'If you hadn't, there are times when I think I might have crawled all the way to your grandfather to beg his permission to marry you. That's how completely you had me under your spell,' Judd told her, and rubbed his mouth against her temple. 'But it's something we'll never know for sure.'

'No,' Valerie agreed. 'And I wouldn't want to turn back the clock to find out. Not now.'

He couldn't seem to stop slowly trailing kisses over her face. His gentle adoration was almost worshipful, while Valerie felt like a supplicant begging for his caresses. This freedom to touch each other with no more self-imposed restraints was a heady elixir to both of them.

'When I made love to you that first time and realised no other man had ever touched you, I was filled with such a self-contempt and loathing that I swore I'd never come near you again,' Judd murmured. 'I felt like the lowest animal on earth. Then you confronted me with your justifiable accusations that I'd abused you for my pleasure and dropped you, and I was lost.'

'I thought you were avoiding me because I was so inexperienced,' Valerie remembered, her fingertips reaching up to explore his jaw and curl into his hair. 'Because I hadn't satisfied you.'

'It was never that,' Judd denied. 'You were a wonder to me. I wanted you to know the same feeling of fulfilment that you gave me.'

'Judd, there's something I want to ask.' Valerie

hesitated, hating to ask the question, yet after his revelation it troubled her.

'Ask away,' he insisted, lightly kissing her cheek-bone.

Her hands slid down to his chest, her fingers spreading over the hard, pulsing flesh. Eluding his caressing mouth, she lifted her head to see his face, and the contentment mixed with desire that she saw reflected in his eyes almost made her dismiss the question as unimportant and as trivial as all that had gone before them.

'Why didn't you ever take me anywhere, ask me out on a date?' she finally asked the question, her look soft and curious.

Judd winced slightly, then smiled. 'You were my private treasure,' he explained. 'I wanted to keep you all to myself. I wanted to be the only one who knew about you. I guess I was afraid if I took you somewhere someone might steal you from me. So I kept trying to hide you, but I ended up losing you anyway.'

'Only for a time,' she reminded him and sighed. 'I thought it was because I was just Elias Wentworth's granddaughter, not worthy enough to be seen in the company of a Prescott.'

'I know. Or at least, I realised it that last time we met,' he qualified. 'I was angered by that. But I was more worried that someone at the party you were so anxious to attend might take you from me. And I suddenly questioned whether you hadn't been meeting me just to eventually obtain an invitation to one of the Prescotts' parties in order to meet someone else. I was enraged at the thought that you might be using me.'

'Judd, you didn't!' Valerie breathed the incredulous and frowning protest.

'Jealousy is an ugly thing, darling,' he admitted, 'especially the obsessively posessive kind. Mine was almost a terminal case.'

'You don't need to be jealous. Not now and not then,' she told him, her throat aching from the love she felt. 'There's never been anyone else but you. Oh, I've dated a few times these last seven years,' she admitted in an offhand air that said they meant nothing. 'But it seemed that if I couldn't have you, I didn't want to settle for second best.'

Judd kissed her hard, as if grateful for the reassurance and angry that he had needed it. 'The week after we argued and you stormed away, I practically haunted our place. Then I went into town and overheard someone mention that you'd gone away. For a while I told myself I was glad you'd left because I could finally be in control of my own life again. When I found myself missing you, I tried to make believe it was because you'd been such a satisfactory lover.'

'And it wasn't that?' she whispered hopefully. Her hands felt the lifting of his chest as Judd took a deep breath before shaking his dark head.

'No, it wasn't that,' he agreed. 'After six months, I finally accepted the fact that mere lust wouldn't last that long. That's when I rode over to your grandfather's to find out where you were. Remember that filly I told you I bought from him?'

'Yes,' Valerie remembered.

'That's the excuse I used.' There was a rueful

twist of his mouth. 'It took me a week of visits to get the subject around to you. When he finally did mention you, it was to tell me you'd eloped with some man.'

'But——'

'I know.' Judd staved off her words. 'It wasn't true, but at the time I didn't know it. I almost went out of my mind. Half the time I was calling myself every name in the book for letting you go. Or else I was congratulating myself on being rid of a woman who could forget me in six months. But mostly I was insane with jealousy for the man who now had you for himself.'

'And I was trying so desperately to hate you all this time.' Her voice cracked and she bit at her lip to hold back a sob. 'Seven years.' So much time had been wasted, unnecessarily.

'Everybody pays for their mistakes, Valerie,' he reminded her. 'What we did was wrong and we both had to pay. My price was seven years of visiting your grandfather and listening to him talk about your happy family and his grandchild and all the places your husband was taking you to see. I had seven years of endless torture picturing you in another man's arms. While you had to bear my child alone and face the world alone with him.'

'In Tadd, I had a part of you. I loved him even more because of that.' Valerie hugged him tightly to share the pain they had both known.

'When your grandfather died and Mickey told me you were coming for the funeral, I vowed I wouldn't come near you. I didn't think I could stand seeing you with your husband and child. But I couldn't stay away from the house.' His voice was partially muffled by the thickness of her tawny hair as his mouth moved over it, his chin rubbing her head in an absent caress. 'I think I was trying to rid myself of your ghost. I was almost hoping that having a child had ruined your figure and being married would have turned you into a nagging shrew—anything to rid me of your haunting image. Instead you'd matured into a stunningly beautiful woman who made the woman-child I loved seem pale in comparison.'

'When you walked out of that door, I nearly ran into your arms,' Valerie admitted. 'It was as if those seven years we were apart had never existed.'

'If I hadn't believed you had a husband somewhere, that's exactly what would have happened,' he said, and she felt his mouth curve into a smile against her hair. 'It wasn't until that night that I found out you didn't have a husband. It was as if the heavens had just opened up and I tried to rush your surrender.'

'Before I came back, I thought I'd got over you. All it took was seeing you again to realise I hadn't,' she confessed. 'I fought it because I knew how much you'd hurt me the last time and I didn't think I could stand it if it happened again. And I ... I thought all you wanted was to have me back as your lover.'

'My lover, my wife, my friend, my everything,' Judd corrected fiercely. 'It was after the funeral that I told my mother about our affair seven years ago and that this time I was going to marry you no matter how I had to make you agree. But first I had to try to convince you to stay.'

'I thought you were trying to set me up as your mistress when you offered to lease the farm,' Valerie remembered.

'I was,' he admitted. 'I knew you still felt a spark of desire for me.'

'A spark?' she laughed. 'It was a forest fire!'

'I didn't know that,' Judd reminded her. 'I was simply desperate to try anything that would re-establish what we once had. Later I could persuade you to marry me.'

'But when you found out about Tadd——' Valerie began.

'Yes, I had the weapon,' he nodded. 'I knew that for his sake I could persuade you to marry me. That's when I realised that if you married me without loving me, the hell of the last seven years would be nothing compared to what the future would hold. I had to find out first whether you felt more than sexual attraction for me.'

'Have I convinced you?' She gazed into his face, her eyes brimming with boundless love.

His mouth dimpled at the corners. 'I'll be convinced when you stand in front of a minister with me and say, "I do". And if I can arrange it, that day will come tomorrow.'

'The sooner the better,' Valerie agreed, and couldn't resist murmuring the title, 'Mrs Judd Prescott, Valerie Prescott. It sounds beautiful, but I'm not sure it's me.'

'You'd better get used to it,' he warned. 'Because it's going to be your name for the rest of your life.'

'Are you very sure that's what you want?' Just

for an instant, she let herself doubt.

'Yes.' Judd kissed her hard in punishment. 'As sure as I am that our next child is going to be born on the right side of the blanket.'

'What about Tadd?' Valerie began.

Only to be interrupted by Clara ordering, 'Tadd! Come back here this minute!' from inside the house.

A pair of stampeding feet raced to the screen door and pushed it open as Tadd came rushing out, staring wide-eyed at the embracing pair. 'Clara said we might not be leaving after all!' he declared. 'Is it true, Mom? Are we going to stay?'

'Yes,' Valerie admitted, making no effort to move out of Judd's arms, not that he would have permitted it.

'Till summer's over?' he questioned further.

'No, you're going to live here,' Judd answered him this time.

Clara came hustling to the door, scolding, 'Tadd, I thought I told you not to come out here until I said you could.' Her shrewd blue eyes glanced apologetically at Valerie. 'He bolted out of the kitchen before I could stop him.'

'It's all right,' Valerie assured her, smiling into the twinkling eyes.

'Does that mean I can have a puppy?' Tadd breathed in excited anticipation.

'You not only can have a puppy, you're also going to have a father,' Judd told him. 'I'm going to marry your mother. Is that all right with you?'

'Sure.' Tadd gave his permission and switched the subject back to a matter of more urgent interest. 'When can I have my puppy?'

'In another couple of weeks,' Judd promised. 'As soon as it's old enough to leave its mother.'

'That long?' Tadd grimaced in disappointment.

'It's better than seven years,' Judd murmured to Valerie as his arm curved more tightly around her waist.

'It will go by fast, Tadd,' Valerie told him. 'In the meantime, you can choose the one you want and play with it so it will get to know you.'

'Can I go over now? I know which one I want,' he said eagerly.

A wicked light began to dance in Judd's green eyes. 'Clara might be persuaded to take you,' he suggested. 'While you're playing with the puppies, she could be helping my mother make arrangements for the wedding reception tomorrow.'

'And leave you here alone with Valerie?' Clara scoffed at the very idea of it. 'As virile as you are, Judd Prescott, there'd be a baby born eight months and twenty-nine days after the wedding!'

Judd chuckled and Valerie felt her cheeks grow warm at the thought. He glanced down at her, his gaze soft and loving.

'She's right,' he said. 'After seven years, I can wait one more night. Because it's the last night we're ever going to be apart. I promise you that, Valerie.' Unmindful of the small boy and the older woman looking on, his dark head bent to meet the toffee gold of Valerie's.

HEART OF STONE

HEART OF STONE

BY
JANET DAILEY

MILLS & BOON LIMITED
15–16 BROOK'S MEWS
LONDON W1A 1DR

First published 1980
Australian copyright 1980
Philippine copyright 1980
Reprinted 1980
This edition 1984

© Janet Dailey 1980

ISBN 0 263 74708 5

Set in Linotype Pilgrim 12 on 14 pt.
09—0584

Made and printed in Great Britain by
Cox & Wyman Ltd, Reading

CHAPTER ONE

THERE was a sudden flurry of activity outside Stephanie's office. Located in the heart of the luxurious New Hampshire inn, it gave her ready access to all phases of the operation. Through the open doorway Stephanie had a partial view of the front desk, which gave her a feeling of the comings and goings of the guests. Across the hall was the housekeeping department. The office next to hers belonged to her brother, Perry Hall, the manager of the inn, and her boss.

When Mrs Adamson, the dining room hostess, went hurrying past Stephanie's door, her curiosity was throughly aroused. Something unusual was going on. Even though she had actually worked in the White Boar Inn a short three months, Stephanie felt the accelerated tempo of the inn's pulse, a tense quickening of interest.

The unbalanced ledger sheet on her desk was forgotten as she speared the lead pencil through the chestnut hair above her ear and rose from her chair. Bookkeeping was invariably the last department to know anything if she allowed routine to run its normal course. Since Perry was her brother, she didn't choose to sit back and wait to be informed. She had been isolated from the mainstream of life for too many years to let it continue now that she had rejoined it.

In the hallway, she glanced towards the front desk. Her blue eyes noted the expressions of harried excitement in the faces of the usually unflappable pair manning the registration counter. It was rare indeed for the arrival of an important personage to create such a disturbance, since the inn catered to the wealthy and the notable. Besides, every room was already taken, occupied by guests on hand to view the autumn splendour of the White Mountains, and there were reservations all the way through the winter season to spring.

Puzzled by the unknown cause of all this barely subdued commotion, Stephanie absently fingered the scarab pendant suspended by a gold chain to nestle in the valley between her breasts, the loose weave of her white rollneck sweater providing the backdrop for the jewellery. The slight frown remained in her expression as she walked the few feet to her brother's office. The door was standing open and she paused within its frame, not wanting to interrupt her brother's consultation with Mrs Adamson.

'Get a bottle on ice right away,' he was instructing the woman, who was hastily making notes on a pad. Perry, too, was consulting the papers in front of him, not glancing up to see Stephanie in the doorway. His brown hair was rumpled as if he had run his fingers through it many times. 'Fix a tray with a selection of cheeses and fresh fruits to go with it. You'd better re-check the wine cellar and make sure you have an ample supply of his favourite wines in stock, too. Alert your staff. I want them on their toes in case he decides to dine in the restaurant this evening. I don't want—— Flowers!' Perry interrupted himself to exclaim. 'I nearly forgot the damn flowers.' He punched the buzzer to summon his secretary.

For once, the young girl appeared within seconds. She looked pale and anxious, more timid than usual. Despite her youth, Connie York was highly skilled and competent. Her chief flaw was a marked lack of self-confidence, which was blatantly in evidence at the moment.

'Yes, Mr Hall?' She made a question of her response to his summons, her small face pinched into tense lines of unease and framed with dark hair.

His upward glance took note of Stephanie in the doorway, but he didn't acknowledge her presence in his office beyond that. 'Call the florist. If they can't have a bouquet of roses delivered here within ninety minutes, I want you to pick them up.'

'Yes, sir.' Her head bobbed in quick agreement, but she didn't make any move to follow through with the order.

Perry, who was usually extraordinarily patient with his self-effacing secretary, sent her an irritated look. 'You aren't going to get it done standing there, Connie. Go on!'

'I know, but——' She wavered uncertainly.

'What is it?' he demanded in short temper. 'I haven't got time to coax it out of you.'

Stephanie's gaze wandered over her brother's face in surprise. Six years older than herself, he rarely allowed stressful situations to shake him. He had been more than just her big brother; he had been her idol for as long as she could remember. Life hadn't been easy for him . . . or for her either. Their mother had died when Stephanie was only four. Perry had played surrogate mother to her, fixing meals and keeping house while their father worked long hours, skilled only as a ski instructor and bartender, to make ends meet.

Five years ago, when Stephanie was seventeen, it had seemed the world would become their oyster. Perry had obtained a scholarship to attend a prestigious post-graduate law school and Stephanie had been accepted by a prominent women's college. Then a freak skiing accident had left their father a paraplegic, and Perry had given up his scholarship to take the position of assistant manager of this inn while Stephanie stayed home to take care of their father. A virulent pneumonia virus had claimed their father four months ago. In many ways, his death had been a blessing—for him and for them.

Stephanie hadn't completely adjusted to the freedom from responsibility that had matured both of them beyond their years while it deprived them of the pleasures of youth. The night course she had taken in accounting to supplement their income by doing bookkeeping at home for small businesses had provided her with the experience to take the post as bookkeeper at the inn when her predecessor had retired with few grumblings about nepotism because her brother had become the manager in the last year.

She liked working at the inn, being with people and being part of things. Most of all, she liked working with her brother. She had come to respect his competency in a position whose duties were far-ranging and varied. Perry always appeared to be totally in control whether dealing with a crisis in the restaurant kitchen or organising the staff. Which was why Stephanie was surprised by his harried attitude at the moment. It didn't seem in character.

'It's just that . . . I was wondering . . .' Connie

was stumbling over the reason for her hesitation.

'I don't have all day. Please get to the point,' Perry ordered.

'It's your appointment,' his secretary began, intimidated by his abruptness.

'I told you to cancel them.' His mouth thinned with impatience.

'Yes, but——' She bit her lower lip.

Perry appeared to mentally count to ten, in an effort to control his temper. 'But what, Connie?' he asked with forced evenness.

'You're supposed to speak at a luncheon this noon.' She rushed the explanation. 'It's been on the agenda for two months. They couldn't possibly get anyone to take your place at such late notice.'

Perry groaned. 'Is that today?'

'Yes, sir.' Anxiety tortured Connie's expression. 'What should I do?'

'Do? There's nothing you can do,' he sighed. 'I'll have to attend the luncheon, but cancel everything else. And get those flowers.'

'Yes, sir.' With a nod of her head, the girl disappeared inside her adjoining office.

Returning his attention to the woman in front of his desk, Perry raked a hand through his dark hair again, adding to its disorder. 'You know the routine, Mrs Adamson. I trust you to handle it.'

He cast a glance at his wristwatch, in effect dismissing the hostess.

Stephanie stepped to one side so the woman could exit through the open door. From the conversation she had overheard, she had a general idea what was happening. With the exception of the private suite, the inn was fully booked. And the suite was reserved exclusively for the owner or his personal guests. Before she had a chance to ask whose arrival was anticipated, Perry was addressing her.

'Whatever your problem is, Stephanie, it will have to wait—unless someone has absconded with the receipts. In that case, I don't want to know about it for three days,' he declared with a tired shake of his head.

'I don't have any problem,' she assured him. 'I'm just trying to figure out what's going on. Who's coming? The place is in a quiet uproar— if there is such a thing.'

Sighing, Perry rocked back in his swivel chair. Eyes the same blue as her own skimmed her slender figure in its white sweater and green tartan skirt. A faint smile touched his mouth when his gaze returned to her face with its soft frame of sleek chestnut hair.

'Brock is making another one of his impromptu visits. He called a half an hour ago to say he'd be here by two this afternoon. He's driving up from

Boston,' he explained as tension etched lines in his strong face.

'Aha!' Stephanie mocked him to ease his concern. 'Now I understand why everyone is jumping at the slightest sound. The big man himself is coming to inspect his property.'

'It's all right for you to joke about it. Canfield expects the best and I am the one who has to explain why, if he doesn't get it.' Perry rubbed his fingers against a spot in the centre of his forehead.

'I don't know what you're worrying about.' Stephanie walked to the back of his chair and let her hands knead the taut cords between his neck and shoulders. 'Don't forget I've been keeping the books for the past three months. I know how very well the inn has been doing. Brock Canfield can't possibly have any complaints about your work or how you run the inn.'

'We have done well,' he admitted, relaxing under the massage of her hands. 'If that trend continues through the winter ski season, we should have our best year ever.'

'That proves my point, doesn't it?' she reasoned.

'The point will be proved only when it's accomplished,' Perry reminded her. 'In the meantime, Brock is going to judge by what he sees on this trip.'

'He won't have any complaints.' Stephanie was certain of that. The service at the inn was flawless. Even the hard-to-please guests found little to grumble about. 'Do you know this will be my first opportunity to meet this paragon of all manhood, Brock Canfield?' she realised. 'You've worked here what? Five years? Everybody talks about him like he was God. Depending on their sex, they either tremble or quiver when they hear his name.' She laughed. 'I've heard him alternately described as a ruthless tycoon or a gorgeous hunk of man. Now I'll be able to find out for myself which is the real Brock Canfield!'

'He's both, plus a few other things.' Her brother took hold of one of her hands to end the rubdown and pull her around to the side of his chair. Handsome in an attractive kind of way, he studied her for a quiet second. 'I have this luncheon to attend, so I'll have to deputise you to stand in for me in case I'm not back when Brock arrives.'

'Me?' Stephanie frowned her surprise.

'Somebody has to be on hand to welcome him. Connie practically cringes every time he looks at her,' Perry explained with a wry grimace. 'And Vic is home sleeping after being on duty all night,' he added, referring to the night manager. 'I can't think of anyone else. Do you mind?'

'Of course not. What do I have to do, besides

be on hand to greet him?' Despite her willing agreement, Stephanie experienced a shiver of unease at some of the more formidable descriptions she'd heard applied to the inn's owner.

'Show him to his suite and make certain everything is in order. Connie is getting the flowers and Mrs Adamson will have a bottle of champagne on ice, along with some cheese and fruit. In general, just see that he has everything he wants.'

'That sounds simple enough,' she shrugged.

'Watch your step, Stephanie,' her brother advised, suddenly serious.

She was confused by the warning. 'I'm not likely to say anything that would offend him.' She wasn't the outspoken type. Most of the time she was very tactful, able to curb her tongue despite the provocation.

'I know you wouldn't.' He dismissed that possibility with a wave of his hand. 'I was trying to say that you should stay clear of Brock Canfield. He goes through women the way a gambler goes through a deck of cards. He's rich, good-looking in a way, and can be both persuasive and forceful. I'm told that can be an irresistible combination.'

'I've heard a few stories about him,' Stephanie admitted.

'I wouldn't like to see you get mixed up with him, because I know you'd be hurt. Honestly, Steph, I'm not trying to play the heavy-handed big brother.' Perry seemed to smile at himself. 'It's just that I know he's going to take one look at you and get ideas. You haven't had all that much experience with men, especially his kind.'

'Experienced or not, I think I can take care of myself.' She didn't mind that Perry was worried about her. In fact, she liked the idea that he cared enough about her to try to protect her. A smile hovered around the corners of her mouth. 'Is that why you never brought him home to dinner when I suggested it during his other visits?'

'Partly,' her brother admitted. 'But mostly it was because Brock isn't your home-cooked meal type. He's smooth and finished, like a diamond that's been cut into the perfect stone, hard and unfeeling.'

'And diamonds don't sit down at a table set with ironstone flatware,' Stephanie concluded in understanding.

'Something like that,' Perry agreed. 'Now, off with you,' he ordered in a mock threat. 'I have to find my notes for the luncheon speech.'

She started for the door and hesitated short of her goal. 'When will you be back—in case Brock asks?'

'Between half past one and two.'

'Maybe he'll be late,' she suggested, and walked to the door.

Forty-five minutes later, Perry stuck his head inside her office to let her know he was leaving to keep his luncheon engagement. 'Take care of Brock if he arrives before I get back,' he reminded her, unnecessarily.

'I will,' she promised. 'Good luck with the speech.'

He waved and left. A few minutes later Stephanie closed her office to have lunch. Her appetite was all but non-existent, so she chose a salad plate and picked at it for twenty minutes before giving up. A few minutes before one, she obtained the key to the private suite from Mary at the front desk and checked to be certain all was in readiness for Brock Canfield's arrival.

There had been no occasion for Stephanie to enter the private suite before. It consisted of a spacious sitting room, an equally large bedroom with a king-sized bed, and an enormous bath. Stephanie explored it with unashamed curiosity.

Bronze-tipped double-paned windows offered an unparalleled view of the White Mountains cloaked in their rust and gold autumn colours. Sunlight streaming through the glass laid a pattern of gold on the stark white floor of Italian ceramic, set in a herringbone design. There was nothing about the sitting room that resembled New England except for the scene outside its windows.

The furnishings included a white leather armchair and ottoman. A pair of short sofas were upholstered in natural Haitian cotton with coffee tables of antique white. The walls were covered with grass cloth in an ivory shade. A floor-to-ceiling cabinet had been built into one wall, which included a shelf for a television to be rolled out. A glass-topped rattan table and four chairs were the only natural wood pieces in the room; besides an eight foot high secretary, hand-carved in walnut. A gold leaf Coromandel screen opened to reveal a bar. In total, it was an eclectic blend of periods and designs.

Stephanie took note of the bouquet of long-stemmed roses on the coffee table. The arrangement had an oriental touch with bare branches rising above the blood-red blooms. A vintage bottle of champagne was on ice in a silver bucket supported by a stud. A tray of cheese as well as an attractive bowl of fresh fruit was on the rattan table.

When Stephanie ventured into the bedroom, she stepped on to thick, shrimp-coloured carpeting. The same colour was repeated but dominated by black, in the patterned bedspread and matching drapes. An ornate ebony headboard adorned

the king-sized bed and was flanked by carved
night stands of the same dark hardwood. A hunt-
ing scene was depicted on an elephant tusk and
a second was repeated in a massive collage. They
gave the room the masculine accent.

The bathroom was a bit overwhelming in its
luxury, with the shrimp carpeting extending into
it. A white Jacuzzi bathtub was set in a platform
faced with Italian marble that continued all the
way up to the ceiling. The wall area not covered
with marble was hung with black silk, a collec-
tion of framed South American butterflies making use of its back drop. The bath towels were all
a very sensual black velour material, thick and
rich-looking.

Leaving the suite was like stepping into another
world. The inn was luxurious, but it attempted to
give its guests the flavour of New England. It was
obvious that Brock Canfield had decorated the
suite to please himself. Stephanie wasn't certain
if she liked the result or whether she was indulg-
ing in a little inverted snobbery.

As she entered the lobby, she thought she preferred the wide spaciousness of the white-painted
woodwork and its massive stone fireplace with
the welcoming warmth of the flames emitting the
pungent aroma of woodsmoke. Expensive Currier
and Ives lithographs adorned the white walls and
added the flavour of New England to the lobby.

The brass chandelier suspended from the ceiling was a nuisance to clean, Stephanie knew, but the hurricane globes were attractive and homey.

She stopped at the front desk to return the key. 'Any sign of Mr Canfield yet, Mary?'

The mere mention of the owner's name seemed to unnerve the usually calm woman. 'Mr Canfield? No, not that I know of. Ben, have you seen him?' She suddenly didn't trust her own answer, and sought the confirmation of the bellboy.

'No. He hasn't arrived yet.' He was much more positive.

'I'll be in my office,' Stephanie replied. 'Let me know as soon as he comes.'

Circling behind the registration counter, she walked down the short hallway to her office. She left the door open so she could be aware of the activity going on outside her four walls. The excited buzzing and whispering hadn't lessened since the news had circulated through the inn's grapevine of the imminent arrival of its owner. There was electricity in the air, and Stephanie wasn't immune to its volatile charge.

Before she put her bag away, she paused in front of the small mirror on a side wall to freshen her lipstick. But the new coat of bronzed pink on her mouth only accented the faint pallor in her cheeks. She stroked on a hint of blusher, then retouched her long lashes with mascara. By the time she was finished, she had completely redone her make-up.

Studying her reflection, she decided she was attractive but definitely not a raving beauty. The combination of thick chestnut hair and Corinthian blue eyes was pleasing, but not startling. Her figure was slender with all the proper curves, but not eye-popping. There was a certain freshness about her, although she looked twenty-two.

All the while, she assured herself that this assessment had nothing to do with Brock Canfield or the warning Perry had given. Still, there was a little part of her that was wondering what it would be like if someone like Brock Canfield made a pass at her—a passing curiosity, no more than that, she insisted, just a flattering thought.

'Stephanie!' Mary hissed from the doorway. '*He* just drove up out front. Ben's going out to get his luggage now. And he has a woman with him.'

Initially Stephanie smiled at the woman passing the information in such a frantic whisper. Who would hear? And what would it matter? But the last sentence wiped the smile from her face. Too late, she remembered that in the past, Perry had mentioned that Brock Canfield often brought his current girl-friend with him.

But what was the procedure? Did the woman stay in his suite? There wasn't any choice, was there? There wasn't a single other empty room in the entire inn. But she was attacked by the same uncertainty that Mary had suffered earlier, and the need to have someone back up her conclusion.

'Was Perry informed that Mr Canfield was bringing a guest?' she asked the desk clerk.

'He didn't say anything to me about it,' Mary replied with a negative shake of her head.

'Mr Canfield wouldn't expect us to . . . have a separate room for her, would he?' There was no longer any need for the blushes on her cheeks. Mother Nature was doing an excellent job of providing colour for Stephanie. 'I mean, he didn't give us any warning.'

'I seriously doubt if he wants her in a separate room.' Mary's voice was both dry and suggestive. She glanced towards the lobby and quickly hissed, 'He's coming through the door now!'

Stephanie took a deep breath to calm her suddenly jumping nerves and mentally crossed her fingers. Be calm, cool, and collected, she told herself as she started towards the lobby. What did she have to be nervous about? Brock Canfield was only a man.

CHAPTER TWO

ONLY a man. That phrase Stephanie instantly revised the minute she saw the tall, dark-haired man in the lobby. Lean and virile, he was all finished masculinity. The planes and contours of his tanned face had been chiselled into the final product of total manliness. An expensive topcoat hung from a set of broad shoulders and tapered slightly to indicate narrow hips before falling the length of his thighs to stop below the knees. Its dark colour was contrasted by the white silk scarf around his neck.

Yet not for one minute did Stephanie believe that the elegant male attire covered a body that was other than superbly fit and muscled. It was evident in his ease of stride and natural co-ordination. Perry's description became very clear —a hard, finished diamond. Brock Canfield was all that, and all male.

Stephanie felt the awesome power of his attraction before she ever walked in front of the counter to greet him. It was even more potent when she came under the observation of his metallic grey eyes. Their lightness was compelling, at odds with the darkness of his brown hair.

His gaze made a thorough appraisal of her feminine assets as she crossed half the width of the lobby. His study was so openly one of male interest that she would have been offended if it had come from another man. But, no matter how hard she searched, she couldn't come up with any sense of indignation. Almost the exact opposite happened. Her pulse quickened with the inner excitement his look had generated.

Seeking a balance, she switched her attention to the blonde clinging to his arm. There was a surface impression of class and sophistication. Yet beneath it, Stephanie noticed the blue cashmere sweater was a size too small. The fine wool was stretched to emphasise the full roundness of the girl's breasts. So was the material in the complementing shade of darker blue pants that was forced to hug her hips and thighs.

Brock Canfield might regard the result as sexy and alluring, but Stephanie thought it was disgusting. Then she wondered if she was being bitchy. She didn't have time to decide as she reached the point where she had to speak.

'Hello, Mr Canfield. I'm Stephanie Hall,' she introduced herself, and offered her hand. 'I hope you had a pleasant trip.'

'An uneventful one.' The grip of his hand was firm, its warmth seeming to spread up her arm and through her system. His gaze had narrowed in sharp curiosity. 'Stephanie Hall,' he repeated her name, his smooth voice giving it an unusual texture to the sound of her spoken name. 'I wasn't aware Perry had got married. When did this happen?'

'Perry isn't married,' she replied in quick surprise, then tried to explain. 'At least, not to me. I mean, he isn't married to anyone.' She regained control of her wayward tongue and managed a more controlled, 'I'm his sister.'

'Ah, yes.' He seemed to step back, to withdraw somehow, yet he didn't move except to release her hand. 'I remember now that he mentioned he had a younger sister. Somehow I had the impression you were much younger.'

Stephanie decided it was best if she didn't comment on that. 'I'm sorry Perry isn't here to meet you himself, but he's a speaker at a club luncheon today. He should be back within the hour.'

'Fine.' His faint nod was indifferent. The blonde arched closer to him as if to remind him of her presence. It earned her a glance that was amused and tolerant, yet Stephanie detected no affection in his look. 'Helen, I'd like you to meet Stephanie Hall, her brother manages the inn for me. This is Helen Collins.'

But he deliberately omitted identifying the blonde's relationship to him. What could he have said? That she was his current mistress, his current lover? Stephanie wasn't certain if she could have handled such frankness. The glint in his eye made her suspect that Brock Canfield had guessed that. She didn't like the idea that he might find it—and her—amusing.

'May I show you to your suite?' Her stilted suggestion sounded as stiff and defensive as she felt.

'I think it would be an excellent idea.' The line of his mouth was slanted in faint mockery.

The action pulled her gaze to his mouth. The firm set of male lips seemed to hint at worldly experience, their line strong and clean. Stephanie's curiosity ran rampant, wondering how expert they were.

Forcing a smile on to her mouth, she turned and walked to the desk to obtain the key from Mary. The woman slipped two keys into her outstretched palm. Out of the corner of her eye, Stephanie noticed Ben struggling with the luggage and knew he would be following them to the suite.

When she rejoined Brock Canfield and his female companion, the couple had already started in the general direction of the hall leading to the private suite. Stephanie would have preferred simply to give the man the keys, since he obviously knew the way, but she remembered

Perry's instructions—take him to the suite and make sure he had everything he needed.

'Do you work here, Miss Hall? Or are you just helping your brother out?' The question came from Helen Collins, her tone on the acid side.

'I work here,' she replied smoothly, and tried not to let her instinctive dislike of the blonde become obvious.

'In what capacity?' The masculine thickness of an eyebrow was arched in her direction, again assessing and appraising, but from an intellectual level.

'I take care of the books.' Her answer was cool, prompted by an uncertainty whether Brock Canfield hadn't actually known or merely forgotten.

'So you're the reason the monthly reports have suddenly become legible these last few months,' he concluded.

Something in the remark had been faintly taunting. Stephanie was spared from replying as they reached the suite. She unlocked the door and quickly led the way inside, anxious to bring the task to an end and regroup her scattered senses.

'It's stunning, Brock!' Helen exclaimed, betraying that it was her first visit to the suite. She released his arm when she saw the roses on the coffee table. 'And roses! They're gorgeous. You knew they were my favourite.' She bent to inhale the fragrance of one of the large blooms, and

Stephanie worried about the seam of her pants and whether the thread could stand the strain.

'There's a bottle of champagne on ice for you,' Stephanie murmured, and made a small gesture with her hand in the general direction of the silver bucket.

Brock Canfield's grey eyes skimmed her face, their look mocking and amused, as if he sensed her discomfort. There wasn't any need for him to comment on the information, since Helen discovered the bottle of champagne seconds afterwards.

'Darling, you think of everything,' she declared, and plucked the bottle out of the ice. She wrapped it in the towel and brought it to him. 'Open it, Brock.'

As he shrugged out of his topcoat, Stephanie saw her opening to be excused. 'if there's anything else, Mr Canfield——' she began.

'Don't leave yet, Miss Hall.' His smooth order stopped the backward step Stephanie had taken to begin her retreat. But he offered no more explanation than the simple command that she remain.

She stood silently by, trying to appear as composed and calm as her jittery nerves would permit, while he tossed his coat and scarf over the white leather chair. A minute later his suit jacket joined them. Then he was expertly popping the cork out of the champagne bottle and filling the two glasses Helen had in her hands.

'Would you care to join us, Miss Hall?' he enquired. 'There are more glasses in the bar.'

'No, thank you,' she refused with stiff politeness. 'I have work to do this afternoon.'

'One glass of champagne would interfere with your ability to function?' he mocked her, but returned the bottle to the ice bucket without re-issuing his offer.

There was a knock at the door. Since Stephanie was closest, she answered it. It was Ben with the luggage. She motioned him inside the room.

'Put it in the bedroom,' Helen instructed, and followed him to supervise.

'I think you'll find everything in order, Mr Canfield.' Stephanie tried again to make her exit. 'I checked the suite myself before you arrived.'

'I'm sure I will,' he agreed.

Her opportunity was lost a second time as Ben came out of the bedroom. She was rather surprised when Brock gave him a tip for bringing the luggage. After all, he was the owner, so it wouldn't have been necessary. Benny thanked him and left.

'Here are your keys, Mr Canfield.' Stephanie crossed the front half of the room to give them to him.

He didn't immediately reach out to take them.

Instead he turned to set the champagne glass on an antique white table. The white of his shirt complemented his supply muscled torso without emphasising it. He looked lean and rangy like a wild animal on the prowl.

Minus the suit jacket, he appeared more casual, more approachable. Her unsteady pulse revealed the danger of such thinking as she dropped the keys in his outstretched hand. The glitter of his grey eyes seemed to mock the action that avoided physical contact.

When Helen Collins appeared in the bedroom doorway, his gaze slid from Stephanie. He didn't wait for the blonde to speak as he issued his instructions. 'Unpack the suitcases, Helen, and make yourself comfortable. I'm going to be tied up for the afternoon.'

He was politely but firmly telling his companion to get lost, dismissing her from his presence until he had time for the toy he had brought along to play with. Stephanie watched the curvaceous blonde smother the flash of resentment to smile and blow him a kiss before shutting the bedroom door.

'You don't approve of the arrangement, do you?' Amusement was threaded thickly through his question.

Stephanie worked to school her expression into one of indifference. 'I wouldn't presume to pass judgment on your personal affairs, Mr Canfield. They have nothing to do with me.'

'Spoken with the true discretion of an employee to her indiscreet boss,' he mocked her reply.

When he absently moved a step closer, Stephanie had to discipline her feet not to move back in an effort to keep a safe distance from him. Her nerve ends tingled with the sexual force of his attraction at such close quarters. The not unpleasant sensation triggered off a whole series of alarm bells in head.

'Will there be anything else, Mr Canfield?' She made a show of glancing at her watch as if she was running late. 'I really should be getting back to my office.'

For a long second he held her gaze. Then his glance slid downward as he turned away and slipped the keys into his pocket. 'You probably should.' He picked up the glass of champagne.

Taking his agreement as permission to leave, Stephanie started towards the door. Relief was sweeping through her, the tension disintegrating with a rush. She could fully understand how curiosity killed the cat.

She was still five feet from the door when Brock Canfield stopped her with a low question. 'Did your brother warn you about me?'

The plaid swirled about her knees as she

pivoted to face him. 'I beg your pardon?'

She felt cornered, trapped like a little brown mouse that almost escaped before a set of claws gently forced it back into the mouth of danger. A faintly wicked smile was deepening the corners of the firm male lips.

'Perry is very conscientious and thorough. That's why I made him manager,' Brock stated, and let his eyes run over her slender figure. 'Surely he told you that I eat little girls like you for breakfast.' He sipped at the champagne and gave Stephanie the impression he was drinking the essence of her.

Her throat worked convulsively for a second before she could get an answer out. 'Actually, I think Perry said you go through women like a gambler goes through decks of cards.' She matched his frankness, but she was shaking inside.

'Very aptly put.' His glass was lifted in a mock salute. 'Because generally I discard them after very little use—sometimes for no greater reason than that I want something new.' Again, he took a drink of champagne and studied her with unnerving steadiness over the rim of the crystal glass. 'After all these years of keeping you hidden away, your brother took quite a risk sending you in his place. Why did he do it? Are you supposed to provide me with a distraction so I won't uncover some current problem?'

'There aren't any problems. Everything is running smoothly.' She denied the suggestion that it was otherwise. 'Perry asked me to meet you because there wasn't anyone else. The night manager is at home sleeping and Perry's secretary is . . . terrified of you. That only left me to represent the managing staff, unless you throw out protocol. Then anyone would do.'

'She's a timid soul. Her name's Connie, isn't it?' Brock Canfield mused, and wandered towards Stephanie. 'Do you suppose she's afraid of sex?'

'She's naturally shy,' Stephanie defended her brother's secretary, and fought the warmth that was trying to colour her own cheeks.

When he reached her, Brock didn't stop but went on past her. She heard him set the glass on a table and started to turn. 'Perry must have told you that if you become involved with me, I would hurt you.'

His constant changing from directly personal to impersonal was keeping her off balance. Stephanie tried to adjust to this current reversal of tactics. He made a leisurely circle to stop on the opposite side of her. Her head turned slightly to bring him into the focus of her side vision. He didn't seem to expect a reply from her, and she didn't make one.

'It's true,' he went on. 'I know your kind. You

eat Yankee pot roast on Sunday while I have Châteaubriand. I live out of hotel suites and you want a house with four bedrooms.'

He reached out to lift the scarab pendant from her sweater and study it. His hand made no contact with her body, but the sensation was left anyway. When he replaced it, his fingertips trailed down, tensing her stomach muscles.

'You want children, a boy and girl to mother, but I have no desire for an heir. It's time the Canfield name died.' His gaze roamed to her breasts. The shallowness of her breathing had them barely moving beneath the ribbed knit of her sweater. 'More than likely, you're the type that would want to nurse your babies yourself.'

Stephanie didn't dispute any of his statements. She couldn't, because she guessed there was a fragment of truth in all of them. Her silence was ruled mostly by the knowledge that she was being seduced.

Brock Canfield was stating all the reasons why an affair with him would never last at the same time that he was persuading her to surrender to his desire anyway. She couldn't raise a single objection when he was saying them all. It was crazy how helpless she felt.

When he moved to stand in front of her with only a hand's width separating their bodies, she was conscious of his maleness. Eye-level with the lean breadth of his shoulders, she lifted her chin to study the strength of his masculine features, the darkness of his hair, and the burnished silver of his eyes. He threaded his hands through the sides of her hair to frame her face.

'You want a man you can snuggle up to in bed and warm your cold feet,' he said. 'And I want to enjoy a woman's body, then sleep alone on my side of the bed. We're oil and water. The combination doesn't mix.'

His gaze shifted to her lips. Her heartbeat faltered, then shifted into high gear, but she managed to control the downward drift of her eyelashes and kept them open, offering no silent invitation. Brock Canfield didn't need any. Her nerves tensed as his mouth descended towards hers with excruciating slowness.

First, the fanning warmth of his breath caressed her sensitive lips. Then she was assailed by the stimulating fragrance of some masculine cologne, the scent tinged with dry champagne. The hint of intoxication swirled through her senses an instant before his mouth moved expertly on to hers.

With persuasive ease, he sampled and tasted the soft curve of her lips, not attempting to eliminate the distance between them. Stephanie didn't relax nor resist the exploring kiss. Of their own accord, her lips clung to his for a split second as he casually ended the contact to brush his mouth against her cheek.

'You're a delectable morsel.' His voice was deliberately pitched to a caressing level of huskiness. 'Maybe I'll save you for dessert.' A light kiss tantalised the sensitive skin near her ear before he lifted his head to regard her with lazy grey eyes. 'If you're smart, you'll slap my face, Stephanie.'

'I'm smarter than that, Mr Canfield.' She was surprised she had a voice—and that it sounded so steady. 'I'm not going to fight you—or in any way heighten your interest in the chase.'

A smile of admiration spread across his face. It gentled the overwhelming virility of his tanned features. Stephanie's heart stopped beating for a full second, stunned by the potent charm the smile contained. He untangled his hands from her hair and stepped away to reclaim his champagne glass.

'Now you've intrigued me, Stephanie,' he murmured, and downed the swallow of champagne.

'Believe me, that wasn't my intention.' Agitation stirred her voice.

'Wasn't it?' Brock challenged with a knowing lift of a dark eyebrow.

'No.' But she couldn't hold his gaze so she looked away, lifting her chin a fraction of an inch higher.

The phone rang and Brock walked away from

it, ordering over his shoulder, 'Answer it.'

Stephanie hesitated, then stepped to pick up the white receiver. 'Yes? Mr Canfield's suite.'

'Stephanie?' It was her brother calling. He sounded surprised that she had answered. 'Connie said Brock arrived fifteen minutes ago. Why are you still there? Any problems?'

'No, I was just leaving.' She was glad her voice sounded normal, and not as emotionally charged as she felt. 'Mr Canfield is right here. Would you like to speak to him?'

'Yes, put him on,' Perry agreed to her suggestion, a little thoughtfully.

She held out the receiver to Brock. 'It's Perry.'

He walked over to take the phone from her hand, without attempting to touch her. His hand covered the mouthpiece. 'It's a pity we have to postpone our discussion just when it was becoming interesting.'

She refused to rise to his bait. 'I hope you enjoy your stay with us,' she offered, as if she was addressing a hotel guest instead of the owner.

As she turned to walk to the door, his voice followed her. 'That remains to be seen, Stephanie.'

His remark held the hint of a promise that their discussion would be resumed at a later time. The part of her that wasn't ruled by common sense was looking forward to it.

Crossing the threshold into the hallway, Stephanie half-turned to close the door. Her gaze was drawn to the leanly muscled man on the phone, but he had already forgotten her. His dark head bent in concentration as he listened to what Perry was saying. Very quietly she shut the door and walked swiftly down the carpeted hallway.

When she reached her office, she closed its door. It was a defence mechanism to prevent her from watching for Brock Canfield. She paused long enough at the mirror to smooth the hair his hands had rumpled, then spread the daily entry sheet on her desk and started to work.

Once she heard Perry and Brock's voice in the hall outside her office. Unconsciously she held her breath, but they didn't stop. She guessed her brother was taking Brock on a brief tour of the inner workings of the inn. It sounded logical although Brock was probably very familiar with all that went on.

Late in the afternoon, Perry knocked on her door and walked in. 'Stephanie, do you have those cost projections on renovating the pool house into a sauna and exercise club?'

Her gaze ricocheted off her brother to be stopped by the masked gleam of Brock's grey eyes. A charcoal pullover had taken the place of his tie, the white collar of his shirt extending over the neckline of the sweater. The casual attire didn't diminish the air of male authority that draped him like a second skin.

'I have a copy.' She dragged her gaze from Brock to open a side desk drawer. 'I believe I saw yours at home.'

'That's right,' Perry remembered. 'It's in the library on the desk.' He took the portfolio Stephanie handed him and passed it to Brock. 'As you can see on page two, the cost of equipping it is within range of the estimate. The main stumbling block is this bearing wall.' He unrolled the architect's drawing on Stephanie's desk to show Brock where the difficulty had arisen in revamping the pool house.

Stephanie leaned back in her chair, unable to work while the two men discussed the problem. The inaction gave her too much freedom to study Brock Canfield. Sitting sideways on the edge of her desk, he listened attentively to Perry's explanations and counter-proposals.

His position pulled the material of his slacks tautly over his thigh as his muscles bunched beneath it. She liked the clean, stong lines of his profile, the vibrant thickness of his dark brown hair, and his lean, well-muscled build.

What bothered her was his innate sex appeal that didn't rely on good looks. He was handsome in a hard kind of way, but it was much more than that. She couldn't look at him without being aware that he was a man.

All the warnings didn't mean a damn, Stephanie realised—not coming from Perry or Brock. It was like being warned against the dangers of getting too close to a fire when she was shivering. She'd take the risk for the chance to be warmed by the flames. Glancing away from the compelling figure half-seated on her desk, she nervously moistened her lips as she realised what she was admitting.

When she looked back at Brock, he was watching her, a smile in the grey depths of his eyes as if he knew what she was thinking and the decision she had reached. It was totally impossible. But she didn't draw an easy breath until he returned his attention to the green portfolio.

'Let me make a suggestion, Perry,' he said. 'I'll study these blueprints and the cost projections and we'll discuss it this evening. You and your sister can join me for dinner.' He straightened from her desk, his glance barely touching her, as he bent to roll the blueprints. 'Have you made other plans for dinner?' The question was an afterthought, addressed to her brother, not Stephanie.

'I'm free this evening, but I can't speak for

Stephanie.' There was a silent warning in the look Perry gave her, that said he would back up any excuse she chose to give.

'You'll come to keep the numbers even, won't you?' The statement was issued in the guise of a question as Brock studied her with knowing certainty. 'You and Helen can gossip while Perry and I discuss business.'

'We could always postpone it until morning,' Perry suggested.

'Business before pleasure,' Brock insisted with a glance in the general direction of her brother before his gaze returned to lock with hers. 'Shall we meet at eight o'clock in the restaurant? That will give you time to go home and change.'

'Eight o'clock will be fine,' Stephanie agreed as she had known she would all along.

Perry gave her a look that said she had taken leave of her senses—but that was precisely what had happened. It didn't matter how foolish or futile it seemed. She was way out of her league with Brock Canfield, and there was no future in pursuing a relationship with him.

But she wasn't ruled by logic. A more powerful force was directing her actions.

CHAPTER THREE

'DID he make a pass at you?' Perry slipped the curly jacket over her shoulders, his hands lingering for a second.

'Of course.' At his muffled curse, Stephanie laughed. 'That shouldn't come as a surprise to you. You did warn me that he would.'

The laughter eased the tension gnawing at her nerve ends. Dining out was a luxury that they had rarely been able to afford. It was rarer still when her occasional dates had taken her out to dinner. Therefore her wardrobe was sadly lacking in dressy clothes.

The simple lines of the rust-coloured dress came the closest to being what Stephanie deemed appropriate to wear. To it she added a plain gold belt and two strands of gold chain to overlap the jewel neckline. She tried to consider her choice as understated elegance as opposed to under-dressed.

Luckily, Perry hadn't arrived at the house until twenty minutes ago, so he didn't know how she had agonised over what to wear. He had barely had time to shower and change into a fresh suit and tie. His brown hair still glistened from the shower spray. She could feel him eyeing her with brotherly concern while she buttoned the short jacket.

'What happened, Stephanie?' he questioned with less anger.

Turning to face him, she made a pretence of straightening his tie. 'I didn't swoon at his feet, if that's what's worrying you,' she joked.

'Will you be serious?' Perry insisted, acting every inch the wise older brother. 'I can assure you that Brock isn't regarding it so lightly.'

'Probably not,' Stephanie conceded, sobering a little.

'Listen, if you want to change your mind, I'll make an excuse for you. One of your friends drove up for the weekend or something,' he suggested.

'And fix something to eat when I can dine out? No, thanks.' She shook her head in definite refusal. 'Besides, you're going to be there to chaperone me. Not to mention the fact that his girl-friend will be with us, too.' The thought left a bad taste in her mouth. She moved to the front door. 'We only have ten minutes to make it to the inn.'

'I forgot about the girl he brought along.' Perry followed her out of the house to the station wagon that belonged to the inn. There was a frown in his expression when he opened the car door for her. 'Are you attracted to him, Stephanie?'

'I wouldn't be normal if I wasn't,' she admitted. 'Don't look so worried, Perry. It's better that I know it and admit it than have it hit me all of a sudden one day when it's too late.'

'I suppose there's some logic in that thinking.' But he didn't sound convinced.

When her door was shut, he walked around the front of the car to slide in the driver's side. Stephanie studied his grim profile as he started the motor. Impulsively, she reached out to touch his arm.

'Try not to worry about me too much, Perry,' she said. 'I know you'd like to fight all my battles, big brother, but some of them I have to face alone.'

'I'm being over-protective,' he admitted. 'But it's become a habit to look after you. It's hard to remember that you're an adult.'

'I know.' And Stephanie did understand. She didn't resent the concern Perry voiced because she knew his intentions were the best.

Tactfully, he switched the subject to the renovation of the pool house, which had been his idea. He was certain it would enhance the overall appeal of the inn and ensure their ability to compete with the newer, more modern ski lodges in the area. So far, Brock hadn't vetoed the plan, which made tonight very important.

The inn possessed two restaurants, but the formal dining room was only open during the evening dinner hour. It was one of the few dining rooms in the area that required proper attire, yet it was rarely empty. After spending the day hiking, skiing, or cycling, guests seemed to welcome the excuse to dress up. Local residents often dined there as well, making reservations almost a necessity. This Friday was no exception.

After leaving her jacket at the coat check, Stephanie let Perry escort her to the table where Brock and his blonde companion were waiting. Brock rose at their approach, his dark elegance reaching out to ensnare Stephanie. A ghost of a smile touched his mouth as he met her look. She felt oddly breathless, but her reflection in the mirrored wall didn't show this inner disturbance.

'Have you been waiting long?' Perry asked, more out of politeness than concern that they were late.

'No, Helen and I have just arrived. I don't believe you've met Helen Collins,' Brock introduced. 'My manager, Perry Hall. Of course, you remember his sister Stephanie.'

Stephanie received no more than a cursory glance from the blonde, who did manage to smile at Perry. It was obvious by the forced pleasure in her expression that Helen resented their presence. She had probably looked forward to having Brock all to herself that evening, Stephanie realised.

That little trill of gladness that sang in her veins was the result of suppressed jealousy. The discovery brought Stephanie briefly to her senses. She wasn't going to spend the entire evening being envious of the slightest attention Brock paid to Helen.

'Sit here, Perry.' Brock indicated the empty chair to his left. 'That way we'll be able to talk without having to shout across the table.'

Which left the chair opposite him for Stephanie. She wouldn't be sitting beside him, but she would be facing him through dinner. She knew she would have to guard against staring at him. Something told her Helen Collins wouldn't be very talkative.

It proved to be a very accurate prediction. Courtesy insisted that Stephanie make some initial attempts to start a conversation by enquiring where Helen was from etcetera. When the other girl made no attempt to keep the conversation going, Stephanie didn't either.

In consequence, she sat through dinner listening to the two men discuss the proposed renovations. She didn't find it boring. On the contrary, she was fascinated by the quickness of Brock's mind, shrewd and astute. And she was rather proud of Perry's ability to keep up with his fast-thinking employer.

But it became increasingly obvious that Helen didn't share Stephanie's appreciation of the conversation. She began smoking incessantly, since it gave her an excuse to interrupt the talk to have Brock light her cigarette. Stephanie was more embarrassed than envious of the way Helen gazed so limpidly into Brock's eyes and bent closer as if inviting his embrace. Brock's reaction was a mixture of aloofness, tolerance, and amusement.

Occasionally his glance did stray to Stephanie, but he made no attempt to flirt with her. She was glad, because it would have made a mockery of the business discussion with her brother if he had.

After the dinner plates were removed, the waiter wheeled the dessert cart to the table. 'Aren't you going to have something, Brock?' Helen protested when everyone ordered something except him.

'No.' He gave her a lazy smile that remained in his expression when he glanced around the table. 'I'll have my dessert later.' His gaze lingered for a fraction of a second on Stephanie.

Her recall was instant and vivid, remembering that he had mentioned saving her for dessert. There was a wild fluttering in her stomach as she quickly dropped her gaze to the bowl of sweetened fresh fruit in front of her.

She was constantly off balance with him. Just when she had become used to being ignored, he had reminded her of that intimate remark. Somehow she had to learn to keep both feet solidly on the ground whenever she was around him. It was the only way she would survive this tumultuous interlude.

'The dining room closes at ten, Mr Canfield,' Stephanie remarked. 'If you want dessert, perhaps you should have it now.'

'Now?' His mouth twitched with a smile as his gaze dared her to repeat that challenge. 'I'd rather have it later. If it happens to be after ten, and the craving is too great, I'll simply raid the icebox.'

'If you'd like, I can arrange to have a selection sent up to your suite,' Perry suggested, and Stephanie nearly choked on a strawberry.

'Can you?' There was a wealth of understated meaning to Brock's droll response. 'I'll try to remember that.' The waiter was at his elbow with the silver coffee pot. 'Yes, black, please.'

While they finished their coffee and dessert, it was decided that Perry would contact the architect and arrange a meeting early on Saturday morning. Brock had changes he wanted made in the plans before he gave his final approval.

Stephanie knew her brother's sense of achievement at Brock's acceptance of his idea and felt proud for him.

'I'm beginning to get the feeling your talents are not being fully utilised at the inn,' Brock remarked, studying Perry with a narrowed look. 'Is this your ambition? To be in charge of a place like this?'

Perry hesitated, darting Stephanie a quick look. His uncertainty was obvious. 'I wouldn't say it's my sole ambition, but I find it challenging, always different.'

'That's a diplomatic answer. Now, what's the truth?' Brock challenged.

'That's the truth,' Perry laughed, but insincerely.

'The truth is, Mr Canfield, that Perry has always wanted to be a lawyer,' Stephanie inserted, disregarding the silencing look her brother sent.

'What stopped you? I've seen your college transcripts.'

'My father had a skiing accident. I was needed at home,' her brother explained simply, and immediately changed the subject. 'The long range forecast for the winter calls for a lot of snow. It's predicted the area will have its best ski season to date.'

'The reservations show it.' Stephanie followed his lead, her way of apologising for bringing up the education he had been forced to abandon. 'We're booked solid all the way to March.'

'I noticed.' Brock went along with the new topic.

'Excuse me.' The brittle words were issued by Helen as she pushed away from the table to stand. 'I'm going to the powder room to freshen my lipstick.'

Brock caught at her hand. 'We'll meet you in the lounge. Don't be long.'

The sullen look was immediately replaced by a bright smile. 'I won't,' the blonde promised, and hurried away with a provocative sway of her hips.

'We should be going home,' Stephanie murmured to her brother.

'Yes, it is late,' he agreed, with a glance at his watch.

'Have one drink with us,' Brock insisted. 'We haven't toasted your new plan. It was a brilliant idea of yours, Perry, to utilise an existing building for the sauna, especially since it's virtually unused. It makes an already attractive package both practical and economical.'

'I'm glad you think so, Brock,' her brother replied modestly. 'But I'm certain you would have come up with the plan if I'd suggested building an entirely new building.'

'I hope so.' Again there was that wide smile,

all lazy charm. 'How about that drink? Will you join us?'

After exchanging a glance with Stephanie, Perry agreed. 'Just one. We don't want to intrude any further on your evening.'

'Just one,' Brock nodded.

He was at her chair when Stephanie rose. His hand seemed to find its way to her waist to guide her to the side door leading to the lounge. His touch was lightly possessive, impersonal yet warm. She could feel the imprint of his fingers through the material of her dress. The sensation seemed to brand her as his property.

The lounge was crowded, as it generally was on the weekends. A dance combo was playing, sprayed by a rotating rainbow of lights in the otherwise dark room. During the off-season, the inn only had live entertainment at the weekends. In the winter, when the White Mountains were filled with skiers, they had a group seven nights a week.

Brock found an empty booth in a far corner of the room. By the time they had ordered a round of drinks, Helen arrived. She ignored his invitation to join them and instead coaxed Brock on to the dance floor. Stephanie watched the blonde become the sultry enchantress, weaving her web around Brock, and knew she could never compete with such tactics.

'Would you like to dance?' Perry suggested.

Stephanie glanced up to refuse, but one look at the challenging gleam in his eyes made her realise how dispirited she had become in the span of a few minutes. A faintly chagrined smile curved her mouth as she nodded acceptance of his invitation.

Once on the dance floor, the swinging music soon made its upbeat rhythm felt. Concentrating on the dance steps distracted her from the sight of Helen with Brock. Also there was the knowledge that she and Perry danced well together, their steps always matching, but he had also been the one who taught her how.

When the song ended, she was breathless and laughing. 'Feel better?' Perry smiled as he guided her off the dance floor.

'Much better,' she agreed, glancing over her shoulders to smile at him. 'Thanks.'

The lights were dimmed to a single blue colour for a slow number. Her eyes didn't adjust immediately to the change of light, and she had to stop for a minute to keep from running into a table or chair in the semi-darkness.

Her gaze saw Brock and Helen on a course parallel with theirs. He bent his head to murmur something to the blonde, who didn't look pleased by his statement. Then he was leaving Helen to make her way back to the booth alone, and crossing to intercept Stephanie.

'You don't object if I have this dance with your sister before you leave, do you, Perry?' Brock asked, although Stephanie didn't know why. He had already taken hold of her arm to direct her back to the dance floor.

She was certain Perry answered him, but she didn't hear what was said. Almost the instant they reached the cleared area, Brock was turning her into his arms. As usual, there were more couples on the floor to dance to the slow tunes, so it became less a matter of dancing and more a matter of avoiding others. They were soon swallowed into the centre of the group.

He folded her arm against his chest while his hand slid up her spine to force her closer. Stephanie could feel her heart thudding against her ribs as they swayed together, moving their feet without going anywhere. Ultimately she became conscious of the hard wall of his chest, the flatness of his stomach, and the leg shifting between hers in rhythm with the music.

When he released her hand to leave it against the lapel of his jacket, Brock seemed to give up all pretence of dancing. Both arms were around her, his fingers spread as they roamed over her shoulders, ribs, and spine, slowly caressing and moulding her to him.

Stephanie could barely breathe. This was what she had wanted all evening, yet she couldn't relax. She felt like a child who had been given a giant lollipop and was afraid to enjoy it too much because she knew it was going to be taken away from her.

His chin rubbed against her temple, his breath stirring her hair. A silent whimper of suppressed delight sighed through her when he turned his mouth against her, investigating the corner of her eye and the curve of her cheekbone.

'I could develop a sweet tooth for dessert.' Finding her ear, he nuzzled aside the silken chestnut hair covering it to let his moist lips nibble at the lobe, shattering her equilibrium.

In another second she was going to melt like a piece of sugar on his tongue. 'You already have.' Her voice wasn't all that strong, the words coming out in a thin, taut whisper.

'Is that right?' His mouth curved against the skin of her cheek.

All she had to do was lift her head and Brock would find her lips, but she lowered her chin a fraction of an inch. Her eyes were closed by the feathery brush of his mouth across her lashes.

'Any member of the opposite sex would satisfy you when you're in an amorous mood,' she insisted, because she knew it was true. Brock was pursuing her because she was new, not because he

thought she was special. It was a fact she acknowledged without bitterness. 'You have such a
healthy appetite that you bring your night-time
treats along with you.'

'But you're the one in my arms. Why don't
you satisfy me?' he challenged softly.

Her heart ran away with itself at the thought
of satisfying him and being satisfied by him. His
virility was a potent force that left her weak.
She could imagine the devastation his practised
skill could wreak if she let herself become carried away by it. Someone jostled her shoulder in
the mêlée of dancing couples and her head lifted
in faint surprise.

In the next second, she was imobilised by the
touch of his mouth against the corner of her lips.
Then she was turning to seek the completeness of
it, mindless of the others around them. It was a
devouring kiss, hard and demanding, ending
within seconds after it had begun. It hadn't
seemed to help that she had both feet on the
floor. Discretion had been swept aside so easily.

'Do you do this with all your women? Make
love to them on the dance floor? First Helen, now
me.' She found the strength to mock him. although her voice was a little shaky.

Her head was still tipped back, enabling her to
look into his eyes. The dim interior of the lounge

had enlarged the black pupils, leaving a thin silver ring around them. They were smiling at her, with an inner satisfaction and supreme confidence, certain of his ability to seduce her.

Stephanie supposed she was transparent. Her pride was injured that she was such an easy conquest for him. But was there a woman born who could deny his attraction for long?

'I've aroused you, despite that cool and composed expression you're wearing,' Brock stated. Cool? Composed? Her? It seemed impossible. His hand moved to caress her neck, stopping when it found her pulse point. She could feel it and hear it hammering against his fingertip. 'Your pulse is racing. Feel what you're doing to me.'

Taking her fingers, he carried them to his neck and pressed them to the throbbing vein. She felt its wild beat, not so far behind the swift tempo of her own. Had she disturbed him? Or was it only desire? She had felt safer with the jacket beneath her fingers rather than the vital warmth of his skin.

'Your hand feels cool,' he murmured.

That seemed impossible when she felt hot all over. When she tried to withdraw her fingers from his grasp, it tightened. He lifted her hand to his mouth and sensually kissed the centre of her palm.

'I want you, Stephanie,' he said as the last note of the song faded and the rainbow of lights came on.

The sudden murmur of voices shattered the intimacy of the moment. Stephanie didn't have to find an answer to that heady comment as the exiting dancers forced them apart. He retained his hold of her hand while she let the crowd lead her off the floor.

Fixing her gaze on Perry in the far booth, she weaved her way through the tables. Before she reached it, she gave a little tug to free her hand from Brock's grip. He let it go without protest. She didn't squarely meet the look her brother gave her when she slid on to the booth seat beside him. Her glance darted across the table to Helen, whose bored and impatient expression spoke volumes.

'I hope you've finally fulfilled all your obligations for the evening, Brock,' Helen voiced her irritation at being left to her own devices for so much of the evening.

'Stop bitching, Helen.' As he sat down, he stretched his arm across the backrest behind the blonde and picked up his drink. 'I warned you this would be a business trip.' It was a lazy reminder, a steel edge cloaked in velvet tones.

Over the rim of his glass, his gaze locked

with Stephanie's. She read his message of dissatisfaction and desire, schooled with patience.
She took a sip of her own drink, but the ice had
melted, diluting it and leaving it flat and tasteless.
She set it down and pushed it aside to glance at
her brother.

'It's getting late, Perry. We should be going.'
Knowing he would agree, she rose and moved
aside so he could slide out.

'I'll see you in the morning, Brock.' He shook
hands with Brock, who was also standing.

'It was a pleasure meeting you, Miss Collins.'
Stephanie nodded at the blonde, not caring that it
was only a polite phrase she offered. Her only
response was an indifferent glance. Then she addressed Brock. 'You're leaving on Sunday, aren't
you?'

'Yes, late in the afternoon,' he acknowledged
with a slight narrowing of his gaze.

'I doubt if I'll see you again before you leave,
so I hope you have a safe trip.' She placed her
hand in his.

Brock held on to it when she would have withdrawn it. 'Aren't you working tomorrow?'

'No.' Conscious of Perry at her side, she sent
him a sideways glance, smiling. 'I have a great
boss. He gives me the weekends off so I can do
his laundry and clean the house.'

He released her hand somewhat absently and smiled at her brother. 'Goodnight. I'll meet you in the morning around eight.'

Before they had taken a step away from the booth, Brock was sitting down and turning his attention to Helen, who was suddenly all smiles. Stephanie tried desperately not to remember that only moments before he had been holding her in his arms. Now someone else was going to satisfy him. She didn't do a very good job of convincing herself that she was the lucky one to be walking away relatively unscathed.

They stopped at the coat-check for Stephanie's jacket and Perry's overcoat. Both were silent as they walked outside into the crisp autumn night to the station wagon.

The only thing that was said during the drive home came when Perry remarked, 'I hope you know what you're doing, Stephanie.'

'So do I,' she sighed.

CHAPTER FOUR

THE dirty breakfast dishes were stacked in the sink. Stephanie paused at the counter to drink the last swallow of coffee from her cup. Her gaze automatically wandered out of the window above the sink to the foothills emblazoned with the reds and golds of autumn.

In the back of the old farmhouse, a brook rushed through the rolling acreage, complete with a romantic stone bridge crossing it. Cords of firewood were stacked near the back door of the house—fuel for the cold New England winter.

Sighing, she turned away from the beauty of the clear autumn morning and set her cup with the rest of the dishes. She'd wash them later. Right now she wanted the hot water for the first load of clothes.

The back porch doubled as the washroom; a washer and dryer were ensconced in one corner. The small floor space was littered with baskets and piles of dirty clothes which Stephanie set about separating into individual loads, tossing the white clothes directly into the washing machine.

It was a nice enough day that she could hang

the clothes on the line to dry. Besides, the clothes always smelled so much cleaner and fresher that way.

She pushed the sleeves of the old grey sweatshirt up to her elbows. It was one of Perry's which meant it was several sizes too large for her, but it was comfortable to work in and it didn't matter if she spilled bleach on it. Her blue jeans were faded and shrunk from numerous washings and snugly hugged her slender hips and thighs, but the denim material was soft like a second skin.

Her hair was pulled away from her face into a ridiculously short ponytail, secured with a piece of blue yarn. She hadn't bothered with make-up. By the time she washed the clothes, dusted the furniture, and swept the floors of the two-storey farmhouse, there wouldn't be any trace of it left anyway. Besides, the only one who came on Saturday mornings was Mrs Hammermill with fresh eggs for the week.

When there was a knock at the front door, Stephanie didn't hesitate over who it might be. 'Come in!' she shouted, and continued separating the clothes. At the sound of the door opening, then closing, she added, 'I'm in the kitchen, Mrs Hammermill,' which was close enough to her location. 'You can put the eggs on the counter. If you have an extra dozen, I'll take them. Perry mentioned he'd like an angel food cake. I thought I'd try my hand at making one from scratch this afternoon.'

There was a movement in the doorway to the porch, but Stephanie didn't glance up. She was busy examining the white shirt in her hand that Perry had somehow managed to mark up the front with ballpoint ink.

'You don't happen to know what I can use to get this ink out of Perry's shirt, do you?' she frowned. 'I've tried just about everything at one time or another and——' When she looked up, she saw Brock leaning a shoulder against the door jamb, his arms crossed. She froze at the sight of him. 'Brock!' His name was startled from her.

'Try hairspray. My secretary swears by it,' he suggested with a trace of teasing amusement in his droll voice. His corduroy pants were desert brown, the same shade as the heavy sweater with the stag's head design on the chest.

Her gaze flew past him to the cat clock on the kitchen wall with its switching tail for a pendulum. It was a few minutes before half past eight.

'What are you doing here?' she asked in confusion, still clutching the shirt and standing amid the piles of dirty clothes. 'I thought you were——'

'The egg lady? Yes, I know.' He finished the sentence for her and uncrossed his arms to stand up straight. 'The answer to your question should be obvious. I came to see you.'

'Yes, but . . . you were supposed to meet Perry this morning,' Stephanie said in vague protest.

'I did . . . for a few minutes. Are you going to come here? Or am I going to have to wade through all those clothes to get to you?' He both challenged and mocked her.

Stephanie laid the shirt over the side of the washing machine. In doing so, she became conscious of her appearance. Her gaze slid down the front of her sloppy sweatshirt and faded jeans. She felt the nakedness of her face, minus even lipstick.

'You should have called before coming over.' Raising a hand to the hair tied back, she stepped over the pile of clothes blocking her path to the doorway and Brock.

'If I had, I wouldn't have got the chance to see this domestic scene.' Brock reached out to take the hand she was balancing with and pulled her into his arms, locking his hands behind her back while he studied her upturned face. 'And you know you look like a sexy little girl in that outfit.'

It wasn't exactly the compliment she wanted to hear as she turned her head away to let his kiss land on her cheek and pushed her way past him into the kitchen. The floor seemed to roll under her feet, but she knew it was only her knees quaking.

'I don't want to look like a little girl,' she declared, and lifted both her hands to untie the knotted yarn around her hair. But she had tied it tight and the knot defied the attempts of her trembling fingers to loosen it.

When she felt Brock's push hers out of the way, she tried to move away, but he clamped a hand on her shoulder to keep her in place. 'Hold still,' he ordered, and Stephanie stood quietly while he worked the yarn free of the knot. When it was untied, he turned her around and combed her hair into place with his fingers. 'Now you just look sexy. Are you happy?' he asked with a lazy glint in his grey eyes.

But he didn't wait for her to answer he bent his head to cover her lips with his mouth, skilfully parting them as he curved her into his arms. Her fingers curled into the wool of his sweater, clinging to the only solid thing she could find in the deepening intensity of his kiss. She was exposed to a whole set of raw, new emotions that had her straining towards him in trembling need. He dragged his mouth roughly across her cheek to her ear.

'Did you really think you wouldn't see me again before I left?' He sounded almost angry.

'I'm not sure if I believed it or not,' Stephanie

admitted with her eyes closed as he nibbled his down her neck to her shoulder.

'Where are your parents? Who else are you expecting besides the egg lady?' he demanded.

'My parents are dead,' she whispered, and wondered why he didn't know that. 'There's only Mrs Hammermill. She usually comes before nine.'

She felt as well as heard the deep shuddering breath Brock took before he lifted his head to smile tightly at her. 'In that case, why don't you fix me some breakfast? I didn't bother to eat before I came over. I thought you might do your shopping in the morning and I didn't want to miss you.'

Not knowing how much she dared into that statement, Stephanie decided not to commit on it. 'Do you want bacon and eggs?' she asked instead.

'What I want, I can't have at the moment.' His hands slid up her back, suggestively pressing her closer to him before he released her and stepped away. 'Bacon and eggs will do.'

'How do you like your eggs?' She walked to the refrigerator, glad to have something to do. She took out the package of bacon and the last two eggs from the shelf.

'Sunny-side up, and crisp bacon.'

She spied the pitcher of orange juice on the refrigerator shelf. 'Juice?'

'No, thanks.' Brock came to stand beside her while she laid the bacon strips in the skillet.

When it began to sizzle, she walked to the cupboard on the other side of him and took down a place setting. She glanced uncertainly at the kitchen table, then at him. 'Would you like to eat in the dining room?' she suggested.

'No,' he said with a decisive shake of his head. 'I have no intention of letting you out of my sight.'

His look as well as his answer was disturbing, but it also gave her such much-needed confidence. She was smiling as she arranged the plate and cutlery on the gingham-clothed kitchen table. She walked back to the stove to turn the bacon.

'When was the last time you had breakfast in somebody's kitchen?' she asked curiously, eyeing him with a sidelong glance.

'Probably not since I was a child,' he admitted what Stephanie had suspected. 'Are you a good cook?'

'Not as good as Perry, but he's had a lot more practice than I have.' The bacon was beginning to brown nicely, so Stephanie kept turning it.

Brock took up a position behind her, his hands caressing the curve of her shoulders, while his thumbs rubbed the hollows of her neck. 'Why did he have more practice?' He didn't really sound interested in the subject.

'Our mother died when I was only four. Since our father had to work two jobs to support us, Perry had to do the cooking and look after me.'

It was difficult to concentrate on what she was doing under the caress of his hands. She managed to rescue the bacon before it was burnt and set it aside to drain on a paper towel.

'What did your father do?'

'He considered himself a ski instructor, but mostly he earned money as a bartender and cutting firewood . . . until his accident.' She cracked the eggs and slipped them into the hot bacon fat.

'The accident that forced your brother to give up his law career,' Brock guessed.

'Yes, he was crippled in a skiing accident.' She looked over her shoulder, a curious frown knitting her forehead. 'Perry has worked for you for over five years. Surely you knew that.'

'No. I don't bother to enquire about the personal lives of my employees unless it affects their work. There's never been any reason to fault your brother's work.' There was an indifferent and dismissing shrug of his shoulders.

'But surely you want to know something about their backgrounds,' Stephanie insisted.

'Only their qualifications for their particular position. As long as I get the results I want, I couldn't care less who or what they are as individuals.' There was a curve to his mouth, but it wasn't a smile. 'You think that's a very callous attitude, don't you?'

She concentrated her gaze on the eggs in the skillet, the bright yellow yolks staring back at her. 'Yes, I do.'

'White Boar Inn represent half of one percent of the gross business Canfield Enterprises earns annually. Maybe that will give you an idea of how many Perry Halls I have working for me,' he suggested. 'I couldn't possibly become involved or have knowledge of their personal lives without losing perspective of my overall responsibility. By rights, I should sell the inn.'

'Why don't you?' She could see the logic in his argument, but she mentally recoiled from this evidence of his lack of feeling. The eggs were done, so she moved away to fetch his plate from the table and scoop them on to it with the spatula.

'For personal reasons,' Brock answered. Stephanie didn't think he intended to explain what they were, but she was wrong. 'My parents spent their honeymoon at the White Boar when they eloped. He bought it for her on their sixth anniversary. He was the one who decreed that the honeymoon suite would be reserved only for Canfields.'

'No wonder you're reluctant to sell it.' Her

smile was soft and radiant when she gazed at him, touched by this unexpected display of sentiment.

'Six months after he bought it, they went through a messy divorce that lasted two years. My mother has since remarried several times. My father, wisely, contented himself with a stream of mistresses.' Brock watched her smile fade almost with satisfaction.

'Is . . . Is he living?' Averting her gaze, Stephanie walked past him, carrying the plate of eggs and bacon to the table.

'Yes. He's retired to the South of France. I believe his current lover is a twenty-year-old model.' Brock followed her. 'Of course, he refers to her as his protégée.'

'Coffee?' When she set his plate down, she searched for an excuse to find something else to do.

'Black with no sugar.'

Stephanie moved away from the table as he sat down to eat. 'You must not have had a very happy childhood,' she guessed.

'That depends on your definition of happy. My grandfather raised me even before my parents were divorced. They were always vacationing in some exotic resort in a far-off corner of the world. The divorce had little effect on me. Most of the time I was away at school, or else with my grandfather. From the day I was born I was groomed to take over the company, and when my grandfather died a few years ago, that's exactly what I did.'

Stephanie poured two cups and carried them to the table. 'And the last time you ate in somebody's kitchen, that was with your grandfather?'

'Hardly.' Brock laughed shortly. 'He had all his meals at his desk unless it was a business dinner. No, I spent a week at the home of one of my classmates.'

'Why don't you sell the inn?' Stephanie watched him, half afraid to hear his answer. 'It's obvious that you feel no sentimental attachment to it.'

Brock was slow to answer, but it wasn't due to any hesitancy. 'It reminds me that intimate relationships don't necessarily last for ever no matter how strong the attachment appears on the surface.'

'You make the trip here on an average of four times a year. Yet I've never heard of you bringing the same woman twice. Is that why?' But that question simply prompted another. 'Why did you come this morning when Helen is back in the suite?'

'Because I didn't want to be with her. I wanted to be with you.' His sharpness dissolved into a chuckle. 'You are having a hard time trying to understand me, aren't you? The Helens of this world go in and out of my life all the time. I have the sex drive of any normal male. There's no pretence, on either side, that we're together for any reason other than the purely physical—or sexual—if you prefer. She understood the ground rules going in—no emotional claims on me or my time. In return, I treat her with respect and courtesy. I'm not attempting to brag or shock you; I'm only trying to explain the circumstances that dictate my life style.'

Stephanie was trying, but it all sounded very cold-blooded. 'I am sure you can rationalise any behaviour,' she replied stiffly.

Leaning forward in his chair, Brock reached for her hand and gripped it firmly in his. The intensity of his gaze was piercing. 'What I'm not making clear to you, Stephanie, is how difficult it is for me to have the kind of relationship you regard as normal, with any woman. I don't have time to carry out a courtship.' A muscle was working convulsively along his jaw. 'Tomorrow I'm driving to New York. When I arrive, there might be a phone call that will take me to the West Coast. I could be there a month, maybe two. Or I might be there a day and leave for Zurich—I have hotel suites in a dozen cities. I'm with you today, but it might be six months before I can see you again. How can I build a relationship on that? How can I ask a woman to wait for me without being able to tell her when I'll see her again?'

'It's really quite hopeless, isn't it?' Her voice was choked, the futility swamping her.

He released her hand with controlled irritation, pausing a second before he resumed eating the rest of his breakfast. 'Sometimes I forget that it is, but the inn reminds me ... every month when I see the name on the report.'

'That's why you said you didn't want an heir —that it was time the Canfield name died,' she realised.

'No one should have this responsibility unless he wants it,' Brock stated.

'You ... You could sell?' Stephanie suggested hesitantly.

'This is what I was trained for—what I'm good at.' His mouth slanted in a half-smile. 'I doubt if I can make you understand that. I wouldn't change my life and what I do, even if I had the choice.' He wiped at his mouth with a napkin. 'That was a very good breakfast. Is there more coffee?'

'Yes, of course.' A little numb, Stephanie stood up to take his cup. After all he had explained, she was still trying to figure out and where she might fit into his life.

Brock must have read the bewilderment in her

eyes, because he reached out to stop her when she started to pass his chair, his hand resting lightly on her forearm. 'When I find something I want, I reach out and grab it, Stephanie, because it might not be there the next time I come back. I live hard and fast—and I love the same way. If I forget to say you're beautiful or that your eyes are the colour of the morning sky, it isn't because I don't think of it. I just don't waste precious time.'

'Yes, I——' Her reply was interrupted by a knock at the front door. It startled her until she realised who it was. 'It's Mrs Hammermill.'

'The egg lady,' Brock nodded, and dropped his hands to leave Stephanie free to answer the door.

Setting his cup down, she walked toward the living room. 'Yes! Come in, Mrs Hammermill!' she called, and the front door opened to admit a short, stout woman in a dark pillbox hat. Two dozen eggs were balanced under one short arm.

'I'm sorry I'm late, but the Mister's been sick with the 'flu. I've been doin' his chores as well as my own.'

'I hope he's feeling better soon,' Stephanie murmured, and led the way into the kitchen. The woman stopped short at the sight of a strange man and eyed him suspiciously. Stephanie quickly introduced them.

Mrs Hammermill was instantly all smiles. 'Maybe you can talk to Perry about letting me supply the eggs for the restaurant. I would have to buy some more layers, but——'

'I'll talk to him about it,' Brock assured her.

Taking the egg money out of the jar on the counter, Stephanie paid the woman and tactfully hurried her on her way. She almost regretted identifying Brock, but the gossip about a strange man would have been worse.

After she had shown the woman out, Stephanie returned to the kitchen. 'I'm sorry Mrs Hammermill tried to persuade you to let her have the egg account at the restaurant inn,' she apologised to Brock with a wry smile. 'What she really wants Perry to do is finance it. She would have to buy more laying hens, which means she'd need to build a new coop, as well as the initial cost of more grain. She's a marvellous, dependable woman, but I don't think you want to go into partnership in the egg business.' At the table, she stopped to stack the dishes and add them to those in the sink waiting to be washed.

'You're right, I'm not interested in the chicken business—or the dishes. In fact——' Brock took hold of her hand and pulled her to his chair and on to his lap, 'I only have one merger on my mind. The one with you.'

Off-balance by the move, Stephanie was dependent on the supporting steel of his arms. There was a wild flutter of her pulse as he made a sound under his breath, almost like a groan. Her hands encircled his neck, fingers seeking the vibrant thickness of his dark hair.

The kiss was sensual and exploring, their mouths mating in delighted discovery; the slow, heady joy of it insulating Stephanie from all thought. In the hard cradle of his lap, she felt the burning imprint of his thighs beneath her, the flatness of his stomach, and muscled breadth of his chest and shoulders. So male, so virile! It stirred her already disturbed senses.

As he kissed her, Brock mouthed her lips and cheek, the angle of her jaw and the hollow under her ear, setting afire the urgent yearning of her body. Arousing as his kisses were, she was stimulated by the chance to let her lips wander intimately over his smooth jaw and cheek, tangy with the astringent flavour of after-shave. It was a wildly novel experience to have this freedom to reciprocate the sensuous exploration.

His caressing hands became impatient with the thick, loose folds of the large sweatshirt she was wearing. When he lifted the hem to expose her bare midriff, Stephanie drew in a breath of startled surprise that was never quite completed. Her flesh tensed under the initial touch of his hand, then melted at its firm caress.

He seemed intent on personally exploring every naked inch of her ribs and shoulders. She was quivering, her white breasts straining against the lacy material of the confining bra. When he covered one with his palm, there was a rushing release of tension that was wildly gratifying.

Yet, as his fingers sought the back fastener of her bra, sanity returned a fragment at a time. She had let herself be carried away without knowing for certain it was what she wanted. She drew away from him, pressing her hands against his chest for breathing space while she tried to clear her head of this heart-pounding passion.

'Stephanie.' His voice both coaxed and commanded as he planted a kiss on an exposed shoulder bone.

'No.' She gulped in the negative and swung off his lap, taking a couple of quick steps away from his chair while she pulled her sweatshirt down to her hips. 'The first time I saw you, I knew I had to keep both feet on the ground or you'd knock me right off of them. I should have meant that literally.' Stephanie laughed, shakily, trying to make a joke out of it even though she knew it was the absolute truth.

'I want you, Stephanie. I told you that last night,' Brock reminded her, and Stephanie walked to the kitchen counter, keeping her back to him, in a weak attempt to escape the heady seduction of his voice. 'If anything, it's more true at this moment.'

At the scrape of the chair leg indicating he had risen, she grabbed hold of the edge of the counter, needing to hang on to something. 'It's all happening too fast for me,' she tried to explain without sounding as desperate as she felt. 'You don't understand, Brock. I can't be as casual about sex as you are.'

'How much do you know about sex, Stephanie?' When he spoke, she realised he was directly behind her, his tone steady with patience and confidence.

Her knuckles were white from gripping the counter edge in an effort to keep from turning around. If she did, she knew she would be lost.

To counter his sureness, she became sharp and defensive. 'I'm sure I don't know as much as you do, Mr Canfield.'

'Mr Canfield?' His voice was dangerously low. His fingers gripped her shoulders and forced her to turn around. She was rigid in his hold, but she didn't resist him. Under the narrowed regard of his grey eyes, her head was thrown warily back. 'Hey, what is this?' Brock demanded.

'Sex is just a physical act to you, like kissing. I don't treat it that lightly,' she defended her hesitation and uncertainty.

He studied every particle of her expression for such a long time that she felt herself growing hot.

'Are you a virgin, Stephanie?' He seemed to doubt the accuracy of his conclusion.

Her gaze fell to the neckline of his sweater. 'Should I apologise for my inexperience?' The challenge was a little angry, a little hurt, and a little defiant.

'How old are you?' His fingers dug into the flesh of her shoulders.

'Twenty-two,' she answered stiffly.

'My God, where have you been all your life? In a convent?' Brock was dryly incredulous and mocking. 'Twenty-year-old virgins went out with hula-hoops.'

His remark ignited her temper. 'It's too bad if you think I'm an oddity. My father's skiing accident left him almost completely paralysed. I had to feed him, bathe him, dress him, read to him, do everything for him, for five years. Daddy never complained for himself, but he used to cry because I didn't go out and have fun. Perry took care of him whenever he was home, but he never knew when an emergency would come up and he'd have to go to the inn. I dated now and then.' She was angry and didn't attempt to conceal it. 'But who wants to get serious about someone with a sick father? We couldn't afford to hire anyone to take care of him full time. I'm not complaining about those five years. I don't regret a single one of them, because they brought me closer to my father than I'd ever been. So you can make fun of me if you want——'

He covered her mouth with two fingers to check the indignant tirade. His chiselled male features were etched in sober lines. 'I'm not making fun of you.' He traced the outline of her mouth and became absorbed with the shape of it. Her anger vanished as if it had never been. 'It's simply rare to meet someone with your passionate nature who hasn't been around. It doesn't change anything.' His gaze lifted to catch her look and hold it. The silver-dark glitter of his eyes dazzling her. 'I'm going to keep trying to get you into bed. Knowing I would be the first just makes you a prize I'm more determined to have.'

Very slightly, his fingers tilted her chin. Then his mouth closed on to hers in consummation of his promise. A fluttering surge of desire rose within her, like a slow-burning flame fanned to burn hotter.

Brock gathered her into his arms, unhurriedly, arching her backwards, his hips pinning her to the counter. The wayward caress of his hands was keenly pleasurable. He shifted his attention to the pulse quivering so wildly in her throat.

'Whose sweatshirt is this?' he muttered when a hand became tangled in the loose folds.

'Perry's.' It was a husky admission, shattered

by her vivid awareness of his stark masculinity.

'*This* has got to go.' He pulled at a shoulder inseam, saying the words against her neck, punctuating them with kisses. 'From now on, if you wear a man's clothes, they're going to be mine.'

'Whatever you say,' she whispered with a throbbing ache in her voice, boneless and pliant in his arms, her forehead resting weakly against his shoulder while he rained havoc on the sensitive skin of her neck and throat.

'You know what I say.' Brock seized on the submissive response, his tone fiercely low and urgent. 'I've been saying it every time I looked at you or touched you. I want to make love to you —here and now. You have both feet on the floor. What do you want?'

But it wasn't that simple. Not for Stephanie. Not even with the twisting, churning rawness knotting her insides. The awful confusion kept her from answering him, but he must have felt her stillness and chose not to press the point. Instead he loosened his arms, letting his hands move in a series of restless caresses over her shoulders.

'I've postponed everything until after lunch so we could spend the morning together,' he informed her in a slightly thick voice. 'But there isn't any way I'm going to be able to stay in this house alone with you and not——' He took a deep breath and released her entirely. 'We'd better go for a drive somewhere. At least with my hands on the steering wheel, I'll be able to keep them off you. Go and change, fix yourself up—whatever you want to do. I'll wait for you down here.'

Stephanie looked at him, reluctant to agree to his suggestion, but his grey eyes warned her not to protest unless she was willing to accept the alternative. That was something that still confused her.

'I'll only be a few moments,' she promised.

CHAPTER FIVE

THE roads were crowded with cars of tourists, eager to see the spectacle of the autumn foliage and catch a glimpse of the lore that personified Yankee New England—wooden covered bridges, white church steeples, antique shops, and village squares. The route Brock took became less a planned drive and more a matter of choosing a path with the least resistance.

Stephanie relaxed in the contours of velour-covered seats, enveloped in the luxury of the blue Mercedes. The radio was turned low, its four speakers surrounding her with the serene sounds of the music. A riot of colour exploded outside the window; reds and yellows against the back-drop of dark green pine forests climbing the slopes of the White Mountains, and a crisp blue sky.

Traffic thinned in the lane ahead of them as Brock made the turn that would take them on the road south through Franconia Notch. An outcrop-ping of granite loomed into view, and a contented smile curved Stephanie's mouth when she saw it.

'There's my friend,' she murmured, unconsciously breaking the companionable silence.

'Which one?' Brock's gaze narrowed on the rear view mirror, trying to identify which of the cars they had passed that had contained her friend.

'Not that kind of friend.' Her smile broadened as she pointed. 'Him. The Old Man of the Mountains.' She gazed at the jagged profile Mother Nature had carved into the granite millenniums ago. 'I used to make up stories about him when I was a child—the way some kids do about the Man in the Moon, I suppose.'

'If he's my only competition, I've got it made.' Brock sent her a sidelong glance that was warm and desiring, beneath its teasing glitter.

'At least your heart isn't made of stone like his.' They had passed the granite profile, immortalised so long ago by Nathaniel Hawthorne in his classic *The Great Stone Face*. Stephanie settled back into her seat again, letting her gaze roam to Brock's profile, much more virilely alive and vigorous. Just to look at him made her feel warm. 'When I was little, I was certain there was a way that I could make him come to life, some magic I could perform the way the fairy godmothers did with their enchanted wands. And he would tell me all the secrets of the world.' She laughed softly at her whimsy.

'Now?' Brock sounded curious, speculative.

Stephanie shrugged. 'I grew up, I guess.'

'No. All you have to do is touch me and I come to life.' His low delivery was heavy with its sexy intonation, repeated by the languid yet serious gleam of his look. 'I can prove it whenever you want.'

Swallowing, Stephanie glanced away, feeling the feverish rise of heat in her veins. Her gaze made a restless sweep outside the window at the passing scenery, seeking escape without wanting to find it. The interior of the luxury car seemed suddenly very small and intimate. The click of the turning signals startled her, pulling her gaze to Brock.

'I think we could both use some air,' he offered by way of explanation.

Before they reached the end of the mountain pass, he turned off and parked at the visitors' lot to the Flume. When he switched off the motor, Stephanie opened the passenger door, not waiting for him to walk around the car to do it for her. The invigorating briskness of the autumn air immediately cleared her head, freeing her senses to notice other things around her.

As she waited for Brock to join her, she zipped the front of her Eisenhower jacket, a combination of dyed white and grey rabbit fur and tan leather. The legs of her deep burgundy corduroys were tucked into her high boots. The short jacket added to her clean-limbed look. The air was cool enough to turn her breath into a frosty vapour.

When Brock reached automatically for her bare hand, she automatically placed it in his, the warmth and firmness of his grip filling her with a pleasant sensation of belonging. He crooked her a faint smile before setting off to join the band of tourists lining up to get on the bus that would take them to the Flume.

The endless chatter of the tourists negated the need for them to talk. Stephanie didn't mind. It left her free to savour the sensation of being squeezed close to Brock on the bus seat so a third passenger would have a place to sit.

His arm was around her, her shoulder resting against the unbuttoned front of his parka, the muscled length of his thigh and hip imprinted on her own. There was safety in the knowledge that she was surrounded by people, allowing her to simply enjoy the closeness with the temptation removed to take it to a more intimate degree.

As the bus slowed in approach of their destination, Brock murmured in her ear, 'If you turn out to be a damned tease, I'm going to wring your lovely neck—after I take a bite of it.'

Her head pivoted sharply in alarm. She looked up, relieved to see he was smiling. The remark had been aimed to let her know he was deriving his own kind of pleasure from having her body crushed to his side. He lightly brushed his lips across the wing of her eyebrow in a fleeting kiss.

An older woman behind them twittered in a whisper to her companion. 'Isn't it wonderul—a pair of lovers!' Which deepened the corners of Brock's mouth without curving them. Stephanie glanced to the front, feeling a little self-conscious.

When the bus stopped to let them out, neither of them rushed to join the mass exodus. They let the other tourists hurry on ahead of them while they followed more slowly. Stephanie wasn't as comfortable with the silence between them as she had been. When Brock removed his hand from the back of her waist to button the middle buttons of his coat, she paused with him. Ahead was the railed boardwalk winding through the cool shadows of the gorge.

'It's really better to come here in the summer when it's hot,' she said to fill the silence. 'Then you can appreciate the coolness and the shade.'

'If you want to get warm, just let me know. I'll only be too happy to oblige.' When her gaze fell under the lazily suggestive regard of his, he reached out to lace his fingers through her chestnut hair, pulling her towards him and lightly stroking her cheek with his other hand. He smiled gently. 'You don't know how to handle all this sexual bantering, do you?'

'I've never been with anyone . . . who alludes to it as constantly as you do,' she admitted, trying not to be embarrassed.

'I'm just saying what's on my mind,' Brock stated, gazing deep into her blue eyes. 'On my mind every time I'm near you.' The vibrancy of his low voice caught at her breath, cutting it off in her throat. 'Does that disturb you?'

'Yes.'

'I'm glad.' It was said gently, his mouth swooping down to feel the coolness of her lips against his own. Straightening, Brock took his hand away and wrapped an arm around her shoulders to turn her towards the broadwalk.

They entered the deep ravine in silence, walking side by side until the boardwalk narrowed and Stephanie moved ahead. On both sides of them, a sheer rock wall towered upwards to seventy feet in the air. Moss grew thickly on the moist rock, hugging the striated crevices. In the spring and summer, delicate and rare mountain flowers blossomed in the shadowy darkness of the gorge.

A laughing stream tumbled over the rockbed running alongside and below the boardwalk. The long chasm was carved by nature and the swift waters of the Pemigewasset River centuries before the glaciers of the Ice Age moved across the land.

The cool temperature and the high humidity

combined to pierce the bones with a chilling dampness. Stephanie shoved her hands deep into the pockets of her jacket to protect them from the numbing cold. They strolled along the boardwalk that twisted and curved with the ravine. Red and gold leaves swirled downward from the trees high overhead to float in the little stream like colourful toy boats.

Stephanie paused near the end of the Flume where the boardwalk made a right angle turn with the gorge. Leaning against the railing, she gazed down at the stream. A sodden group of leaves had formed a miniature dam, but the rushing water had found a spillway at one end and was fast eroding the fragile blockage.

'It's peaceful here, isn't it?' She glanced at Brock, standing beside her, leaning a hand on the railing, but it was she who had his undivided attention.

'Have dinner with me tonight, Stephanie,' he said. 'Just the two of us. In my suite—with wine, candlelight, and soft music. I'll hire a car and send Helen wherever the hell she wants to go—Boston, New York, Rome. We'll have the whole night and top it off with breakfast in bed tomorrow morning.'

Stephanie made to move away from him, but Brock blocked the attempt, shifting his position to trap her to the rail, a hand on either side of her. 'I met you less than twenty-four hours ago,' she reasoned helplessly.

When he began brushing kisses over her neck and cheek, Stephanie didn't resist this persuasive tactic of a master. She was conscious of the warmth of his breath and coolness of his mouth against her skin, making her tingle with awareness.

'Pretend that when we met yesterday afternoon, it was two weeks ago. Dinner was a week ago and this morning was yesterday. Time is something I don't have in quantity. We have to make the most of what's available, not waste it on all these needless preliminaries,' Brock murmured. 'Stay with me. We'll have all night to get to know each other—in every way there is.'

She shuddered with exquisite longing and drew back, tossing her head in a wary kind of defiance. 'You don't understand, Brock.' Her voice was tight and soft. 'I want to be more than a virgin you slept with one October in New Hampshire.'

His look became stony as he straightened from the railing. 'All right,' he said grimly. 'Forget about tonight.' His balled fists sought the pockets of his jacket, facing her with nearly a foot between them. 'I have to leave shortly after noon tomorrow. What are you doing in the morning?'

The question caught Stephanie off guard. 'I . . . I usually go to church.'

The muscles along his jaw line tautened, flexing in suppressed anger. There was a bleakness in his grey eyes that chilled her with its wintry blast. 'I suppose you're going to ask me to come with you. My God, Stephanie, I'd be sitting in that pew lusting after you,' he expelled the words in a rush of hot anger. 'Please, spare me the hypocrisy of that!'

Her mouth opened but she couldn't find anything to say. His hand snaked out to grab her elbow and propel her along the boardwalk. The serenely quiet and peaceful ravine suddenly became rife with raw tension.

Not a word was exchanged until they had returned to the car and Brock started the motor. 'Will I see you before you leave?' Stephanie risked a glance at his forbidding profile as she asked the subdued question.

'Not tonight. I haven't got that kind of control.'

He didn't even look at her as he reversed out of the parking stall. Before he turned on to the road, he let the car idle and glanced at her. There was a softening in the hardness of his expression—a surfacing patience that was reluctant.

'We'll get together in the morning . . . before church. In the meantime——' he pushed back the

sleeve of his parka to see his watch, 'it's time I
was back at the inn. Perry and I have an appointment to meet the architect at one.'

At the farmhouse, Brock didn't bother to get
out of the car. When he looked at her, not moving,
Stephanie leaned across the seat to kiss him. His
hands didn't touch her and his response to the
contact of her lips was severely checked, barely
warm.

Vaguely dejected, Stephanie walked to the
house and paused at the door of the two-storey
brick structure to watch Brock drive away. She
didn't really blame him for his attitude, but she
knew that hers was not without justification, too.

On Sunday morning, Stephanie awakened
earlier than usual. Since Brock hadn't given her
any indication when he might call or come, she
didn't take the chance of being caught unaware.
She was dressed complete with make-up when she
went downstairs to make coffee and get the Sunday newspaper the paperboy had delivered to
their doorstep.

Before she drank her second cup of coffee, she
was on pins and needles, waiting for the phone to
ring or the sound of a car driving up the lane. All
the while the knowledge that Brock would be
leaving at noon and she didn't have any idea when
he would come back kept preying on her mind. A

noise in the living room sent her rushing out of
the kitchen, certain she had missed hearing
Brock's car, but it was a bleary-eyed Perry who
had caused the sound.

'Brrr, it's cold in here! Why haven't you
started the fire?' he grumbled, and shivered in his
corduroy robe. His hair was mussed from the
night's sleep and a pair of old slippers covered his
large feet as he moved tiredly towards the Count
Rumford fireplace. 'You're up and dressed very
early this morning. How come?' He waved aside
the question, kneeling to set dried logs on the
grate. 'I remember. You told me at supper that
Brock was supposed to come over this morning.'

'Yes, he is.' While her brother got the fire going,
Stephanie walked to the front window to look out.
'You were late coming home last night.'

'I know. I hope you have the coffee made,' he
sighed. 'Is the Sunday paper here yet?' The fire
was crackling merrily in the fireplace, already
chasing out the chill in the room.

'Yes, to both. I'll bring them to you,' she
volunteered, and retraced her steps to the kitchen
to pour a cup of coffee for her brother and bring
him the newspaper.

When she returned, he was stretched out in his
favourite armchair, his feet on the footstool, his
eyes closed. She set his coffee on the lampstand

beside him and dropped the paper on his lap. Perry stirred, slowly opening one eye, and yawning.

'Why didn't you sleep longer?' Stephanie chided. 'There wasn't any reason for you to get up this early.' Sundays were, theoretically, his days off, except in the winter, but he usually stopped by the inn in the afternoons.

'I'm really bushed,' he admitted. 'But I woke up and couldn't go back to sleep.'

While he sipped at the steaming hot coffee, Stephanie wandered to the hooked rug covering the wide floorboards in front of the fireplace. The living room was large and open, with exposed beams and hand-planed wainscoting. The sliding glass doors were decorated with October frost, partially concealing the hills rising behind the house.

'I always think I'm doing well until I come away from a meeting with Brock.' Which was where Perry had been the night before until well after midnight. 'Now, I feel drained and empty. He's like a sponge, absorbing everything I know out of my brain, asking endless questions,' he sighed.

'About what?' Stephanie turned to study her brother, wondering if Brock had asked about her.

Perry started to answer, then interrupted her look. 'No, he didn't ask about you. Obviously you told him that I gave up graduate school in law when Dad had his accident.'

'Why? What did he say?'

'A lot of nonsense about night school and summer courses.' His mouth tightened grimly. 'Which would take me forever, plus there's the problem of commuting back and forth and keeping the inn operating the way it should. No, it just isn't possible.'

'What else did you talk about?' They had discussed the possibility of Perry resuming his education many times, always with the same conclusion, so Stephanie didn't argue with him now. She was too eager for any snippet of information about Brock.

'Everything from the difficulty of getting and keeping good help to renovating the whole place and turning it into the most famous ski lodge on the continent.' Her brother paused, appearing to consider something. 'You know, Stephanie, most of the time I feel like I'm a pretty experienced guy, but last night, in his suite, he was getting calls from half the world. My whole life is centred around that inn, yet I doubt very seriously if the inn earns enough money to pay his travel expenses for a year. I represent pretty small potatoes to his organisation. The place could burn down and he'd never miss it.'

'Why are you thinking like that?' It didn't

sound like her brother; his attitude was defeated and inferior.

'I don't know,' she shrugged, and sighed. 'Maybe I'm jealous. Hell, I know I am,' he laughed shortly. 'There I am sitting in his suite last night, trying desperately to concentrate on the discussion, and this chick of his keeps waltzing in and out of the the bedroom dressed in this sheer lacy peignoir. I spent more time imagining——' Perry stopped at the sight of the ashen colour that spread over Stephanie's face. 'I'm sorry. Stephanie, don't be a fool.'

'Please, don't say anything,' she protested softly. 'There isn't anything you can say that I haven't told myself already.' She turned, needing a few minutes by herself. 'Excuse me. I'm going to get some coffee.'

When she returned to the living room, Perry was buried in the front page of the newspaper, and the conversation wasn't resumed. Stephanie sat on the sofa to drink her coffee. The minute it was gone she was up, walking to the window to look at the empty scene. Back and forth she went —too nervous to stay seated, while the grandfather clock ticked away the minutes.

'A watched pot never boils,' Perry remarked on her tenth trip to the window.

'I know it.' She walked to the fireplace to add another log to the waning fire.

'It's getting late,' he observed. 'I'd better get dressed for church. Are you coming?'

Rising, she glanced towards the window. 'I——' Then Stephanie saw the blue Mercedes coming up the drive. 'He's here!'

She dashed to the door and was outside by the time Brock stepped from the car. Her smile froze into place when she spied the blonde sitting in the passenger seat. Her gaze swung in hurt confusion back to Brock as he approached, his features grimly drawn.

'I have to leave. With luck, I'll make it to New York in time to catch the afternoon flight to Geneva,' he said.

Stephanie couldn't speak, her throat paralysed. She could only stare at him with her rounded blue eyes. The frosty chill of the October morning wasn't nearly as cold as she felt. He was leaving, and they wouldn't even have the morning together.

'I came to say goodbye,' Brock continued. 'I should have called, but——' His jaw hardened. 'I told you this could happen. Dammit, I warned you!' He grabbed her by the shoulders as if to shake her.

The physical pain was almost welcome. In the next second, he was yanking her into his arms and bruising her lips with a hard, angry kiss, relentless in its punishment. But his savagery aroused an emotion stronger than pain. It engulfed her, leaving her weak and breathless when he broke the contact.

He pushed her away and had already turned to walk to the car before he muttered a rather final sounding, 'Goodbye, Stephanie.'

But she couldn't get that one word out—not even his name. The car had been started and was turning around. Still Stephanie hadn't moved from where he'd left her at the door.

There was no last glance from Brock, no wave, nothing. Tears misted over her eyes, blinding her vision. She didn't see the exact moment when his car disappeared from view down the long lane.

Entering the house, she was aware of Perry's blurred outline near the stairwell. 'He had to leave . . . for Geneva.' Her voice was choked and very small. Her brother looked at her for a long minute, but didn't say anything as he turned to climb the stairs. Stephanie walked blindly into the kitchen where she cried slow, silent tears.

The north winds came to strip the leaves from the trees, exposing the dark skeletons of the trunks and leaving piles of brown leaves to carpet the ground. The first snow flurry of the season came the last weekend in October. November arrived.

Stephanie had written Brock two letters, short ones with news of the inn and the area, minus any personal messages. The only address she had was the one the monthly reports were sent to. She couldn't be sure if they would reach him. Last week, she had sent merely a postcard.

There hadn't been a single reply of any kind, and she was gradually becoming convinced he had forgotten her. She couldn't shake the feeling she had been on the brink of discovering something wonderful, only to lose it.

The ring of her office extension drew a sigh. Unclipping an earring, she answered the phone. 'Miss Hall speaking. May I help you?'

'How are you?' a familiar male voice enquired.

Incredulous, Stephanie tightened her grip on the receiver, the blood singing in her veins. 'Brock?' She could feel her voice choking. 'Where are you?' In the background she could hear a hum of voices.

'Can you believe it?' His short laugh was a quietly harsh sound. 'I'm in the middle of a board meeting. I don't know who the hell they think I'm talking to, but I had to call you.'

'I'm glad.' Her answer was hardly above a whisper.

'The mail packet caught up with me this morning. I got the letter and postcard you sent,' he said.

'I . . . I wasn't sure if I should write,' she admitted.

'These are liberated times, but I'm not surprised that you're behind them,' he mocked, but not unkindly.

A voice intruded from the background. 'Mr Canfield, here's the breakdown report you wanted on the foreign currency exchange this quarter.'

'Good, Frank,' was Brock's partially muffled response, then clearer, 'Are you still there?'

'Yes, I'm here,' Stephanie assured him, her voice regaining its strength.

Brock started to say something, then changed his mind. 'This is the most frustrating means of communication.' His tone was low and charged with irritation. 'I can't see you or touch you.'

'I know.' There was a certain torment in hearing his voice.

'Mr Canfield?' The same voice interrupted Brock again.

'Dammit, Frank, can't you see I'm on the phone?' he demanded. He came back on the line, sighing tiredly. 'I'm sorry. It's no good, I can't talk now. I'm trying to schedule a trip there in December or January.'

That long! Stephanie thought, but didn't say it. Instead she attempted a light remark. 'The heart of the skiing season. Maybe you'll have enough time to spend an afternoon on the slopes. We already have a good snow cover.'

'I don't give a damn about the snow.' He controlled the impatience in his voice to add a promising, 'I'll see you . . . soon, I hope.'

'Goodbye, Brock.'

The line clicked dead before Stephanie hung up the phone. She stared at it until a flicker of movement caught her attention and she looked up to see Perry in the doorway.

'Was that Brock?' He studied her quietly.

'Yes.' She reclipped the earring on her lobe, unwilling to discuss the sweetly short conversation with Brock.

A sadness stole into his features. 'Don't let him break your heart, Steph.' His hand slapped at the door-frame in a helpless gesture as he turned to walk down the hallway to his office.

CHAPTER SIX

THERE weren't any more calls from Brock. Stephanie continued to write him, but not more frequently than she had before. Other than to say she looked forward to his next trip to New Hampshire, she didn't make any possessive references to him. She knew that the next time she saw him it might all be different, and she didn't want any potentially embarrassing letters sent by her.

The forecast for Thanksgiving called for snow. It was falling steadily in fat flakes, accumulating quickly on a ground that was white from previous snowfalls. It was a workday as usual, the Thanksgiving holiday weekend being one of their biggest of the winter season.

When Stephanie entered the kitchen that morning, her brother was at the big door, bundling up with boots, muffler and gloves. 'Let's forget about breakfast this morning. I'm going out to put the snow chains on the wagon. We'll eat when we get to the inn.'

'When the weatherman said snow last night, he meant it, didn't he?' She glanced out the frosty window at the large flakes veiling the grey-white hills.

'We're in for a storm,' Perry prophesied. 'It wouldn't hurt if you grabbed a clean shirt and my shaving kit, and something for yourself. If this keeps up, we'll just sleep at the inn tonight. Our road is always the last one the snow-ploughs hit.' He grimaced and ducked out the back door amidst a whirl of snowflakes and cold air.

The drive from the farmhouse to the inn usually took ten minutes, but the limited visibility and the slippery roads caused by the falling snow increased it to twenty-five. The car radio forecast worsening conditions.

Before breakfast was over the area slopes were closed to skiers. The inn suddenly seemed more crowded than usual because all the guests were virtually confined to the inn. They congregated in the lobby around the fireplace, the games room, the lounge, and the restaurants. There was even a line to use the recently completed sauna and exercise room. Almost any flat surface was commandeered for a game of cards. Impromptu chess and checkers tournaments were held.

Shortly after twelve noon there was a mild panic when it was discovered two cross-country skiers hadn't reported in from an overnight trip. Perry and Stephanie had just sat down to the restaurant's turkey dinner. The adventurers were finally located at another lodge, but their dinners were cold when they returned to them.

Then the deluge of stranded motorists began. Although they were full, Stephanie temporarily doubled up rooms where she could, shifting all the members of one family into a room, helped Household figure out how many spare blankets, sheets, cots, and pillows were on hand and how many motorists they could handle, and fill in wherever she was needed.

'Don't forget to save us a place to sleep,' Perry reminded her at one point when she was working out the capacity of the sofas in the lobby.

'There's always the floor,' she retorted with a laugh.

It was almost a relief when the storm knocked the telephone lines out late in the afternoon and the switchboard finally stopped buzzing. The dinner hour didn't bring a let-up in the frantic pace. With all the extra people, both Perry and Stephanie lent a hand in the restaurant kitchen, doing everything from helping fix the food to running the dishwasher.

At nine-thirty Perry laid a hand on her shoulder.

'You've done enough, Steph. Why don't you call it a night?'

'Yessir, boss,' she agreed readily. 'What about you?'

'I'm going to the lounge. Freddie needs some

help behind the bar. And,' he breathed in tiredly, 'I'd better be around in case someone gets rowdy.'

Stephanie was tempted to insist he let someone else do it, but Perry took his responsibility as manager too seriously to shrug it on to someone else. 'Okay. I'll see you in the morning.'

'Wait a minute!' He called her back when she started to turn away. 'Where do I sleep tonight?'

'On the couch in your office . . . unless it's already occupied,' she joked. 'In that event, you're on your own.'

'Thanks a lot, Sis,' he retorted in a mock-growl.

Stopping at her office, Stephanie picked up the small overnight bag she had packed and started down the hallway. She didn't know which sounded more divine—a shower or sleep? With luck, she would be able to have both.

Before she knocked at the door of the suite, she heard the childish giggles coming from inside. Her knocks produced some shrieks and more giggles. The door was opened by a young woman, barely a year older than Stephanie. She looked tired, harassed and exasperated, her smile growing thin.

'Hi. It's me, your room-mate for the night.' Stephanie struggled to sound cheerful.

'Of course, come in, Miss Hall.' But she was diverted by the impish little five-year-old girl who appeared in the connecting doorway to the bedroom. 'Amy Sue, you get back in that bed before

I spank you!' the woman threatened, and the little nightgowned figure fled in laughter. 'I'm sorry. I've been trying to get the girls asleep for the last hour. They think this is some kind of a party.'

'It's all new. They're just excited, Mrs Foster. And please, call me Stephanie,' she insisted.

'I'm Madge.' She walked to the bedroom. 'And these are my daughters, Amy five and Marsha four.'

Amy, the oldest, quickly scurried under the covers. The king-sized bed seemed to swallow up the two small girls with their dark hair. The pair eyed Stephanie with bold curiosity.

'Hello, Amy and Marsha,' she smiled. The two looked anything but sleepy with their bright brown eyes.

'Hello. Who are you?' The youngest asked, exhibiting no shyness because Stephanie was a stranger.

'My name is Stephanie,' she replied.

'My friend in Day Care has that same name,' Amy piped.

'Will you read us a story?' Marsha dived for the storybooks on the nightstand beside the bed. 'Read mine.'

'No, mine!' Amy protested.

'Girls!' Madge Foster attempted to intervene with some measure of authority.

'I don't mind,' Stephanie murmured. 'I'll read

to them while you relax in the tub.' When the woman hesitated, obviously tempted, Stephanie repeated, 'Really, I don't mind.'

'Thank you. I don't know what to say,' the woman faltered. 'All day long, trying to drive in that storm, with those girls bouncing all over, then being stranded here ... my nerves could use a rest. But I won't leave them with you for long, I promise.'

'Read my story, please?' Amy pleaded.

'I'll read them both,' Stephanie promised. 'But we'll start with Marsha's first.'

She set her overnight case on the floor by the bed and walked over to sit on the edge where the bed lamp was lit. Marsha immediately pressed her book into Stephanie's hands. They grumbled when she insisted that they had to crawl under the covers and lie down before she would read to them. They didn't give in until she had agreed to show them the pictures on each page.

Her ploy worked. By the time she had read the first story for the third time, both girls had fallen asleep. When the bathroom door opened Stephanie held a silencing finger to her lips. Madge Foster smiled and shook her head in disbelief.

'You must have my husband Ted's kind of voice. I can read until I'm hoarse, but they go right to sleep for him,' she whispered. 'I don't think my head is even going to have a chance to touch the pillow before I'm asleep. The bathroom is all yours, and it's like heaven.'

'Good.' Stephanie flexed her shoulders as the fatigue began to set in. She picked up her night case and started towards the marble bathroom.

'Oh, Miss H . . . Stephanie, do you mind if I leave the lamp burning on my side of the bed? The girls don't like to sleep in the dark. I've been trying to break them of it, but this is a strange place and . . . if it wouldn't bother you . . .'

'No, it won't bother me. I'm like you,' Stephanie explained. 'I'll probably be asleep before my head's on the pillow.'

'The girls don't toss and turn very much, so I don't think they'll disturb you.'

'I'm sorry we weren't able to provide you with a room of your own,' Stephanie apologised.

'Listen, I'm just grateful for a bed to sleep in. And heaven knows, this one is big enough to hold two more,' Madge smiled. 'Go and take your bath. And goodnight.'

'Yes, goodnight.'

The hot bath water made Stephanie realise how mentally and physically exhausted she was. It was an effort to towel dry and pull on her nightdress. All three were asleep when she re-entered the bedroom. She moved quietly to the far side of the bed on the fringe of the pool of light cast by the lamp.

She, too, drifted into sleep within minutes.

A coolness roused her, a vague sensation of a draught. Stephanie tried to pull the covers tighter around her neck, but something held them down. She started to turn on to her side, only to become conscious of something heavy weighing the edge of the mattress down.

Her lashes opened to a narrow slit, then widened at the outline of a person sitting on the bed beside her. It was a full second before she realised who the man in the white shirt was.

'Brock!' Was she dreaming? She said his name softly in case she scared his image away.

But his hand touched her face in a light, cool caress and she knew it wasn't a dream. 'Hello.'

'What are you doing here?' she breathed, keeping her voice low.

He looked tired and drawn; she could see that in the half-light from the lamp. But the glint in his grey eyes was anything but weary.

'Here you are finally in my bed, and there isn't room for me.' His gaze danced to the sleeping children in the centre of the bed, their faces illuminated by the soft glow spilling from the lamp.

'The storm——' Stephanie started to explain in a whisper.

'Yes, I know. I stepped over bodies in the lobby.'

Without warning, Brock straightened to fold back the covers and slide his arms beneath her, picking her up.

Stephanie clutched at his neck, too stunned and sleepy to struggle and too conscious of the possibility of waking the children or their mother. 'What are you doing, Brock?' The question was issued in confused excitement, her pulse accelerating at this contact with his leanly muscled frame.

'I'm taking you into the other room with me,' he stated, and carried her through the connecting door to the sitting room. 'We have an hour of Thanksgiving left and I mean to spend it with you.'

Brock didn't put her down until they were inside the room and the door was shut. A single light burned in the far corner. Outside the window, the snow was still falling, but slower and not as thickly as it had been earlier.

Not quite able to believe he was really there in the flesh, Stephanie gazed at his manly features, the darkness of his hair and the melting greyness of his eyes. His hands spanned her waist, gliding over the silken material of her nightgown to bring her slowly closer as if he enjoyed the feel of her.

When his mouth began a downward movement towards her, Stephanie went on tiptoes to meet it.

He took possession of the yielding softness of her lips with a gentle sensuality. It was so different from any other kiss that she could hardly understand what was happening to her.

His hands were at the small of her back, caressing but firm against her silk-covered skin and holding her close to the hardening contours of his thighs. Her blood ran with fire as he practised the subtle art of seduction so expertly and so effortlessly. Stephanie was lost to his skill and she didn't care.

When at last he released her lips to seek the bareness of a shoulder, she sighed her enchanted contentment. It gradually dawned on her that the coolness she was feeling against her scantily clad body did not come from any draught in the room. It was Brock who was chilled.

'You're cold,' she murmured in concern.

'So?' His mouth was against her ear, his tongue circling its sensitive hollows. 'Warm me up.'

Taking him literally at his word, Stephanie pressed closer to him in an effort to warm him with her body heat. 'How did you get here in this storm?' she wondered, her mouth brushing the coolness of his shirt at his shoulder. 'I still can't believe you're really here,' she sighed at the miracle of being in his arms.

'Neither can I!' His arms tightened fiercely for

an instant. 'There were times when I wondered whether I would make it,' he admitted in a tired and rueful sigh.

'Why did you come? With this storm and all . . .' Stephanie lifted her head, shuddering when she thought of him out there in that blizzard.

She was frightened by what might have happened. Her hand glided along the smoothness of his jaw and he rubbed his cheek into her palm.

'Why did you take such a risk?' Her voice was choked by the dangerous chance he had taken.

'I wanted to be with you.' He gazed deep into her eyes, letting his look add a heady force to his statement. 'I didn't want to spend the holiday without you.'

'You should have called. You should have let me know you were coming,' Stephanie admonished, but she knew she would have been worried sick about him.

'I wanted to surprise you.' His mouth twisted in a wry line. 'It's been an eighteen-hour obstacle course—closed airports, diverted flights, trains not running, highways closed. When I finally admitted there was a distinct possibility I wouldn't make it, the telephone lines were down. I couldn't get through to tell you I wanted to be here.'

'Brock . . .' The frustration he had suffered was very real to her.

'I know.' The circle of his arms tightened as he pressed a kiss to her temple.

'How did you get here?' She still marvelled that he had actually made it.

'I rented a car and bribed a maintenance crew to let me follow their snow-plough,' he explained.

'How did you guess I'd be here at the inn?'

'I didn't. I went to your home first,' Brock told her.

'But the lane——' Stephanie's eyes widened in alarmed protest.

'—was blocked,' he finished the sentence for her. 'I had to leave the car on the road and walk back to the house. It's a good thing you and Perry are the trusting sort and left the back door unlocked. When I discovered the house was empty, I guessed you'd decided to spend the night at the inn, so I came here. Of course, I never expected to find you sleeping in my bed. Lucky for me, the night clerk knew where you were bunking and I didn't have to go around knocking on doors in the middle of the night trying to find you. Perry would have had some irate guests on his hands come morning.'

She was shaken by his single-minded determination to find her, to be with her. Surely it had to mean something? Mere sexual attraction couldn't be all it was they shared. The thought left her feeling slightly euphoric and dazed by the fiery surge of emotion rushing through her system.

'Come.' Moving, Brock took hold of her hand and led her to the side of the room. 'I took the seat cushions off the sofa and the spare pillows and blankets from the closet to make us a bed on the floor in here.'

Stephanie stared at the blanket-covered cushions on the floor and the two pillows lying side by side at the top. Brock was studying her, waiting for her reaction. But there was none— at least, not a negative one.

'I'll turn out the light.' Releasing her hand, Brock moved to the opposite side of the room where the lamp burned.

Stephanie watched him. There wasn't any conscious decision on her part. She was only aware of how very close she had come to losing him to the winter storm. All arguments for and against going to bed with him paled in comparison to that unshakeable fact. It was truly the only thought in her mind.

When the click of a light switch buried the room in darkness, she sank on to the hard foam cushions. A sublime calmness settled through her as she folded back the blanket to slide beneath it.

She loved Brock. The quiet knowledge wasn't a rationale for her action, but the simple truth. Implausible as it seemed, as short a time as she had known his, she loved him. The unshakeable strength of this emotion made her feel mellow and warm, ripe with fullness of it.

Brock was a dark shadow as he approached the makeshift bed. Not until he had joined her under the covers did he take form and substance. Lying on his side, he reached for her to draw her into his embrace.

Her hands encountered the muscled bareness of his chest, its dark hair sensually rough beneath her palms, his legs shifting to tangle with hers. The sweet intimacy twisted its knife-sharp blade into her stomach, a heady desire building.

His mouth sought and found hers, covering it with a softly bruising force and demanding a response that she had no wish to suppress. He mastered her with a fiery hunger, possessing her heart and soul which she was only too willing to give into his keeping. With a surrendering sigh, she slid her arms around the smooth skin covering his hard shoulders to bring more of his weight on to her.

The blanket slipped to a position over their hips as Brock pushed the silken strap of her nightgown off a shoulder. His mouth explored the rose-crested top of a breast that had been exposed to his dark grey eyes. It heightened the taut desire curling her toes and knotting her insides. Then his

mouth returned to crush her lips while the sensually abrasive hair on his chest brushed across the
sensitive skin of her naked breast.

A moaning sound came from his throat, his
warm breath filling her mouth with suffocating
sweetness. The thin barrier of her nightgown
didn't keep out the sensation of the growing limp-
ness of his body.

Reluctantly, Brock drew away from her to roll
on to his back, an arm flung above his head on to
the pillow. Stephanie was confused and aching
by this withdrawal. Turning on to her side, she
levered herself on to an elbow to gaze at him.

His gaze slid to her, the vibrant glitter fading
from his eyes. He reached out to slide the strap of
her gown on to her shoulder, his hand remaining
to silently caress her. A half-smile was lifting one
corner of his mouth. Even that seemed to require
a lot of effort.

'What's wrong, Brock?' Stephanie asked uncertainly, wanting to curl herself into his arms,
but refraining to obey the impulse because of the
lack of an invitation.

'I've been working some long hours the last few
days, trying to clear up any business that might
come up at the last minute and keep me from
coming here to be with you.' His hand moved to
rest on the curve of her neck beneath the curtain
of chestnut hair. 'I've had six hours of sleep in the

last fifty-two. That's what's wrong.'

She heard the weariness in his voice, but in the dimness of the darkened room she could only guess at the strain of fatigue etched in his features. When he chuckled softly, she frowned in confusion.

'Don't you see the irony of this, Stephanie?' Brock murmured. 'After all this time you're finally beside me—here in this bed, just the way I imagined it. And now I'm too damned tired to do anything about it,' he sighed in irritation.

Her personal dissatisfaction was forgotten in a rush of loving concern for him. Leaning forward, she kissed his lips with infinite tenderness. A loving smile curved her mouth when she straightened.

'You'd better get some sleep before you collapse,' she advised, and turned to sweep back the covers to return to her own bed.

'No.' Brock waylaid her action with an outstretched hand. 'Stay with me tonight.'

Her hesitation was fractional. Accepting his invitation, she lay down once more beside him. Brock turned her on to her side, with her back to him and curled her against his length. His arm was around her waist, a hand possessively cupping a breast.

Stephanie was warmed by the memory that Brock had once insisted that he preferred to sleep alone. He shared this need to be close—a need that transcended every thought and feeling that might have been true in the past. What they had unique. Stephanie knew it, and she suspected Brock did too.

Hugged close to him, she heard his breathing grow deep and heavy as tiredness carried him quickly to sleep. She closed her eyes, not certain that she would drift off so quickly, but the utter contentment soon whisked her away. Thus they slept spoon-fashion, enfolded in an embrace of passive desire.

Morning light infiltrated the room through the large windows, pricking at Stephanie's eyelids. She became conscious of a heavy weight across her legs and stomach. A delicious heat was radiating from something and she snuggled closer to it. When she realised the heartbeat she was hearing did not belong to her, she opened her eyes.

A pair of broad shoulders were in front of her, tanned skin stretched across sinewy muscles and darkened with rough, curling hairs. The weight across her stomach was Brock's arm, his hand cupped to her hipbone in firm possession, while a leg was hooked across her knees. Peering through the top of her lashes, she studied the unrelenting strength of his face in sleep. Lean and powerful, he stirred her senses.

There was a very strong impulse to kiss him

awake, but the amount of sunlight streaming through the windows and the muffled voices of others in the outer hall warned Stephanie of the lateness of the hour.

Reluctantly she slid out of his hold and out of the makeshift bed on the floor. Her bare feet made no sound as she entered the bedroom where the young woman and her two children were still sleeping. With her overnight bag in hand, she slipped into the bathroom to wash and dress.

There wasn't a sound from anyone when she came out. She hesitated in the sitting room, but Brock was still sound asleep. He had left the key to his suite lying on an end table. Stephanie slipped it into her pocket and quietly left the room through the hall door.

She went directly to the restaurant kitchen. The inn was already astir with early morning breakfasters. Outside, the sky was clear—almost too blue against the pure snow white of the ground. She laid a tray with china cups and a pot of coffee to take to the suite.

As she was passing through the lobby, her brother appeared. 'Stephanie!' he called out to stop her. 'Brock's here,' he said when he reached her side. 'He arrived last night.'

'Yes, I know,' she nodded. 'I'm taking him some coffee now. He's still sleeping. He made a bed on the floor of the sitting room.' She didn't mention that she had shared it with him. It wasn't an attempt to conceal the knowledge from Perry. Rather, she preferred to choose her own time to tell him when there weren't others around who might overhear and misinterpret her action.

Perry glanced at the tray, then at her, studying her closely. 'Why is he here? Did he say?' he questioned.

'He wanted to have Thanksgiving here.' She hesitated over carrying the explanation farther, but she needn't have.

Her brother did it for her. 'With you,' he identified the reason specifically.

'Yes,' Stephanie nodded, unable to keep the radiance from shining in her eyes.

Perry shook his head in absent amazement. 'In that blizzard . . .' he murmured. He bit at his lip in a second of pensive silence. 'Maybe I was wrong about him . . . and his interest in you,' he offered. Whatever else he was about to add, he changed his mind and flashed her a wry smile. 'You'd better take that coffee to him before it gets cold.'

'I'll be back shortly,' she promised.

'No rush,' Perry insisted. 'After the long day you put in yesterday, you can be as late as you want this morning.'

Her smile was full of affection for her brother. 'Thanks, boss.'

At the door to the suite, Stephanie had to set the

tray on the floor to have her hands free to unlock the door. The cups rattled on their china saucers as she entered the sitting room, but the delicate noise didn't waken Brock, who was still sleeping soundly on the floor. Only silence came from the bedroom where the young woman and her two little girls were.

Stephanie carried the tray to the rattan table and set it there. Knowing how little sleep Brock had in the last few days, she didn't pour him any coffee yet, only a cup for herself. The thermal pot would keep the coffee hot for a long time. She walked to a chair, unconsciously choosing one that would permit her to watch Brock in sleep.

The blanket was down around his hips, exposing his lean, untanned torso to her inspection. Briefly she was fascinated by the button roundness of his navel, a dark hollow in his flat stomach. He was lying on his side, facing her.

Stephanie let her gaze wander upward to his strongly defined mouth and the thickness of dark lashes resting against his cheekbone. His brows were thick and malely arched. Across his forehead was a thatch of rumpled dark hair. Even in sleep, Brock exuded an incredible virility. She wanted to touch him so much, it was almost a physical pain.

When he stirred, she unconsciously held her breath. His hand moved across the empty cushion beside him, as if instinctively seeking something. Was he in search of her? What a wondrous thought! His hand froze for a full second, then instantly he was awake, turning on to his back and alarm flashed in his expression.

'Stephanie!' He called out for her in an impatient voice a fraction of a second before he saw her seated in the chair. His expression changed immediately to one of satisfaction.

'Good morning.' Her voice was husky with the knowledge that he had missed having her sleeping from beside him.

'Not so good,' Brock denied her adjective in describing the morning. 'You should have awakened me when you did.'

'Would you like some coffee?' Stephanie rose, conscious of his gaze taking in her fully dressed appearance, detail by detail. Without waiting for his acceptance, she walked to the table and poured a cup for him.

'Why did you get dressed right away?' he questioned before his gaze flickered past her to the sunlight that drenched the room. 'What time is it?'

'Nearly nine o'clock.' She carried the cup to him.

The blanket had slipped a little farther downward, giving her a tantalising glimpse of the elastic waistband of his white jockey shorts. It was crazy the way her pulse reacted to the sight, yet she had entered her brother's bedroom many times to waken him when he slept through his alarm, and found him similarly clad. She hadn't even blinked an eye then.

'I suppose you have to work this morning.' His mouth was grim as he looked up when she stood beside the crude bed. He was still supported by his elbows and forearms in a half-reclining position.

'No. Perry said it was okay if I was late,' she assured him, and knelt down to give him his coffee.

But Brock didn't reach for it. 'In that case, come back to bed.' His gaze became obsessively attached to her lips, sending her heart knocking against her ribs.

Stephanie couldn't find her voice. She recovered it after he had sat up and circled one arm around her waist while his hand curved itself to the back of her neck, pulling her towards him.

'I'm going to spill the coffee,' she warned a breath before his mouth covered her lips to hungrily remind her of the volatile attraction they shared.

Her hand gripped his hard shoulder for balance while the cup of coffee jiggled in its saucer in the opposite hand, the steaming liquid sloshing over the china rim. But she offered no resistance to his kiss, melting under his heady domination.

'Get rid of that coffee and those clothes, and come back to bed with me,' Brock ordered against her mouth, and proceeded to outline her lips with his tongue.

He kissed her thoroughly and sensually before drawing away. Stephanie was drugged in a euphoric state, barely capable of thought when she met the grey darkness of his eyes. A sound intruded, a mere irritation until a movement entered her vision, drawing her glance.

Five-year-old Amy was standing in the doorway, wearing her flannel nightgown, one bare foot on top of the other, eyeing the pair of them curiously. Stephanie was brought sharply to her senses. Brock turned to look behind him, and barely stifled a curse of frustration rather than anger. There was a glitter of ironic amusement and profound regret when he glanced back to Stephanie.

'Who's that man?' Amy wanted to know. 'Is he your husband?'

Brock rescued the cup of coffee from her shaking hand and arched a mocking brow in her direction. 'No. He's a friend,' Stephanie explained a little self-consciously.

The little girl padded quickly across the room as if invited. 'Why are you sleeping on the floor?' she asked Brock, and bounced on to the cushions to sit on a pillow with her legs under her.

'Because there wasn't any place else for me to sleep,' he replied, regarding the little girl's intrusion with a patience and tolerance that faintly surprised Stephanie.

'There was lots of room in the bed,' Amy insisted.

'It looked a little more crowded than I wanted.' His glance darted to Stephanie, heavy with secret meaning.

A drowsy Marsha entered the room, rubbing her sleep-filled eyes and hugging her storybook in front of her. She pattered quickly to her older sister's side and curled on to the edge of the pillow, sitting cross-legged and yawning.

Brock took a sip of his coffee and murmured to Stephanie, 'This bed is nearly as full as mine was last night.'

'Were you going to wrestle?' the oldest brunette girl enquired innocently.

His look was amused, yet narrowed. 'Why do you ask?'

'Because Mommy and Daddy do that sometimes in the mornings,' she explained. 'Daddy tickles and tickles her. It makes Mommy laugh so hard she cries. Then Daddy kisses her like you were doing.'

'I see.' The corners of his mouth deepened with the containment of a smile. 'Then what happens?'

Stephanie gasped in sharp embarrassment, drawing the wicked glint of his gaze.

'Then Mommy's cheeks get pink like Stephanie's are,' Amy admitted with guileless charm. 'She shooes us to our own rooms and helps us get dressed so we can go outside and play.'

The answer didn't put Stephanie any more at ease under Brock's disturbing and mocking look. 'Is your mother awake?' she asked, hoping to change the subject.

'Not yet.' It was obvious it didn't matter much to either of the girls. 'Do you have any children?' Amy directed the question to Brock. Like any female, she was drawn to the male of the species.

'No,' he replied as his gaze roamed over the two little girls.

'Wouldn't you like to have a little girl of your own?' Amy seemed puzzled. 'Daddy says it's wonderful, especially when you have two.'

'He does, does he?' Brock was deliberately non-committal although he glanced almost automatically at Stephanie.

'Yes. You can have little boys, too,' Amy hastened to add.

'But they can be mean sometimes,' Marsha piped in for the first time. 'Jimmy Joe Barnes stepped on my doll and broke its head on purpose.'

'But Daddy fixed it,' Amy reminded her, before

turning back to Brock. 'Which do you think you'd rather have?'

'I don't know. Do little boys crawl in bed with their parents in the morning, too?' he asked with his tongue in his cheek.

'I think so.' Amy's frown revealed she didn't understand the relevancy of that question.

'Which would you rather have, Stephanie?' Brock eyed her with deliberate suggestiveness, stealing her breath. 'Boys or girls? Or one of each?'

'I——' She was spared from answering that provocative question by the interruption of Madge Foster's voice coming from the bedroom.

'Amy? Marsha? Where are you?' she called in sleepy alarm.

'We're in here, Mommy,' Amy answered immediately.

'What are you ...' The question was never finished as the young woman appeared in the doorway.

The sight of Brock sitting half-naked with Stephanie and her daughters made the woman suddenly and embarrassingly conscious of the revealing nightgown she was wearing. Quickly she stepped behind the door, using it as a shield.

'You girls come here right now,' she ordered. 'You haven't brushed your teeth yet,' she added, as if that was the reason.

The pair hopped blithely to their feet and dashed into the bedroom. Madge sent Stephanie a grimacing look of apology before closing the door.

'Now,' Brock caught at Stephanie's hand to pull her off-balance and into his arms, 'where were we before we were so rudely interrupted?' His mouth had barely touched her lips when there was a knock at the hall door. Releasing her, he muttered, 'This place is turning into Grand Central Station. You'd better hand me my pants, there's likely to be a parade through here any minute.'

Before she answered the door, Stephanie handed him the trousers draped over a nearby chair. It was one of the housekeepers doing a room check. When Stephanie turned around after closing the door, Brock was on his feet, semi-decently clad in the dark pants.

'More coffee?' she suggested.

'Since circumstances don't allow anything else, why not?' he shrugged with a wry smile. She had just started to fill his cup when the telephone rang. Brock motioned her to stay where she was. 'I'll get it.' He answered it, then hesitated, glancing at Stephanie as he responded to the caller, 'Just a minute, please.' He held the mouthpiece slightly away. 'The young woman occupying the bedroom —is her last name Foster?'

'Yes, it is,' Stephanie nodded.

'It's her husband on the phone,' he explained.

'Evidently the telephones are back in service. There's an extension by the bed she can use.'

'I'll tell her.' She handed Brock his cup before she walked over to knock on the connecting door. 'Madge, your husband is on the phone.'

The delighted shrieks of the two young girls came first from the bedroom, then echoed into the sitting room through the phone in Brock's hand. He set the receiver on its cradle and let a glance slide at Stephanie.

'How do you suppose she's going to explain that a man answered?' he mocked.

'With the storm and all, I'm sure her husband will understand.' She dismissed it as a problem and retrieved her coffee cup from the side table to refill it.

As he was pouring the coffee from the thermal pot, Brock came up behind her, sliding an arm around the front of her waist and bending to kiss the side of her neck. 'Believe me, if I called you and a man other than your brother answered the phone, you'd have a lot of explaining to do.'

A delicious tingle danced over her skin at his nibbling kisses. 'I'll remember to always answer the phone myself from now on,' she mocked, 'especially when I'm entertaining male friends.'

His arm tightened with a sudden fierceness. 'I'm not joking, Stephanie. Just thinking of someone else touching you——'

Someone rapped very softly on the hall door. Brock cursed savagely as he broke away from her and crossed the room with long, impatient strides to jerk the door open.

Perry stood outside, briefly startled. 'I wasn't sure if you were up yet.'

Brock's laugh was a harsh sound. 'I'm awake, all right. Thanks to two little girls, then their mother, then a telephone call from their father, and a housekeeper fits in the order of things somewhere. Come in—everybody else does.' Irritation negated the attempt at humour. 'I suppose you need Stephanie.'

'Indirectly.' Perry's gaze was ruefully apologetic when it met hers. 'I need the revised rate schedule we made yesterday afternoon. I looked on your desk, but I couldn't find it.'

'It's in the folder in the top right-hand drawer of my desk,' she quickly supplied its location.

'What's it like getting out of here?' Brock demanded unexpectedly. She stared at him, not wanting to believe the implication of that question. Brock didn't even glance her way.

'The airport is closed still, but the highways are open. The snow is drifting in places, but otherwise it's in good shape, according to the Highway Patrol report we got this morning,' her brother replied.

'You aren't leaving?' Stephanie almost accused.

'I have to.' Then he flashed her an angry look, noting the sharp hurt in her expression. 'Dammit! I don't like it any more than you do!'

Very quietly, Perry slipped out of the room, leaving them alone. Stephanie turned away from Brock, trying to hide her bitter disappointment. She heard him set his cup down and walk up behind her. His hands settled hesitantly on her shoulders.

'Twenty-four hours was all I could spare, Stephanie,' he explained grimly. 'I've already used more than that, most of it trying to get here.'

'I understand that.' She turned and was confronted by the naked wall of his chest. Lifting her gaze, she looked into his face. 'Honestly, I'm glad you came . . . for however long or short it has to be.'

His grey eyes no longer smouldered with a resenting anger, but burned with a sultry fire as they lingered for a long, disruptive moment on her parted lips. There was no longer any hesitation in the touch of his hands as he drew her up to meet his descending mouth.

His kiss seared her with the rawness of his hunger, arousing her to the full awareness of his need and making her ache for male aggression of his wants. Her arms wound around his neck as she was crushed willingly against his chest. Before the embrace erupted out of control, Brock set her from him with a groan.

'You'd better go now,' he advised tightly. 'We aren't going to have any more time alone. And I'd rather say goodbye now.'

'Brock!' It was a silent protest.

'Believe me, it's better this way,' he insisted. 'I'll see you when I can, you know that, don't you?'

"Yes,' she nodded, and tried not to think about how long that might be.

He walked her to the hall door, brushing her lips with a kiss before she left the room. Her throat was raw and her eyes burned, but she didn't cry. An inner voice warned her that these farewells were something she had better accept. They would be very numerous in any prolonged relationship with Brock Canfield.

Perry didn't say anything when she walked into her office to find him going over the schedule he had removed from her desk drawer. There was gentle sympathy in his look, and a suppressed concern.

For nearly two hours she waited, clinging to the hope that Brock would stop by to see her one last time before he left. But he went without seeing her again. Squaring her shoulders, she began concentrating on her work.

Keeping busy was the one sure way to make the time pass faster until she saw him again. The feeling that he cared as deeply about her as she did for him made it seem easier somehow. There was strength to be drawn from that.

CHAPTER SEVEN

'MISTLETOE?' Perry held up the sprig by its red bow and cocked an eyebrow at Stephanie, kneeling in front of the fireplace to arrange the Nativity scene on its snowy blanket. 'What on earth do we need mistletoe for in this house?'

'That's a good question.' She sent him a teasing glance over her shoulder. 'Maybe for that new schoolteacher, Miss Henderson. I understand she came into the restaurant for dinner again last night. I also understand that you just "happened" to take your break at the same time.'

'The restaurant was crowded,' he defended himself, a redness spreading upwards from his neck. 'It seemed logical to ask her to sit at my table.'

'But twice in half a week?' she mocked. 'I didn't realise schoolteachers were paid the kind of wages that would allow them to eat at an expensive restaurant on Monday night and again on Wednesday. Or did she pay for her own meal both times?'

'Pattie really has a big mouth,' Perry sighed in disgust.

And Stephanie laughed at the reference to the

cashier, her source of information that had betrayed the fact that Perry had bought the young, attractive teacher's dinner the night before. 'Pattie is just worried about your single status.'

'It's none of her business.'

'Maybe not,' she conceded. 'But in case you decide to invite Miss Henderson over for a glass of holiday cheer, why don't you hang the mistletoe from that centre beam? It looks like a strategic location to me.'

'Who said I was going to invite her over?' Perry bristled.

'Not me,' Stephanie countered with wide-eyed innocence. 'But if you do, let me know. I can always spend the night at the inn.'

'Hang up your own mistletoe.' Perry tossed it aside in ill-humour and reached into the box of Christmas decorations to take out the wreath for the door.

'Get me the ladder and I will,' she agreed, realising that the new schoolteacher was an unusually touchy subject.

A sigh slipped from her lips as Perry stalked out of the room to fetch the ladder. She regretted ribbing him. It must be more than a casual flirtation for Perry to be so sensitive about it.

She certainly wasn't in any position to make light of someone else's relationship. She hadn't heard from Brock since Thanksgiving which was two weeks ago. And two weeks could seem an eternity.

Perry returned with the ladder, not saying a word as he set it up beneath the beam where Stephanie had suggested the mistletoe be hung. Leaving behind the smaller hammer, he took the heavier one and a couple of tacks as well as the Christmas wreath of evergreen garlands, pine-cones, and red bows and flipped on the outside light. He stepped outside and closed the door to keep the cold night air from chilling the living room.

Finished with the Nativity scene, Stephanie took the sprig of mistletoe, the hammer and a tack, and climbed the ladder. One step short of the top she stopped and stretched to reach the hard-wood beam.

Even though there was only the two of them, they traditionally hung their Christmas decorations after the tenth of December. The Christmas tree wasn't put up until the week before Christmas. Stephanie realised, a little ruefully, that neither of them was in the Christmas spirit on this night.

The phone started ringing before she had the mistletoe tacked into place. Stephanie hesitated, then continued to tap with the hammer, ignoring the commanding ring of the phone. The front door opened and Perry glared at her.

'Can't you hear the phone?' he snapped.

'That's only the third ring,' she retorted just as impatiently.

'Fourth,' he corrected, and walked briskly over to pick up the receiver and silence the irritating sound. 'Hall residence,' he answered with ill-tempered shortness, then paused. 'Just a minute.' He laid the receiver on the table with a thump. 'It's for you.'

The tack bent on the last strike of her hammer, which meant she had to start all over again with a new one. 'Find out who it is and tell them I'll call back.'

'I already know who it is—Brock.' Just for a moment his expression softened. 'Do you really want me to tell him you're too busy to talk right now?'

The mention of Brock's name sent her scrambling down the ladder, nearly upsetting it in her haste to get to the telephone. When she grabbed for the receiver, it slipped out of her fingers and crashed to the floor. Terrified she had broken it, Stephanie clutched it to her ear.

'Brock? Are you there?' Her voice was a thin thread of panic.

'My God, Stephanie! What did you do?' he demanded.

'I dropped the phone. I was on the ladder hanging the mistletoe when Perry answered the phone.'

She hurried her explanation. 'I didn't realise you were the one who was calling until he told me. Then I was . . .' It was too revealing to admit how excited she had been, so she changed her sentence. 'I was in such a hurry to get to the phone that I became all thumbs.'

'Are you glad I called?' His voice changed its texture, becoming warm and searching.

'You know I am,' Stephanie murmured, and noticed her brother slipping out of the room so she could have some privacy. 'It seems so long since I've heard your voice. I . . .' She stopped, unable to actually admit the rest.

'You what, Stephanie? What were you going to say?' Brock insisted that she complete it. 'Have you missed me?' He guessed her words.

'Yes, I've missed you.' Her voice vibrated with the force of it.

'Why didn't you tell me that in your letters?' he demanded. 'I couldn't stand it any longer, not knowing whether you were going through the same torment I've been suffering. The way you write, I get the feeling that everything is white and wonderful back there.'

'Have you really missed me, too?' She hardly dared to believe it was true.

'I've been out of my mind.' An urgency entered his tone. 'Stephanie, I have to see you. I can't wait any longer.'

'I want to see you, too.' Her hand tightened on the telephone, trying to hold on to this moment. 'C-Can you come here?'

'No.' He dismissed it as out of the question. 'I'm in Palm Springs. I don't have a chance of getting away, not until around the holidays, *maybe*.' He stressed the questionable status of that time. 'I want you to come here, honey. I'll make all the arrangements. You can leave tomorrow morning and be here by noon. I'll only be able to spare a few hours in the afternoons to be with you over the weekend, but we'll have the nights—all of the nights.'

'Brock!' She was overwhelmed by the invitation and his determination to see her, whatever the cost.

'Don't worry about packing much or digging out your summer clothes. We'll go on a pre-Christmas shopping spree—just you and me.'

'You don't need to buy me anything,' she interjected swiftly.

'I want to,' he replied. 'I wake up nights, thinking you're going to be lying beside me. I can't describe the hell I go through when you aren't there. Stephanie, will you come?'

A positive answer was on the tip of her tongue when she realised, 'Brock, I can't.' Disappointment throbbed in her voice, acute and painful.

'Why? What do you want me to do—beg?' He

was angry and vaguely incredulous that she was refusing. 'Why can't you come?'

'I have the payroll to finish. Tomorrow is pay-day for the employees at the inn,' Stephanie explained.

'To hell with that! I want you here with me. Isn't that more important?' Brock argued. 'Let someone else finish it.'

'But there isn't anyone else who's qualified?'

'Your brother can do it. And don't tell me he doesn't know how,' he retorted.

'He's overworked as it is, with the inn booked solid and temporary winter help. I couldn't do that.' What Brock was asking was unreasonable and Stephanie tried to make him understand. 'It isn't that I don't want to come, Brock. I can't.'

'You can if you want to badly enough.' Stubbornly he refused to listen to her explanations. 'Tell everybody they'll have to wait until next week for the pay-check. I don't care. Stephanie, I've got to see you. I want you to fly here.'

'It's impossible. I can't do what you're asking. If you'd think about it, you would understand why.' Her voice was growing tight with a mixture of anger and hurt confusion. 'You aren't being fair.'

'Fair? The way I'm feeling isn't fair,' Brock argued. 'I need you.'

'Please don't do this.' She was close to tears. 'I can't come.'

There was a long silence before his voice returned grimly to the line. 'All right, if that's the way you feel about it.'

'That isn't the way I feel. It's just the way it is,' she choked.

'Have it your way.' Brock sounded disinterested and very distant. 'Goodbye.'

Stephanie sobbed in a breath as the line went dead. She stared numbly at the telephone for a long time before she finally wiped the tears from her cheeks. She was sniffling when Perry entered the room a short while later. He handed her his handkerchief, but didn't ask what was wrong.

He didn't say a word when she stuffed the mistletoe in the bottom of the box of Christmas decorations and carried the ladder out to the back porch. Her brother hadn't had any desire to hang it, and Stephanie thought it was highly unlikely that she would have a need for it.

It was almost a week before she gathered the pride to write Brock a short note, saying only that she was sorry he hadn't understood her reason for turning down his invitation. But she subtly made it clear that she still believed she had made the right decision.

After writing that, she didn't write to him

again. He had made it fairly plain that there wasn't any point. Perry had been a rock to her, never once reminding her that he had 'told-her-so'. Instead, he had tried to cheer her up each time her spirits sagged into the pits of despair, which was often.

They had weathered many depressing situations together. His support gave Stephanie the hope that she could do it again. Otherwise she wasn't certain what she would have done.

The week before Christmas their church had a Christmas carolling party. A skiing accident to one of the guests at the inn forced Perry to cancel at the last minute, but he encouraged Stephanie to go without him. Regarding it more as a religious festivity than a social party, she agreed.

He dropped her off at the church with instructions to call him when she was ready to go home and he would pick her up. It didn't prove necessary, however, since one of the first persons she met was Chris Berglund. His parents owned the farm a mile from theirs and the two had virtually grown up together, playmates becoming schoolmates. It had always seemed as though they were related, which they weren't.

Stephanie hadn't seen much of him since they had graduated from high school. Chris had gone on to college, coming back only for term breaks, like this Christmas one.

When Chris learned she was without a lift home, he immediately volunteered to take her since it was right on his way to his parents. They gossiped, exchanged personal news, and recalled funny incidents from their shared childhood days.

As he turned into the lane leading to the farmhouse, Stephanie leaned back in her seat and sighed. She couldn't remember when she had laughed like this and felt so light-hearted. She glanced at Chris, with his curly brown hair and dark-rimmed glasses, a thick parka adding bulk to his slim frame.

'I still can't believe you're going to be a doctor,' she remarked. 'I can remember when you used to squirm at the sight of blood.'

'Thank heavens I outgrew that!' he laughed.

'Doctor Chris Berglund.' Stephanie tried out the sound of the title with his name. 'It has a very professional ring to it.'

'It does, doesn't it?' he agreed with mock smugness. 'But I still have a few years of school left, plus my internship before that's a reality. I have to learn how to say "Open your mouth and say, Aah" with finesse!'

Stephanie laughed, as she was meant to do. 'I'll bet your bedside manner will be impeccable.'

'You know it.' Chris slowed the car as he approached the house. 'It looks like Perry is waiting up for you. Good grief, he even has the front light on for you. Is big brother playing the heavy-handed parent now?'

'That isn't his style. Perry is just Perry. I wouldn't trade him for the world,' she replied, and meant it.

'He is a pretty special guy,' Chris agreed, and stopped the car beside the shovelled sidewalk to the front door.

Stephanie climbed out of the car, joined by Chris as he walked around to see her to the door. 'Why don't you come in for a drink?' she suggesed. 'Perry would love to see you.'

'I'd better not.' Chris turned down the invitation reluctantly. 'I just got home this afternoon. With Mom being in charge of the carolling party and all, I haven't got to visit much with the folks. The minister and his wife and a couple of Mom and Dad's friends are coming by the house tonight I think they'd like to show me off.'

'Naturally,' Stephanie understood, stopping at the door and turning to him. 'I'm glad you're home, Chris. It isn't the same when you aren't around.'

'The next time I come, I'll bring a couple of guys from my fraternity. I'll fix you up with one of them,' he winked. 'I don't want my favourite girl turning into an old maid.' He looked his hands behind her waist and pulled her closer. 'You're much too pretty.'

'Flatterer,' she laughed, but there was a tight pain in her breast.

His kiss was a warm, friendly one, innocent and meaningless. It didn't occur to Stephanie to object —any more than it would have if a member of her family and kissed her. It was the same with Chris. Neither of them were hiding any secret passion for the other.

He was smiling when he drew away to leave. 'Tell Perry I'll stop by the inn tomorrow. Maybe we can all have coffee together.'

'Okay,' she agreed, and added with a quick wave as he disappeared down the sidewalk, 'Thanks for the ride!'

Her answer was a wave. Stephanie turned to enter the house as the car door slammed. Hurrying inside out of the cold, she paused to shut the front door and stomp the snow from her boots on the heavy mat inside.

'Hey, Perry!' she called to her brother as she turned and began unwinding the wool scarf from around her neck. 'Guess who's home for Christmas?——'

She had barely taken two steps into the living room when she saw a dark-coated figure standing beside the fireplace. She faltered in surprise before a searing joy ran through her veins.

'Brock!' she cried happily, and started forward with lighter steps.

'Surprise! Surprise!' Sarcasm dripped from his taunting voice, halting her as effectively as a barrier.

His left hand was thrust in the side pocket of his topcoat. In his right, he held a glass of whisky. It had to be whisky since that was the only kind of drink they kept in the house. His legs were slightly apart in a challenging stance. But it was the rawly bleak anger in his grey eyes that froze Stephanie. His masculine features might have been carved out of brown stone.

'When did you get here?' she managed finally. 'Why didn't you let me know?'

'Fifteen minutes ago. What's the matter?' Brock jeered. 'Are you wishing I'd come fifteen minutes from now so I wouldn't have witnessed that tender little scene out front?' His mouth thinned as he downed a swallow of whisky. Angry disgust and contempt flared his nostrils. 'I'll bet you would have liked to know I was coming. You would have done a better job of juggling the men in your life so they wouldn't meet each other coming and going.'

'Brock, that's not how it is,' she protested in a pained voice.

'You mean that's not an example of how you wait for me?' he challenged with open scorn. 'I saw you kiss him.'

Stephanie half-turned to glance at the glass

pane on the top half of the front door, the outside light illuminating the entrance. If Chris had kissed her in the living room, they wouldn't have been more visible. Out of the corner of her eye she saw her brother appear in the kitchen opening, drawn by Brock's angry voice.

'It was Chris.' She unconsciously appealed to her brother to make Brock understand how innocent the kiss had been.

'He's a neighbour——' Perry began, trying to come to her rescue.

'That's convenient,' Brock snapped.

'You don't understand,' Stephanie insisted helplessly.

'I understand all right.' His voice was savagely low. 'I understand that I was a fool to think you were different.'

With unleashed fury he hurled the glass into the fireplace. Stephanie flinched at the crash of splintering glass and the subsequent small explosion of flames from the alcohol that splattered on the logs.

It all happened so quickly she didn't notice Brock was moving until he swept past her. By the time she turned, the front door was slamming in her face. She wrenched at the doorknob, the lock momentarily jamming from her haste.

She managed to jerk it open in time to see Brock striding around the station wagon to where his car was parked. The boxy bulk of that station wagon had previously hidden it from her view, but then she hadn't been looking for it either.

As she ran down the sidewalk after Brock, she heard the car door slam and the motor start. Before she reached the driveway he had reversed on to the lane. Stephanie had a brief glimpse of his profile and the forbidding grimness of his expression before the car accelerated down the long drive.

'Stephanie?' Her brother was calling to her from the open front door.

She paused long enough to ask, 'Are the keys in the wagon?'

'Yes. Where are you going?' he asked, already guessing.

'I've got to explain to him. I can't leave it like this.' The answer was tossed over her shoulder as she ran to the car.

She lost sight of the Mercedes' tail lights when she turned on to the main road. Judging by the direction Brock had taken, she took a chance that he was going to the inn.

His car was parked in the section reserved for employees, steam rising from the hood, when she arrived. She parked the station wagon beside it and hurried inside, slowing her steps to a fast walk through the lobby. Ignoring the questioning look she received from the night clerk, she didn't stop to explain what she was doing there at that hour of the night.

Her heart was pounding and she was out of breath when she reached the door to Brock's suite. Before she lost her nerve, she knocked rapidly three times. She felt a tense kind of relief when she heard hard strides approaching from the other side of the door. It was jerked open by an impatient hand. Brock's eyes narrowed on her with icy anger.

'I deserve the chance to explain what you saw,' Stephanie rushed before he could order her to leave.

Minus his topcoat and suit jacket, he had on a white shirt, his tie askew from an attempt to loosen the knot. His hand returned to finish the job as he pivoted away from the door, not closing it. Stephanie moved hesitantly into the room, shutting the door behind her and watching the suppressed violence in the way he stripped the tie from around his neck and tossed it on to a seat cushion.

Without looking at her, he walked to the gold-leafed Coromandel screen and opened it to reveal the bar. She watched him splash a couple of jiggers into a glass from a whisky decanter. He took a quick swallow and moved away, not speaking, not looking at her.

'I——' It was difficult to know how to begin

when she was being so frigidly ignored. 'Chris Berglund and I grew up together. We played as kids, we were in the same grade in school. He's studying to be a doctor and I haven't seen him in ages. He arrived home this afternoon for the Christmas break.'

'You must have had a very joyous reunion,' Brock remarked caustically.

'It was wonderful to see him again.' Stephanie refused to deny that. 'Chris and I are old friends. That's all we've ever been. It's more like we're brother and sister. I know how it might have looked——'

'Do you?' Brock spun around, withering her with the fiery blast of his anger. 'Do you have any idea at all what it's like to break appointments, to tell important executives to go take a running jump into a lake because there's this woman you can't get out of your head—and if you don't see her, you're likely to go crazy? So you take off, drop everything. Then you're there, in her home, waiting for her to come back from church—from *church*!' he emphasised with biting contempt. 'You hear a car drive up and voices. You're so anxious to see her that you nearly go flying out the door. But there she is—kissing someone else.'

'But it didn't mean anything.' Her voice was hoarse, scraped by the rawness of the emotions he had displayed, his feeling of betrayal. 'You've got

to understand it was no different from kissing
Perry.'

'Am I supposed to believe that you missed me?'
he challenged, unconvinced. 'That you wanted to
see me again?'

'Yes.' She was astounded that he could doubt
it.

'Then why haven't you written me?' Brock demanded, setting his glass down with a thump to
punctuate the question.

'Because I thought ... When you called me and
I couldn't come to California ...' Stephanie was
so confused she couldn't finish one sentence before
starting another. 'You said goodbye ... I thought
it was final. You were angry because I refused,'
she reminded him.

'Yes.' He began to cross the room. 'I was
furious—with you and with myself. When those
letters stopped, I thought I'd lost you. I came all
this way to apologise for being such a selfish,
arrogant bastard.' He stopped in front of her,
reaching out to dig his fingers into the tender flesh
of her shoulders. 'Then, to find you in that man's
arms, I——'

The male lines in his face were more deeply
etched as he struggled to control his warring emotions. With a smothered curse he crushed her lips
beneath his, grinding them against her teeth. The
brutality of his kiss bruised and punished, shock-

ing Stephanie into the stillness of silent endurance until the moment of wrath passed.

Lifting his head to view her swollen and throbbing lips, Brock permitted her to breathe for a minute. Then his hands were forcing their way inside her parka and crushing her into his tortured embrace. Rough kisses were scattered over her hair and temples as anguished sounds moaned from his throat.

'Do you blame me for going a little crazy?' he groaned. 'For wondering——' He raised his head again, anger still smouldering in his eyes. 'How many men are there? How many men would fly half-way across the world to be with you?'

'Brock, there's only you,' Stephanie whispered, lifting a trembling hand to let her fingertips trace the iron line of his jaw.

'That's what you say.' Rueful cynicism flashed across his expression. 'But I don't know what you do when I'm not here. My God, I don't even know if you're still a virgin!'

She was stunned that his doubt ran that deep. 'You don't mean that!'

'Prove it,' Brock challenged with a new urgency in his voice. His hands tightened their hold to draw her closer to the hardening contours of his body, making her vividly aware of his need. 'Stay with me tonight.'

'You expect me to go to bed with you just to

prove I'm still a virgin,' she accused, her hands straining against his chest to keep some distance between them. 'What kind of a reason is that?'

'It's a damned good one!' he flared. 'Because you're going to have to convince me that I haven't been going through this hell for nothing!'

'No!' A sudden surge of strength enabled her to wrench free of his arms and she backed quickly towards the door. 'I shouldn't have to prove anything to you. Do I ask you how many women you've slept with since you met me? Don't forget I know about Helen! What kind of things do you think I imagine when you're gone? You can't have lain awake as many nights as I have wondering who you were with. But I promise you, tonight it isn't going to be me! Not for a reason like yours!'

Pivoting, she raced out the door into the hallway, but her haste was unnecessary. Brock made no attempt to follow her. The demons that pursued her were from her own imagination. She slowed her flight to walk swiftly through the lobby and outside to the station wagon.

A sense of justifiable indignation and pride kept her eyes dry and her chin steady. It wasn't until she was at home and alone in her bedroom that she began to think about some of the things Brock had said and the implications that he cared for her—even loved her.

Her temper cooled quickly when she realised she might have rejected the very thing she wanted most of all. The next question was whether she could swallow her pride and admit that to Brock.

CHAPTER EIGHT

ALL night long Stephanie wrestled with her dilemma. She awakened on Saturday morning no nearer to a solution than she had been the night before. Perry noticed the faint circles under her eyes at the breakfast table.

'How did it go last night? Did Brock listen to you?' He pushed his empty plate back and leaned on the table to finish his last cup of coffee.

'He listened.' But she didn't say whether he had believed her.

'And?' her brother prompted.

'We argued,' Stephanie admitted, and rose from the table. 'Do you want anything else before you leave?'

'No.' He shook his head and downed the coffee. 'It's late, I'd better be going. Are you going to wash clothes this morning? My basket of laundry is still in my room,' he remarked on her change of routine. Usually she brought the dirty clothes downstairs before she fixed his breakfast.

'Yes . . . I'm going to wash. I'll get them later.' At the moment, the laundry was the farthest thing from her mind. 'I'll see you tonight,' she murmured absently.

After Perry had left, Stephanie decided to leave the laundry until later in the afternoon. Instead she chose to dust and clean the living room. Secretly she was hoping that Brock would make the first move to patch up their argument, so she didn't want to stay far from either the telephone or the front window.

The morning passed without a phone call, and she began to worry that Brock might have left. She couldn't stand the thought that they had parted on a bitter and angry note. Suddenly it seemed that she was being childishly stubborn by silently insisting that Brock had to be the first to say he was sorry they had argued.

She hurried to the phone and dialled the inn, asking to be connected to Brock's suite. Unconsciously she held her breath as she listened to his extension ring once, twice, three times, then——

'Yes?' It was Brock. She recognised his voice instantly.

'It's Stephanie,' she said, and waited for some kind of favourable reaction.

His response was a long time coming. Then it was a disappointing and noncommittal, 'Yes?'

The telephone became a very impersonal and inadequate means of communication. 'I'd like to talk to you. May I come and see you?' she requested, trying to be calm and not as anxious as she felt.

Again there was a pulse-beat of silence. 'When?'

'Now.' Before she got cold feet.

Brock's pause was several seconds long. 'I have some overseas calls I'm expecting. Perhaps later . . . say, about five o'clock,' he suggested in a completely emotionless tone.

'That will be fine,' she answered, because there was nothing else she could say.

'Good. I'll expect you then,' he replied, clipped and to the point. 'Goodbye.'

'Yes . . . goodbye,' Stephanie responded, then there was a click and the line was buzzing its dead signal in her ear. She slowly replaced the receiver, wondering if she had made the right decision after all by contacting him first. Brock couldn't have sounded more indifferent.

The dirty laundry was forgotten. Stephanie spent the afternoon taking a bath, washing and setting her hair, and trying on a half a dozen outfits before finally deciding on the rust-coloured dress she had worn when she and Perry had dined with Brock and his blonde companion that first day she had met him.

Without transportation since Perry had the station wagon, she had to call the local cab. Precisely at five o'clock she was standing in front of the door to Brock's suite. Mentally she rehearsed the speech she was going to make, then knocked on the door.

Brock opened it within seconds. There was a moment of silence as their eyes met. Stephanie thought she saw a flicker of something in the grey depths, but it was too quickly veiled for her to identify it. Her senses reacted to the coral silk shirt he was wearing, half unbuttoned to give her an inviting glimpse of sunbrowned skin and his dark chest hairs.

'You're right on time. Come in.' A smile curved his mouth, but it lacked warmth.

'Thanks,' she murmured as he stepped to one side to admit her. She nervously fingered the metal clasp of her purse, ill at ease with him and not understanding why.

His sharp gaze noticed the way she was fiddling with her purse. 'Would you like a drink?' he suggested.

'Please.' She felt in need of some kind of fortification. At the questioning lift of a male eyebrow, Stephanie added, 'A whisky and soda will be fine.'

As Brock walked to the concealing gold-leafed screen, her gaze made a nervous sweep of the room. The room was immaculate. Except for his briefcase sitting on the floor near the phone, there wasn't any evidence that the sitting room had been used. The door to the bedroom was shut, but

Stephanie suspected the same would be true in there.

Yet the atmosphere in the living room was teeming with invisible and dangerous undercurrents. She could feel them tugging at her.

Her gaze ran back to Brock, so aloof and so compelling. He had fixed two drinks, one for her and one for himself. Carrying them both, he crossed the room to hand Stephanie hers. The drink was not accompanied by an invitation to sit down and make herself comfortable.

Realising that, she held the glass in both her hands and stared at the ice cubes floating in the amber liquid. She was rapidly beginning to regret coming to see him. She heard the ice clink in Brock's glass as he took a drink, but she knew her hands would start shaking if she lifted her glass.

'You said you wanted to see me,' he reminded her.

'Yes.' Stephanie lifted her gaze. 'Last night I was offended by some of the things you suggested,' she began, and searched his expression, hoping for perhaps a hint of remorse.

But his face was an impassive mask. She realised he had no intention of making this easier for her. The speech she had so carefully rehearsed was suddenly and completely forgotten.

Everything was thrown out as she made one last attempt to reach him. 'If you want me to, I'll stay with you tonight. I love you, Brock.'

Her confession didn't seem to make any impression on him. There wasn't even a flicker of an eyelash. 'You'll get over it,' was his cool response.

Stephanie couldn't believe that he could shrug it aside with that much disinterest. She stared at him, too stunned to hear the connecting door to the bedroom open. It was only when a voluptuous blonde in a see-through peignoir waltzed into her vision that she realized she and Brock weren't alone. It was Helen, the same girl Brock had been with the first time he had come.

'Darling,' she linked her arms around Brock's and pouted very prettily, 'you promised we'd be alone for the rest of the evening.'

'Stephanie, you remember Helen, don't you?' Brock drawled. Her gaze was transfixed by his mockingly cold smile. No colour remained in her face. She was as white as one of his white leather chairs. 'Fortunately Helen was able to join me for the weekend, otherwise I might have had to endure a night of amateur entertainment.'

His taunting words rolled out to strike her. The glass slipped out of her numbed fingers, but she didn't hear it crash to the floor. She reeled from the stinging blow, turning to rush blindly from the room. Hot tears rolled down her cheeks in an avalanche of pain.

Shame and humiliation consumed her with a

burning heat. Conscious only of the desperate need to escape, she wasn't aware of the stares or turning heads as she ran through the lobby and out through the front door.

Not even the zero temperature cooled the scalding heat of her pain. Sobbing, she realised she had no place to run, except home. The station wagon was parked to one side in front of the entrance. Hurrying to it, she glanced inside and had to wipe the tears away before she could see the keys dangling out of the ignition.

Climbing behind the wheel, she started the engine and reversed out of the parking stall. The tears refused to stop falling, now that the deluge had begun. As she turned on to the main road, she nearly sideswiped an incoming car, swinging the wheel to avoid it just in time.

Shrugging free of Helen's hold, Brock walked over and shut the door Stephanie had left open. His shoes crunched on the broken glass around the liquor stain on the floor. He gulped a swig of his own drink, trying to wash down the bad taste in his mouth. His gaze flicked uninterestedly to the near-naked girl.

'The show is over. Put a robe on, Helen,' he ordered in a flat voice.

Her gaze swept him with a disapproving look. With a swirl of gauzy nylon, she disappeared inside the bedroom. He finished the rest of his drink and waited for its deadening effect to begin. It didn't work with its usual swiftness and he walked to the bar to refill his glass.

He walked away, carrying the decanter of whisky as well as his glass. Stretching his long frame in a chair, his legs spread in front of him, he stared broodingly out the window at the snow-covered mountains.

He barely glanced up when Helen returned, covered from neck to ankle in an ermine-trimmed robe of black. It was a perfect foil to her perfectly bleached platinum hair. Without waiting for him to suggest it, she walked to the bar and poured herself a gin and tonic.

'Do you want me to call a maid to clean up this mess?' she asked, gesturing towards the broken glass and the spreading pool of liquid.

'No.' Brock shut his eyes. His lungs felt as if they were about to burst.

'Did you have to be so rough on her?' Helen complained. 'Couldn't you have let her down with a little more class?'

'It was the best way I knew to be sure she got the message.' She heard the weariness in his voice, the utter fatigue.

'There are times when I'm not sure that you have a heart, Brock Canfield,' she retorted.

'There's such a thing as being cruel to be kind.'

He lifted his glass and studied its contents in the waning light of the winter afternoon. 'I'm not the four-bedroom type.'

A wall of tears blocked Stephanie's vision. She couldn't see where she was going or even if she was driving on the road. It had ceased to matter. When the station wagon began to skid on the slippery road, she stopped trying to control it and let it go wherever it wanted. It spun and bumped, coming to an abrupt halt. The suddenness of it catapulted her forward against the steering wheel.

It didn't occur to her that she had had an accident. She simply took advantage of the steering wheel's support, folding her arms to rest her forehead against them and cry. There was an ocean of pain dammed up behind her eyes. Tears seemed the only way to relieve the unbearable pressure.

'Are you planning to get drunk, Brock?' Helen questioned from her reclining position on the sofa. 'Or is that whisky decanter you're holding just a security blanket?'

Brock glanced at the crystal decanter with its glass stopper in place and his empty glass that hadn't been refilled. 'I'm considering it.'

But it didn't seem worth the effort. The stupor

would eventually wear off and he'd be back to square one. A knock at the door tipped his head back as he lifted a hand to cover his eyes.

'Answer that,' he told Helen. 'Send whoever it is away. I don't want to see anyone.'

With a soft rustle of material, the girl swung her legs off the sofa to rise and walk to the door in her satin mules. She opened the door with a secretive little flourish. 'I'm sorry, but Mr Canfield can't see anyone just now,' she murmured coyly.

'He'll see me.' Perry Hall pushed his way into the suite.

'Oh dear, Brock, it's the brother,' Helen declared in mock dismay.

Brock let his hand drop to the armrest. He could do without a confrontation with Stephanie's brother, but he had been expecting it. 'What do you want, Perry?' he sighed.

'I want to know where Stephanie's gone.' He stopped in front of Brock's chair, square-jawed and stern.

'How should I know?' His gaze narrowed faintly. 'She isn't here.'

'But she was here. And I'm betting that *she*'— Perry gestured towards Helen—'is the reason Stephanie ran out of here crying.'

'That's a question you'll have to put to Stephanie.' Brock unstoppered the decanter and filled his glass.

'When I find her,' Perry replied. 'She drove off in my station wagon.'

'Then she probably went home,' Brock shrugged.

'She didn't. I've called and called, but there wasn't any answer. Finally I got hold of our neighbours. They went over to the house, but she wasn't there.'

The announcement rolled Brock to his feet. 'Are you saying that she's missing?' The demand came out as a smooth question.

'Yes. I don't know what happened here or what was said, but I do know the kind of state Stephanie was in when she ran out of the lobby,' Perry retorted. 'And she wasn't in any condition to be driving. Since you were responsible, you owe me the loan of your car so I can go and look for her.'

'I'll get the keys.' Brock walked into the bedroom and came out wearing his parka. 'I'm coming with you.'

'I don't need you along,' her brother rejected his offer.

'I'm not asking your permission.' Brock moved towards the door. 'Since, as you say, I'm responsible for your sister's overwrought condition, I'm going along to make certain she's all right.'

'You should have thought about that before,' Perry accused.

'I'm aware of my past mistakes,' Brock countered. 'What happened today will ultimately turn out for Stephanie's own good. You and I both know that, Perry.'

'I warned her that you would hurt her, but she wouldn't listen,' Perry sighed.

'I didn't hurt her as much as I could have.'

Stephanie felt drained and empty, without the strength to even lift her head. Her throat was dry and aching, scraped raw by the last sobs. Her eyes burned with aridness. There wasn't even any relief when she closed them. She hurt; she hadn't realised it was possible to hurt so badly that being alive was agony.

There was a noise, then an influx of fresh, cold air, but she didn't welcome its reviving attempt. Something gripped her shoulders. A voice called her name. It sounded so much like Brock's that Stephanie was convinced she was dreaming. She moaned in protest when she was gently pulled away from the support of the steering wheel and forced to rest against the seat back.

'Are you hurt, Stephanie?' It still sounded like Brock. 'Can you hear me?'

'Yes,' she rasped thinly, but didn't bother to open her eyes. None of this was real anyway.

The familiar and caressing gentleness of Brock's hands was exploring her face, smoothing the hair away from her forehead. The sensation was sweet torment.

'I can't find any sign of a cut or a bruise.' It was Brock's voice again, low and concerned.

'Stephanie, do you remember what happened?'

The second voice made her frown. It belonged to her brother. 'Perry?' Mustering her strength, she opened her eyes.

Again there was a sensation of being in a dream. Brock was half sitting on the driver's seat and facing her. A deep furrow ran across his forehead, pulling his eyebrows together. She felt weepy again, but there weren't any tears left. Something made her glance sideways. There was Perry, bending low and trying to crowd into the car.

'I'm here, Stephanie,' her brother assured her. 'Do you remember what happened? How long have you been here?'

'I don't . . . know.' The last question she could answer, but the first meant pain. Stephanie looked back at Brock. None of it was a dream. She knew exactly where she was and why. She pushed his hand away from her face. 'Why are you here? You should be back at the suite being entertained by your sexy friend,' she accused in a breaking voice. 'Go away and leave me alone!'

But he ignored her. 'Did you hit your head when the car spun into this snowdrift?' His hand went back to her head, feeling for bumps on her scalp.

'No. No, I wasn't hurt at all,' she insisted huskily, and pushed his hand away again. 'I lost control of the car—on a patch of ice, I guess. Is that what stopped me—a snowbank?'

'You're lucky it wasn't a telephone pole,' Brock muttered, and reached for her arm. 'Come on, let's get you out of the car.'

'No!' Stephanie eluded his hand and turned to her brother. 'I want to go home, Perry,' she said tightly, edging along the seat to the passenger side.

She had a glimpse of her reflection in the rear view mirror. Her face was pale and colourless, her eyes swollen and red from the tears, and her cheeks stained with their flow. She looked like a washed-out mop. It wasn't fair that Brock had seen her this way.

She hadn't wanted to give him the satisfaction of knowing how his callousness had crushed her. That was why she had run. She stared at her hands, twisting white in her lap as Brock stepped away from the driver's side to let her brother slide behind the wheel.

After he had started the motor, he shifted the car into reverse. The tyres spun, then found some traction and they were bouncing backwards out of the hard-packed snow. Brock stood by the road-side, his hands in his pockets, watching them. For a moment he was outlined there, alone, his gaze lingering on her. Then the station wagon was moving forward.

'Why did you have to bring him along with you?' Stephanie choked painfully on the question, her eyes misting with tears again.

'It was his car. He insisted.' His gaze left the road, swinging to her. 'Are you okay?'

'No, I don't think so.' She stared sightlessly out of the window at the bleak landscape of snow and barren trees. 'All those lines always sounded so melodramatic before—but, Perry, I wish I could die.'

When they reached the house, Stephanie went directly to her room. Without changing clothes or turning on a light, she lay down on her bed, huddling in a tight ball atop the covers. It was nearly nine when Perry knocked on her door and entered the room carrying a tray with a bowl of hot soup and crackers.

'Go away, please,' she requested in a flat voice.

Setting the tray on the bedside table, he switched on the lamp. 'You have to eat, Stephanie.'

'No.' She rolled away into the shadows on the opposite side of the bed.

'Just a little, Stephanie,' he insisted in that patient voice of his. She rolled back and he smiled gently. 'Sit up.' He fixed the pillows to prop her up and set the tray on her lap. For his sake, she ate a few spoonfuls, but it had no taste for her. When she handed it back to him, Perry didn't attempt to coax her into eating more.

It was nearly midnight before she roused herself sufficiently out of her stupor to change into her nightdress and crawl beneath the covers. She didn't sleep, at least not the kind of sleep she normally knew.

With dull eyes, she watched the dawn creep into her bedroom through the east window. She heard the church bells ring their call to early service, but didn't leave her bed to respond to them. Perry came in with orange juice, coffee, and toast. She sampled a little of each of them . . . for him.

All morning she stayed in her room. When Perry came to tell her he was going to the inn for an hour or so, Stephanie merely nodded. She heard him come home in the middle of the afternoon, but she didn't leave her bedroom.

At the supper hour, Perry came in. 'The food's on the table.'

'I'm not hungry.' She sat in the centre of her bed, hugging her pillow.

'Stephanie, you can't stay in this room for ever,' he pointed out. 'It was rough. It hurt like hell, I know. But it's over. You've got to pick up the pieces and start again.' She stared at him, hearing this truth that was so difficult to put into practice.

'Come on.' He offered his hand. 'The longer you stay here, the harder it will be to leave.'

Hesitantly, she placed her hand in his and let him help her off the bed. Together they went downstairs to the kitchen. She sat down at the table with its platter of Yankee pot roast, potatoes, onions, and carrots. The irony of it stabbed her as she remembered Brock had said she was pot roast while he was Châteaubriand.

'Has . . . has Brock left?' she faltered on the question.

The carving knife was poised above the meat as Perry shot a quick glance at her. 'Yes.'

A violent shudder quaked through her, but she made no sound.

The next morning she was up before Perry. She discovered that routine was something solid to cling to in her shattered world. She made coffee, got their breakfast, dressed, and drove to the inn with Perry. There was one difference. She closed her office door when she went to work. She was no longer interested in the comings and goings of the inn's guests.

There were questions, kindly meant, from her fellow workers, but she turned them aside. She knew they were making their own guesses about what might have transpired, but she didn't offer them any information that would fuel more gossip.

All around her were the festive decorations of Christmas, cheerful voices calling holiday greetings, and the merry songs of the season drifting through the halls. This time, no spirit of glad tidings lightened her heart.

Chris Berglund came over several times while he was home for the holidays. Stephanie suspected the frequency of his visits was at her brother's instigation. But mostly he talked to Perry while she made certain there was plenty of cocoa, coffee, or beer for the two of them to drink. She appreciated that Perry was trying to keep the time from stretching so emptily. In a way, his methods worked.

The coming of the new year brought changes. Stephanie's appetite was almost non-existent. She ate meals because they were necessary, but she lost weight. She rarely slept a whole night through. In consequence, there was a haunting look to her blue eyes, mysterious and sad. She rarely smiled, and laughed even less frequently. Her chestnut hair was worn pulled away from her face, secured in a neat coil. The style was very flattering and sophisticated, adding to her touch-me-not air.

Unless she was escorted by Perry, Stephanie didn't attend any social function. Even long-time friends saw little of her. Except to shop or go to the inn to work, she rarely left the farmhouse.

New Hampshire natives clicked their tongues

when she walked down the streets, prophesying that she would surely become an old maid. With Perry seeing more and more of the young schoolteacher, they wondered among themselves what she would do if her brother got married.

But Stephanie couldn't look ahead any farther than the next day. It was the way she had got through January, February, and March. It hadn't been easy. She wondered if it ever would. But the worst was over . . . over.

CHAPTER NINE

PRECARIOUSLY balanced on a metal folding chair, Stephanie reached as far as she could, but she still couldn't reach the square of dust taunting her from the rear top of the filing cabinet. Sighing, she straightened to stand on the unsteady chair.

The door to her office opened and Perry entered. 'Hi.'

Affection warmed her eyes, although the curve to her lips was barely discernible. 'Hi, yourself. Your timing is excellent.' She carefully stepped down from the chair. 'I need your long arm to dust the back of the cabinet.'

'What's this? Spring-cleaning time?' Good-naturedly, he took the duster she handed him and stepped on to the chair, easily reaching the rear of the metal top.

'It's the right time of year,' Stephanie pointed out. The calendar on the wall was opened to April. 'Besides, I didn't have anything else to do this afternoon.'

'Mud season is always the slow time of year,' he joked. 'Want me to dust the top of the other cabinet?'

'As long as you're here, be my guest.' Taking a spare duster, she started towards the metal storage cabinet where the extra stationery and forms were kept. The shelves looked as if someone had been fingerpainting in the dust.

'Brock's coming,' said Perry.

She had lived in dread of those words. They hit her, spinning her around towards Perry. Accidentally she knocked the wooden cylinder filled with pens and pencils off her desk, scattering them on the floor.

'Damn!' She choked out the word and bent hurriedly to pick them up, grateful for a reason to hide the tears that sprang into her eyes.

She had forced the tears all inside by the time she had gathered all the pencils. Her hands were shaking when she returned the cylinder to the desk. Perry was feigning interest in the sharpness of her letter opener, giving her a chance to recover.

'When . . .' She had to swallow the lump in her throat and try again. 'When is he coming?'

'This weekend. On Friday,' he tacked on to be more specific.

'Oh.' The duster was twisted into a tight ball in her hands.

'Are you going to run and hide?' His question was really a challenge.

It made her feel like a first-class coward, because it was exactly what she wanted to do. 'No.' But it was a very small sound.

'Good girl,' her brother praised. She lifted her head, letting him see the tortured anguish in her eyes. 'Come on,' he cajoled, 'let's see some of that stiff New England backbone.'

'Sure.' She took a deep breath and turned away.

He clamped a hand on her shoulder in a firm display of affection. 'There isn't much happening around here today. We'll leave early this afternoon, around four, okay?'

'Do you have a date tonight with Joyce?' she asked, trying to follow his change of subject.

'No, not tonight. See you later.' He moved towards the door.

Stephanie walked back to her desk and sat down. Brock was coming. It twisted her inside until she wanted to cry out, but she didn't. She had been bracing herself for this moment. Now it had come—her first true test. After nearly four months, surely she would survive it.

Friday. Friday. Friday. Each beat of her pulse seemed to hammer out the word. When she arrived at the inn that morning she was a nervous wreck, despite her well-disciplined outward show of calm.

It took her twice as long as usual to get the payroll checks ready for Perry's signature. Especially the last few, because that was when Perry stuck his head in the door to tell her Brock had just driven up. After that, she mentally jumped at nearly every sound, expecting him to walk in.

She skipped lunch to finish payroll, finally getting it done at two o'clock. Gathering them into a folder, she walked down the hall to Perry's office. The door was standing open, but he wasn't there.

Probably with Brock, Stephanie surmised, and walked in to leave the folder on his desk. Out of habit, she paused to straighten the leather desk set that had belonged to their father.

'Excuse me, miss.' Brock's voice ran through her like a lightning bolt. 'Could you tell me where I could find Mr Hall?'

It gradually dawned on her that the question was being addressed to her. She turned slowly to see him framed by the doorway. Tall, dressed in a grey suit, he was every bit as compelling as she remembered him, if not more so. She watched the disbelief of recognition flash across his expression.

'Stephanie,' he murmured her name and took a step into the office. 'You've changed. I didn't recognise you.'

His grey eyes seemed to examine every detail from her willowy figure to the new, sophisticated way she wore her hair. His inspection left the sensation that he had physically touched her. Inside, she was a quaking mass of nerves.

'Yes, I've changed,' she admitted, but not where he was concerned. The love she felt was just as strong, if not tempered by the separation. She turned away, pretending to straighten some papers to keep from giving into the impulse to throw herself into his arms. 'I'm afraid I don't know where my brother is. Perhaps you should check at the desk.'

'How are you?' Brock enquired, his voice coming from only a few feet behind her.

'I'm fine.' That was a lie. She was dying inside. But she turned to face him and lend strength to her assertion.

At closer quarters she could see the changes time had made on him. Still vital, still vigorously masculine, he looked leaner in the face. The hollows of his cheeks were almost gaunt. More lines were carved into his skin, or else previous ones had grown deeper, especially around his eyes here they fanned out. And he seemed harder.

'From all the reports I received, the inn did exceptionally good winter business,' he remarked.

'Yes. It seems quite empty now, but spring is generally slow.' Why was she letting this conversation continue? Why didn't she leave? Stephanie was angry with herself for not possessing the will power to walk out the door. With a defiant tilt of her chin, she flashed him a cold look. 'But I'm sure that won't bother you, since you bring your entertainment with you.' Then she was angry for referring even indirectly to his female companions. 'Excuse me, I have work to do.'

She brushed past him, hurrying from the room before she made a complete fool of herself. She met Perry in the hall.

'Brock's looking for you. He's in your office.' Her voice was brittle with the force of her control.

Concern flashed quickly. 'Are you okay?'

Her answer was a silent, affirmative nod. He touched her arm as he walked by her to his office. Stephanie slipped quickly into her own and leaned against the door, shaking in reaction. It was several minute before her legs felt strong enough to carry her to the desk.

At five o'clock Perry came to take her home. As they drove away from the inn, he said, 'You don't have to worry about getting dinner tonight.'

'I suppose you're eating out tonight.' With Brock, she added silently.

'You're half right,' he replied cheerfully, and she realised he had been in a good mood when he picked her up. '*We* are eating out tonight.'

'Perry, I——' Stephanie started to refuse.

'It's in the way of a celebration,' he inserted, and glanced at her. When he saw the look in her eyes, he smiled. 'Brock isn't going to be there. At least, he isn't invited.' Her brother actually laughed. 'Just you, me, and Joyce. She's meeting us at the inn.'

Celebration. Joyce, the schoolteacher. 'Are . . .' There was a quick rush of gladness at the implication. Stephanie turned in her seat, her eyes wide and shining. 'Perry, are you and Joyce getting married? Are we celebrating your engagement?'

'That isn't exactly what we're celebrating, at least not yet,' he hedged. 'I haven't even asked her yet. Do you like her, Stephanie?'

'Yes, and I rather fancy the idea of having her for a sister-in-law,' she admitted. 'But let's get back to this dinner. What are we celebrating tonight if it isn't your engagement?'

'That's a surprise. I'm saving it for dinner,' Perry declared with a secretive complacency. 'And you haven't got all night to dress. I promised Joyce we'd meet her a little after six, so you have to hustle.'

One other change her weight loss had made besides slenderising her appearance was that her closet was filled with a whole new wardrobe. It wasn't nearly as difficult to choose what to wear since Stephanie liked them all. In view of Perry's insistence that tonight's dinner was a celebration, she picked an aquamarine dress of whipped silk.

Joyce Henderson was waiting for them when they returned to the inn. A petite and pert brunette, she was naturally outgoing and intelligent.

Stephanie thought she was a perfect choice for her brother, who tended to be too serious at times.

'What's this all about, Perry?' Joyce questioned immediately. 'You were so mysterious about it on the phone this afternoon.'

'Just wait,' he insisted, taking her arm and guiding her to the restaurant entrance.

'Has he told you, Stephanie?' She looked around Perry's bulk at Stephanie.

'He hasn't given me so much as a hint,' she replied.

'You'll both find out soon,' he promised. After they were seated at a table, he waved aside the dinner menus. 'We'll order later. Bring us a bottle of champagne.'

'Champagne?' Stephanie frowned. 'You really meant it when you said this was going to be a celebration! How much longer are you going to keep us in suspense?'

'Wait for the champagne.' Her brother was enjoying the secrecy.

The champagne arrived. Because the waiter was serving his boss, there was a little extra pomp and ceremony attached to popping the cork and pouring a sample for his approval. Finally the three glasses were filled with the sparkling wine.

'All right, the champagne is here. Now out with it,' Joyce demanded.

Perry lifted his glass and started to speak, but

his gaze focussed on a point to the left of Stephanie, then ran swiftly to her. It was the only warning she received before Brock spoke.

'I find myself dining alone this evening. Do you mind if I join you?' he asked.

They were seated at a table for four, and the chair that was vacant was next to Stephanie. She wanted to cry out to Perry to refuse permission, but her voice failed her. Or perhaps she knew Perry wouldn't listen to her anyway.

'Of course, Brock. Sit down,' her brother invited with subdued enthusiasm, and motioned to the waiter to bring another place setting.

Stephanie sat silently through Perry's introduction of Joyce to Brock, aware of the dark-suited shoulder and arm next to her. But she wouldn't look at him. She couldn't look at him.

It didn't seem to matter. Her senses were filled with his presence—the vigorously male smell of his cologne, the warm, rich sound of his voice, and the sensation that she only had to reach out to touch him.

Another glass of champagne was poured for Brock. 'Have you told them the news?' he asked Perry.

'Not yet,' he admitted.

'You know what it is?' Stephanie sent Brock a surprised look and her gaze was caught by the enigmatical greyness of his.

He held it for an enchanted instant, then his gaze slid to Perry. 'I know about it.'

'Will one of you tell us?' Joyce suggested with faint exasperation.

Perry hesitated, bouncing a glance at Stephanie. 'Brock is selling the inn.'

'That doesn't come as a surprise.' Although it was possibly a cause for celebration even if she didn't feel it at the moment. She fingered the stem of her wine glass, darting a look in Brock's direction. 'The inn was really a nuisance to you anyway. I'm sure you'll be glad to get it off your hands.'

'I will, but not for your reason,' Brock replied, but didn't explain what his reason was.

'Is this what we're celebrating?' Joyce was confused.

Perry glanced at her and smiled. 'He's selling it to me. You're sitting with the future owner of the White Boar Inn.'

'What? I don't believe it!' Joyce was incredulous and ecstatic at the same time. She was laughing while tears glittered in her eyes. 'Perry, that's wonderful!'

'I think so,' he agreed.

'I'm glad for you,' Stephanie offered. For herself, she knew how much she would miss the previous owner.

But her brother didn't seem to notice her lukewarm congratulations as glasses were raised in a toast. Stephanie barely sipped at her champagne, not needing its heady effects when Brock was sitting beside her, disrupting her composure and destroying her calm.

'Perry didn't explain the proposal I offered him,' said Brock, glancing at Stephanie over the rim of his glass. 'Actually I gave him two choices.'

'Yes, well, I made my choice,' her brother shrugged. 'It's what I really want. There isn't any question in my mind.'

'What was the other choice?' Stephanie glanced from her brother to Brock. She sensed there was something significant here.

'I explained to him this afternoon that I'd decided to sell the inn,' Brock began. 'If he wanted to buy it, I agreed to personally finance it for him or——' he paused, 'I offered to give him a full year's pay plus a bonus—more than enough to pay his tuition through law school.'

'But——' She stared at her brother. 'I don't understand——'

'Neither did I, until Brock offered me the choice.' He shook his head, as if a little amazed by it himself. 'But when it was there, in front of me, I knew that what I really wanted was this place. All my life I thought I wanted to be a lawyer, but when it came right down to it, I couldn't give up this place.'

· 'I know the feeling,' said Brock. 'The inn isn't the only thing I'm selling. Quite a few of my other companies are on the market. And I'm consolidating the rest of my holdings.' He set his wine glass down, watching the bubbles rise to the surface. 'As a matter of fact, I'm looking at some four-bedroom homes.'

Stephanie's heart stopped beating. She was afraid to breathe or move, terrified that she was reading something into that statement that Brock didn't mean. Her wide blue eyes stared at him. Slowly he lifted his gaze to look at her.

'Would you be interested in helping me pick one out, Stephanie?' he asked huskily. 'I don't want there to be any question about my intentions, so I'm asking you in front of your brother—will you marry me?'

'Yes.' Where was her pride? Quickly Stephanie retracted it. 'No.' Then she wavered, 'I don't know.'

'You need a more private place than this to convince her, Brock,' Perry suggested.

'Will you let me convince you?' He studied her.

'Yes,' she whispered.

'Excuse us.' Brock rose from his chair and waited for her to join him.

She felt like a sleepwalker lost in a marvellous dream as Brock escorted her from the restaurant, his hand lightly resting on the small of her back, faintly possessive. She stiffened in mute resistance when she realised he was guiding her to his suite.

It was the scene of too many conflicting and painful memories. Anywhere else and she might have melted right into his arms the minute they were alone. But when he closed the door, she put distance between them.

'Why, Brock? Why, after all this time?' she asked, remembering the days of hell she'd been through.

'Because I made the same discovery Perry did. I always thought I had the way of life I wanted, until I met you. Even then I didn't recognise what was happening. I didn't see the choice that was in front of me. In these last few months, I've had my way of life, but I finally realised that it could all go down the drainpipe and I wouldn't care, if I had you.'

'But——' Stephanie turned, searching his face, wanting desperately to believe him, '—here ... Helen——' It was such a painful memory that she couldn't put it into words.

'I know how much I hurt you.' A muscle flexed in his jaw as he clenched it. 'I wanted you from the moment I met you. I fooled myself into believing we could have an affair—a long affair— even later I thought our marriage could survive my life style,' he said. 'Then that night, when I made a jealous idiot of myself over that neighbour of yours, and you pointed out the uncertainties and torment you felt when I was away, I knew that constant separations would ultimately kill what we had. I was being ripped apart by them already. I can only imagine what you were going through.'

'Why didn't you explain that?' she questioned, aware that he was moving towards her.

'Because, my lovely Yankee, we might have convinced each other we could make it work. So when you called, asking to see me, I knew you were coming with the intention of making up. I put you off and called Helen in Boston.' His hands began to move in a series of restless caresses over her shoulders. 'I wanted you so much I couldn't trust myself alone with you—I couldn't trust myself to resist your possible arguments. So I staged that scene with Helen, arranged for her to walk in within minutes after you arrived.'

'How could you?' It was a tautly whispered accusation, ripe with remembered pain.

'It was cruelly vicious, I admit it.' His eyes glittered with profound regret. 'But I never for one minute thought that one of the first things you would say was that you loved me. The hardest thing I've ever done was reject you and your love.

I thought it might be easier for you if I made you hate me.'

'You nearly succeeded!'

'Nearly?' He cupped her chin in his hand and raised it to study her face. 'You mean you don't hate me?'

'No. Brock, I love you. I've never stopped loving you,' Stephanie admitted.

His arm curved her slender form to the muscular hardness of his body as he bent his head to seek her lips, parting them hungrily, needing her as desperately and completely as she needed him. Love flamed wild and glorious, sweeping them up in its radiant heat. Breathing shakily, Brock lifted his head before the embrace turned into an inferno.

'Why did you wait so long?' Stephanie sighed.

'Because nobody was there to offer me a clear-cut choice—you or the Canfield legacy. I was too much of a fool to realise it was that simple. But you can believe this.' He framed her face in his hands, gazing at it as if it was the loveliest work of art in the world. 'I love you, Stephanie. And I don't care if I never have another glass of champagne, sleep in another hotel suite, or eat Châteaubriand for the rest of my life.'

'I never thought I'd be this happy again,' she confessed, beaming with the joy filling her heart.

'Everything I said tonight—about selling and

consolidating, you realise that it can't happen overnight,' Brock cautioned. 'It'll take at least a year. In the meantime I'll still have to travel a lot. After that, it will only be a few times a year. Then you can come with me.'

'Whatever you say,' Stephanie murmured.

'Just let me love you, let me make up for all the pain I've caused you.' His mouth moved on to hers, gently at first, then with increasing ardour. Long minutes passed before either of them recovered sufficient control of their senses to come up for air. 'How much time will your brother need to find a new bookkeeper so I can marry my bride?'

'This is the slack season.' She smoothed her hand over his richly dark hair, enjoying the feel of its thickness against her fingers. 'And I do have some influence with the boss. Maybe a week, two at the most.'

'Where would you like to spend your honeymoon? The Caribbean? The Virgin Islands maybe?' he taunted affectionately. 'What about Europe? Or maybe right here in the honeymoon suite where it all started?'

'Here.' Stephanie didn't even hesitate over the choice.

'I think I'll arrange to have that king-sized bed replaced.' His hands familiarly tested the slimness of her build. 'I could lose you in that.'

'Think so?' She brushed her lips across the corner of his mouth.

'I'm not going to take the chance,' Brock murmured before he fastened his mouth on to her teasing lips in a kiss that branded her forever his.